*"I didn* [barcode]

Laura whispered.

Delaney looked at the woman half-asleep in his arms. "Mean to what?" he asked.

Her reply was so low, he barely heard it. "Fall in love with you."

He stared at her in shock. Laura seemed sound asleep now, and he wondered if she even knew what she'd just said. She was in love with him? It was the last thing he wanted. Laura believed in love and families and sticking together, no matter what. To him, love didn't exist, and the idea of families sticking together was something he knew nothing about.

He knew he should get out of here, just disappear from her life, leaving a cold trail behind him. But he couldn't. Not yet.

Dear Reader,

What a lineup we have for you this month. As always, we're starting out with a bang with our Heartbreakers title, Linda Turner's *The Loner*. This tale of a burned-out ex-DEA agent and the alluring journalist who is about to uncover *all* his secrets is one you won't want to miss.

Justine Davis's *The Morning Side of Dawn* is a book readers have been asking for ever since hero Dar Cordell made his first appearance. Whether or not you've met Dar before, you'll be moved beyond words by this story of the power of love to change lives. Maura Seger's *Man Without a Memory* is a terrific amnesia book, with a hero who will enter your heart and never leave. Veteran author Marcia Evanick makes her Intimate Moments debut with *By the Light of the Moon,* a novel that proves that though things are not always what they seem, you can never doubt the truth of love. *Man of Steel* is the soul-stirring finale of Kathleen Creighton's Into the Heartland trilogy. I promise, you'll be sorry to say goodbye to the Browns. Finally, welcome new author Christa Conan, whose *All I Need* will be all *you* need to finish off another month of perfect reading.

As always, enjoy!

Yours,

Leslie Wainger
Senior Editor and Editorial Coordinator

Please address questions and book requests to:
Silhouette Reader Service
U.S.: 3010 Walden Ave., P.O. Box 1325, Buffalo, NY 14269
Canadian: P.O. Box 609, Fort Erie, Ont. L2A 5X3

# BY THE LIGHT OF THE MOON

## MARCIA EVANICK

Published by Silhouette Books
**America's Publisher of Contemporary Romance**

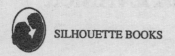

SILHOUETTE BOOKS

ISBN 0-373-07676-2

BY THE LIGHT OF THE MOON

Copyright © 1995 by Marcia Evanick

This edition published by arrangement with Harlequin Books S.A.

Printed in U.S.A.

## MARCIA EVANICK

is an award-winning author of numerous romances. She lives in rural Pennsylvania with her husband and five children. Her hobbies include attending all of her children's sporting events, reading and avoiding housework. Knowing her aversion to the kitchen, she married a man who can cook as well as seemingly enjoy anything she sets before him at the dinner table.

Her writing takes second place in her life, directly behind her family. She believes in happy endings, children's laughter, the magic of Christmas and romance. Marcia believes that every book is another adventure waiting to be written and read. As long as the adventures beckon, Marcia will have no choice but to follow where they lead. She hopes that you will join her for the journey.

For Joan Hohl, whose support has always encouraged
me, and whose friendship is priceless

# Prologue

Delaney Thomas heard the gunshot blast half a mile away from his father's place and pressed the accelerator of his Jeep to the floor. His father, Nevil Thomas, wouldn't be firing his gun unless his life was in jeopardy, or he had sunken once again into the bowels of a drunken stupor and was taking potshots at imaginary pink elephants. Delaney gritted his teeth as the front wheels of the jeep hit another hole in the dirt lane that led to his father's place. He heard the two bags of groceries topple over behind him and cursed as he remembered the dozen eggs in one of the bags. His father's life had better be in danger. Otherwise, there was a distinct possibility it would be if he was drunk again.

For the past five years, since Delaney had retired from the military, he had been delivering food and lectures to his father every Saturday afternoon. And every week his father's health, both mental and physical, had deteriorated further. Both doctors and Delaney had given up hope of ever helping Nevil Thomas regain his strength. Alcoholism was an ugly and debilitating disease that could be cured only if the patient wanted to be cured.

Nevil Thomas did not want to be cured. He was system-
ically, and slowly killing himself bottle by bottle, drop by
drop.

The Jeep took the last bend on the dirt lane practically on two wheels just as another shotgun blast filled
the air. Delaney's heart slammed into his throat as he saw
his father, near the pasture with a small herd of sheep,
slump to the ground. Delaney drove as close as he could,
slammed on the brakes and hit the ground running.

Within an instant he was cradling his father's head and
examining his body for injuries. He ignored the frenzied
baaing of the sheep and lightly ran his hand over his
father's body. He half prayed that the old, drunken fool
had accidentally shot himself. He knew what to do for
gunshot wounds. A heart attack, which he feared his father was having, was another matter. They were too far
from help. The nearest hospital was over a hundred miles
away, and doctors in this area were as scarce as miracles.
Delaney gently brushed back a wave of gray hair falling
across his father's forehead. "Dad?" He hadn't called his
father "Dad" in years.

Nevil slowly raised his eyelids to reveal bloodshot gray
eyes filled with pain, anger and sorrow. "Did you kill
that son of a bitch?"

"Who?" Delaney glanced around the place. He had
been so concerned about his father that he never had
given a thought to what the old man had been shooting
at.

A trembling hand grabbed the front of Delaney's shirt.
"The wolf!" The old man's grip tightened, and he caught
a patch of thick curls covering his son's chest underneath the shirt. Nevil raised his dull eyes to his son's face.
"The son of a bitch killed one of my sheep."

Delaney lowered his head to catch his father's slurred
words. The smell of alcohol on his father's breath nearly
knocked him over, and he wondered who had brought
him the whiskey this time. "Easy, Dad, save your
strength." He pulled his father's frail body closer and
feverishly thought about the fastest way to get medical

help. In his father's small cabin was a shortwave radio. He could either call for help or drive him into Moosehead Falls, the nearest town, and pray that Doc Wyman was around.

Nevil's unfocused eyes widened in pain and a small stream of drool slipped down his unshaven chin. "Kill that son of a bitch for me, Son...."

Delaney watched as the last glimmer of life faded from his father's sightless eyes. He'd seen men die before. Good men who'd served beside him in the name of Uncle Sam. He thought about performing CPR but knew it was hopeless. An old line from a Kenny Rogers song filtered through the pain of losing his only family. *You got to know when to fold 'em.* There was no help on the way and his father's heart was weak and damaged from the years of abuse. Maybe now Nevil Thomas could find peace. He reached down, gently closed the lids over the old man's eyes and folded his father's hands.

The hysterical baaing of the sheep finally penetrated Delaney's mind. He glanced around the enclosure and then toward the woods near the back of the pasture. His gaze narrowed and his breath froze in his lungs. There on the edge of the woods stood the largest black wolf he had ever seen. Golden eyes glared back at him from the shadowy depths. His father hadn't been hallucinating; there had been a wolf.

His glance shifted toward the shotgun lying next to his father. In one lithe movement he grabbed the gun, stood up and fired at the animal. The shot went wide, and the wolf disappeared into the thick underbrush of the woods. It was then that Delaney spotted the carcass of a sheep lying near where the wolf had been standing.

Delaney raised the shotgun again and waited for the wolf to return and claim his dinner. This time Delaney wouldn't miss. His father's shotgun was old and neglected, but he knew how to compensate for those flaws. For thirteen years he had been one of the best sharpshooters in the marines.

He stood there and waited, tears rolling down his cheeks. He was now truly alone in the world. His father, such as he was, had been his only living relative. Delaney Thomas now could say he had nobody. His father had called him "Son" at the end. He wasn't a son any longer. He wasn't a husband any longer. Hell, he wasn't even a sergeant any longer.

Delaney Thomas not only had nobody, he was a nobody. The gun wavered for a second as he rapidly blinked away tears he would not shed. This time he had someone, or something, to blame. The wolf had taken the last member of his family and left him utterly alone. It didn't matter that his father was months, if not weeks, from the end anyway. The wolf was going to pay, and pay with his life.

He would honor his father's last request. He would kill the wolf even if it took the rest of his life to hunt the creature down. Finally he had something to seek revenge on. Something to blame. Something he could physically get his hands on. He wanted that wolf dead. He wanted that black pelt hanging above his fireplace.

Delaney lowered the gun after a few moments. The wolf wasn't coming back for the sheep. Tomorrow was another day. Hell, he had the rest of his life to kill the creature. He glanced down at his father's body and sighed. "Oh, Dad, why did it have to be like this?"

# Chapter 1

Laura Kinkaid drove through the dusky streets of Moosehead Falls with one eye on the road and the other on the handprinted map beside her. Her brother, Marcus, had drawn and sent her the map about a year ago, the same time he had moved up to this remote area of Minnesota from Saint Paul. In the past year she had been so busy with her new project that she'd never taken the time to visit her baby brother in his new home. At twenty-eight, Marcus couldn't be considered a "baby," but he was her younger—and only—sibling by three years. Now she just prayed she wasn't too late.

She had just returned home to her apartment that morning, after spending the past week in New York, buried in contract negotiations with the world's top-selling skin-care-product producer. She was now a very *well-off* woman, and the wrinkle-reducing cream she had invented was going to be marketed worldwide. After working on the formula for three years, she was finally going to have it pay off. She should be singing at the top of her voice, instead of driving like a madwoman, trying to locate her brother. This morning she'd placed her two suitcases in the middle of the living room, gone into the kitchen to make a decent cup of coffee after suffering through airline brew and pressed the button on the answering machine on the way. The first two messages were from friends; the next was from Marcus.

The coffee had been forgotten as the desperation in his voice reached her ears. Marcus was in trouble! The message was a jumbled mess of sentences that made no sense. Something about how he was tired of trying and sick of butting his head against brick walls. He mentioned something about using an unorthodox method, and the despondency in his voice had sent shivers of terror down her spine. Her brother had needed her, and she hadn't been there. Worst of all, the message was three days old, and when she tried calling him back she was informed his phone was no longer in service. She knew absolutely no one in Moosehead Falls, and in desperation she had called his disconnected number twice since she'd left Saint Paul, half an hour after arriving home. It had taken that long to exchange the suits, panty hose and high heels in her suitcases for jeans, sweatshirts, thick socks and boots, which were more reasonable for the fall season in northern Minnesota.

The two-hundred-seventy-mile trip should have taken her well over five hours. She made Moosehead Falls in a little over four. The closer she got to her destination, the more anxious she became. Marcus wouldn't have called her unless it was important. She had no way of knowing what she would find once she reached his house. That scared the hell out of her. Marcus was her baby brother, the one she used to scare silly in the middle of the night by telling him stories of ghosts, vampires and werewolves.

Laura drove down Main Street, spotted the sheriff's office on the right, thought about stopping in, but knew she would appear ridiculous spouting stories and worries about three-day-old messages left on her answering machine. She continued past, reached the intersection of Wintergreen Road and made a left as Marcus's map instructed. A mile down Wintergreen Road she turned onto White Birch Lane. The few houses that she could see in the gathering dark were well off the road and far apart.

Occasionally she spotted a roadside mailbox at the bottom of a blacktop or gravel lane leading off into the woods. Finally, about two miles down the road, she found her brother's mailbox at the end of a gravel driveway. She turned up the twisting lane and shivered at the sense of uneasiness caused by the towering trees on both sides of the lane. The drive probably was gorgeous in the spring and summer with wildflowers bordering the road and daylight filtering through the trees. Now it resembled something out of a horror film.

She shook off that frightful thought and parked her car in front of her brother's dark house. Not a light was burning. Her headlights played over the brown-brick and tan-sided single-story house. It was exactly how her brother had described it, except she'd expected something more inviting. A matching garage stood a hundred yards away, with its large door open. She could see her brother's car parked inside.

Laura reached into the glove compartment and pulled out a flashlight. She kept her car running with the lights shining on the house, as she slowly got out and made her way up the brick walk to the front door. The drapes across the huge picture window were closed, so it was impossible to see in. Taking a deep breath, she pressed the doorbell and prayed Marcus was inside sleeping.

Three minutes and five pushes on the doorbell later, she stopped praying. Either Marcus wasn't home or for some reason he couldn't or didn't want to answer the door. She reached for the knob, and surprisingly, it turned. Marcus hadn't locked his door! Something was terribly wrong. He always locked his doors, if not to protect himself, then at least to protect his work. Both she and her brother had followed in their parents' footsteps and entered the field of science. Their parents were presently away on a research mission with other scientists. Marcus was currently working on his own, on what she wasn't sure. He'd put off telling her about his latest work the past couple of times she had talked to him on the phone. Now she knew she should have insisted on learning more about it.

She slowly pushed in the door and turned on the flashlight, gasping as the weak beam of light slipped over the room. The room appeared to have been trashed. Laura reached in beside the door and flipped the switch. Light flooded the room from one of the lamps. The other lamp was shattered on the floor. Pillows were off the couch, books and magazines were scattered everywhere and two clay pots lay in a broken pile of rubbish. Laura stood on the threshold and softly called, "Marcus?"

No response. She called his name louder and waited. Nothing. She took one step into the room, leaving the door open behind her, and shouted at the top of her lungs, "Marcus!" Only her voice echoing through the empty house greeted her.

She had two choices. She could drive back to the sheriff's office in town, or she could search the house for her brother. Marcus's safety was more important than her own fears. She stepped farther into the room and glanced toward the kitchen. It appeared to be in the same condition as the living room, but worse. Broken dishes littered the floor and a pot of coffee had been spilled over the counter. She found the light switch and flipped it on. The telephone was practically ripped from the wall, which explained why it had been out of service. Three of the four kitchen chairs were tipped over. She moved one of them out of her way and glanced down the dark hallway.

Laura positioned herself to have a clear run straight out the front door if she needed it and shouted her brother's name again. "Marcus! It's Laura. Answer me!"

Silence.

She found the hall light switch and flipped it on. Light flooded the small area. She glanced at a crooked picture of a mountain scene and suppressed the urge to straighten it. *Don't tamper with a crime scene!* screamed through her mind. She frowned at the thought. Who said this was a crime scene? Marcus's phone message indicated that he was depressed about his work, not worried for his life.

She slowly made her way down the hall, listening for any sound that would signify whoever had done this was still around. Only the still of the night could be heard. She clamped her teeth shut and had to use both hands on the flashlight to keep it still. When she came to the first door she swept it with the beam of light before finding the switch. The room was the spare bedroom, the one that Marcus had promised her a dozen times would be hers when she visited. Right now it wasn't fit for guests. Someone had knocked into the oak dresser, scattering framed pictures, a stack of books and papers everywhere. The bed covers were torn from the mattress and a huge potted fern had been knocked over. The closet was empty except for some old, forgotten coats.

Laura backed out of the room and headed for the next door. Marcus's bedroom was in the same shape, except a little worse. The portable television near the foot of the bed had been knocked off its stand and one of the closet's sliding doors was off its track. But thankfully, Marcus wasn't in the room.

Only one room left—the bathroom. Laura skimmed the small room with her light, looking for Marcus. She breathed a sigh of relief when all she encountered were broken after-shave bottles and the shattered glass from the medicine cabinet mirror. She frowned at the few drops of blood splattered on the white sink and the linoleum floor. Whoever shattered the mirror had cut his hand.

Marcus wasn't in the house. She had checked everywhere except his lab in the basement. She didn't want to go into the basement. Every horror film she had ever seen, in which some dumb coed had gone searching in the basement or attic, came rushing back to her. She had hissed and booed at the stupidity of the coed and the film's director. Now she understood their dilemma. Her brother's life could be in jeopardy. He could be lying down there bleeding to death or seriously injured. She had to go into the basement and see for herself.

The stairs to the basement were next to the laundry room off the kitchen. She opened the door and shone her light down the dark steps. No dead body lay on the wooden steps. She flipped on the light switch and watched as light flooded the room below. Not a sound emerged. She shouted his name down the steps. Nothing.

Laura could taste the drop of blood she had just worried from her lower lip. She was terrified to go down the steps, not knowing what she would find, but she was more frightened not to. Marcus might be down there, needing her. She remembered her promise to her parents right before they'd left on their trip months ago. She and Marcus would be fine—she would see to it. She glanced behind her at the disconnected kitchen phone before making up her mind. Hadn't she promised to see to Marcus? With a determined step she marched over to a drawer and removed the largest knife she could find. Holding the trembling flashlight in her left hand and the lethal-looking knife in her right, she started down the steps.

Marcus's lab had been trashed unmercifully. Beakers, vials and glassware lay smashed everywhere. It looked like someone had been in a rage and had swept the counters clean. Papers, reports and books were everywhere. The only sounds in the large open room, which ran the entire length and width of the house, were her own rapid breathing and the crunch of glass under her boots. She stopped in front of a gun cabinet and frowned. Whoever have done this hadn't touched Marcus's guns. She remembered the two televisions upstairs, a VCR and his expensive stereo system. Nothing had been stolen. That eliminated robbery as a motive, but left his work.

Whatever her brother had been working on must have been very important for someone to have done this to his lab. But if that person was after his work, why had he trashed the lab? She searched everywhere, half expecting to find Marcus's body. Finally she climbed back up the steps, letting out a heartfelt sigh of relief. She realized that since she hadn't found his body, that meant he was alive. Didn't it?

She gave the kitchen and living room one last glance before closing the front door behind her and heading toward the garage. Marcus's car sat empty and abandoned inside. Her flashlight skimmed over rakes, a lawn mower and assorted tools. But not Marcus. So where could he have gone without his car? Nothing was making any sense.

She hurried to her car, and headed back down the eerie drive, which had only gotten scarier as the night had fallen.

Nine minutes later, Laura pulled in front of the sheriff's office and ran inside. She skidded to a halt before the large wooden reception desk, manned by a young deputy. "I need to speak to the sheriff."

"What seems to be the problem, miss?"

"My brother is missing and his house has been ransacked." Laura glanced through the glass doors leading into the main station. She spotted only one other deputy sitting at one of the many desks scattered throughout the large room. But there seemed to be something going on in a back room.

"Sheriff Bennet is tied up for the moment. I'll have Deputy Randal help you." He picked up the phone and Laura saw the other deputy answer his call and then motion her inside.

Laura went into the room and directly up to the sitting deputy. "I want to report my brother missing and his house ransacked."

"I'm Deputy Randal, ma'am." He waved his hand toward the chair in front of his desk but didn't bother to get up. "Won't you have a seat?"

She didn't want a seat. She didn't want pleasantries. She wanted her brother. Laura sat down and gritted her teeth. Deputy Randal looked about as competent as three-day-old oatmeal. The man's stomach was straining every button on his uniform. He needed a shave yesterday, and he had enough grease slicking back his hair to lube every car in the entire state of Minnesota. Two powdered donuts sat on a napkin in the middle of his desk and crumbs from at least a dozen others littered the entire area. If Deputy Randal spent half as much energy watching over the town as he did packing his face, maybe her brother wouldn't have ended up in whatever trouble he was currently in. "My name is Laura Kinkaid. I live in Saint Paul."

"How's the weather down there?" Randal took a bite out of one of remaining donuts.

Laura gritted her teeth again and very slowly said, "I received a message on my answering machine three days ago from my brother."

"Three days ago?"

"I only returned home this morning from a business trip." She watched in disgust as the remainder of the donut disappeared into his mouth. "I drove up here immediately, only to find my brother missing and his house ransacked."

"Who's your brother?" Randal eyed the other donut with relish.

"Marcus Kinkaid. He lives out on White Birch Lane."

Randal's gaze shot up to Laura's. "Crazy Kinkaid is your brother?"

Laura felt her grip tighten on her purse. "What precisely do you mean by 'Crazy Kinkaid'?"

"I didn't mean any disrespect, ma'am." He glanced nervously toward a back room to see if anyone had overheard him. "It's just that your brother is a little strange." Seeing her reaction, he stammered, "I mean *different.*"

Laura slowly got to her feet. Her brother wasn't crazy, strange or different. And she'd be damned if she'd put his life in this baboon's hands. She studied the rear office where four men were gathered. By their dress she figured two of the men were deputies and one was the sheriff. The tall man who was standing in the middle, commanding all the attention, didn't resemble any police officer she had ever seen. He had on camouflage pants and jacket and had a dangerous look about him.

She turned away from the slack-jawed deputy, who started to choke on the last donut as she marched across the room, and without knocking stepped into the sheriff's office. "Sheriff?"

All four men turned their attention on the woman standing in the doorway. Sheriff Bennet stepped forward as he scanned the outer room. His eyes narrowed on Deputy Randal for a split second. "I'm Sheriff Bennet. Is there something I can do for you?"

"I would like to report my brother missing and his house ransacked." Laura stood her ground under the four men's stares. The two deputies were both young and seemingly in awe that someone would dare to interrupt the sheriff. She held the sheriff's annoyed look and refused to meet the fourth man's gaze. Something about the man screamed dangerous, and it wasn't the hard planes and angles of his face, or deep probing way he stared at her, or the fact that he had a rifle strapped across his back and a lethal-looking knife strapped to his thigh. There was an unnerving quietness about him that made her edgy. If ever she was in a fight, she'd want that man on her side. He looked like a modern-day warrior.

"I'm sure Deputy Randal would be more than willing to assist you...."

"You honestly don't want my opinion on Deputy Randal—" one of her eyebrows inched up "—do you?"

The sheriff glared out the door at the deputy in question and muttered something about the white donut powder and exercise. The two deputies in the room glanced up at the ceiling, as if seeing it for the first time. The tall, silent warrior cracked a fleeting smile. It happened so fast Laura wasn't positive the slight movement of his lips had been a smile.

"What's your brother's name and address?" The sheriff maneuvered Laura out of his office and over to an empty desk.

"Marcus Kinkaid and he lives out on White Birch Lane." She saw the recognition in the sheriff's eyes. "And I would think twice before referring to him as *'Crazy Kinkaid,'* too." Laura sat down and delicately crossed her jean-clad legs. She was finally going to get some action.

The sheriff rubbed his hand down his face while glaring at the ceiling. "Tact isn't one of Deputy Randal's sterling qualities."

"Care to explain?"

"About Randal's qualities?"

"No, about why everyone seems to think my brother is crazy." Marcus wasn't crazy. He was the sweetest person she had ever known. His heart was pure gold. No sister could ever hope to have a nicer brother, and now he was missing.

"Your brother has developed a reputation around these parts."

Laura raised her brow again. Marcus was a handsome man, and could easily have been a lady-killer if not for the fact he was fascinated by only one thing in life—his work. Six feet tall, with thick midnight-black hair the same as hers and deep-green eyes, all he cared about was the project he was currently working on. "What type of reputation?"

The sheriff cleared his throat. "How do I put this delicately, Ms. Kinkaid?" He shifted his gaze back to his office, where the three men had resumed their conversation without him. "When your brother first moved here, everything was okay. He came into town a couple times a week. Talked to the locals, the normal stuff. No problems." He returned his gaze to Laura. "Then a couple of months ago things started to change. He became distant, only visited town about once a week and became moody."

"Marcus, moody?" Good Lord! He couldn't be referring to her baby brother.

"Recently he stopped coming into town except to buy groceries occasionally. He stopped talking to anyone and he even ran off a bunch of hunters who were up in the woods surrounding his house." The sheriff tugged at his tie and shifted his bottom more comfortably on the corner of the desk. "A couple of folks heard him mumbling to himself about ghosts or werewolves or some such nonsense. He hasn't been into Jimmy's for a haircut in months and he'd even stopped shaving the last time I saw him. The lights up at his place burn all day and night, which only adds to the speculation about what he's doing in that fancy lab of his. Pete Newman says he spotted your brother hunting a couple times out in the woods in the dead of night."

"You're kidding?"

"Afraid not, ma'am."

"Why didn't you do anything? Talk to him? Call me? Something?"

"He wasn't breaking any laws or harming anyone, ma'am."

"Now he's missing!"

"Maybe he's out hunting again."

"His house is ransacked and all his guns are still locked in the gun cabinet." Laura didn't care if the entire town thought her brother was a crackpot; she knew he wasn't. Marcus's work had taken over his life. She had seen and heard of other scientists experiencing this disregard for reality.

"Maybe he's a sloppy housekeeper and wasn't expecting company."

"And maybe you should do your job and protect the citizens of this town, Sheriff. My brother is a citizen of this town, and he's in trouble."

The sheriff left out a heavy sigh, walked over to a file cabinet and pulled out three pieces of paper. He handed them to Laura along with a pen. "Fill out this missing person report in triplicate and I'll have one of my deputies check out his house, okay?"

"That's it? Fill out a form and check a house that I've already checked?"

"Listen, Ms. Kinkaid, as you pointed out it's my job to protect this town and its citizens. Right now we have a crisis on our hands and I don't have the manpower to go searching for your brother, who is probably out hunting or has found a girlfriend." He turned around and walked back into his office.

Laura glared at the sheriff's back and then at the form in her hand. Great! Some help filling out a form would do. She ignored the tears that were stinging her eyes and carefully started to fill out the report. In between each answer she glanced into the office. The tall, dangerous warrior looked to be in charge. Whatever he commanded, he got, immediately. The young deputies eyed him with a mixture of nervousness and hero worship. Whoever he was, he was the kind of man she needed to find her brother, not some backwoods sheriff who thought Marcus was a crackpot, or some donut-eating overweight deputy who'd be lucky to find his way out of the nearest bakery. She needed action, and she needed it now.

She filled out the last blank and signed the form just as the group inside the office broke up. The warrior stepped out of the office, glanced over his shoulder at the sheriff and said, "I'll keep in touch."

Laura felt the rumbling of his voice ripple down her spine. Just as he started to pass her, she quickly stood up and blocked his exit in the narrow aisle alongside the desk. She stuck out her hand and said, "I'm Laura Kinkaid and my brother is missing."

The warrior glanced at her hand, but didn't take it. "So I heard."

Her hand slowly fell back to her side. "Do you think Marcus is a crackpot, too?"

"I've never met your brother, ma'am." He took a step to the right and tried to go around her.

She stepped to her left and blocked his retreat. "I need help finding him. Will you help me?" She hadn't meant for her voice to break on that last question. Up until then, she thought she had been handling Marcus's disappearance very well. The tears flooding her eyes now told a different story.

She saw his jaw tighten, and he glanced somewhere over her shoulder.

"The sheriff will help you, Ms. Kinkaid. He's a good man." He threw a hard glance at Deputy Randal, still sitting at his desk collecting dust and donut powder.

Laura felt the tears slip down her cheeks and hastily brushed them away. They were a sign of weakness, and she didn't consider herself frail or weak. She bit her lower lip and immediately reopened the small cut she had worried before. The warrior's gaze seemed riveted to the cut as one word tumbled from her lips. "Please."

"Bennet!" barked the warrior as he quickly pushed past the crying woman standing in his way. "Send one of your deputies out to Ms. Kinkaid's brother's place and see what he can find." He glared at Randal. "Someone reliable." With that final command he marched out of the office, through the reception area and into the night.

Laura scowled at the man's retreating back. He didn't offer to help. Somehow that disappointed her. She would have bet a healthy chunk of cash on his helping her; there was just something about him.... She startled as one of the young deputies came up behind her.

"Ms. Kinkaid, I'm Officer Bylic. How can I help?"

She glanced at the young, clean-shaven officer and frowned. He was no more than a boy, obviously straight out of police college, or wherever deputies came from. She jerked her head toward the front doors, and as if the Lone Ranger had ridden away, she asked, "Who was that camouflaged man?"

"That was Delaney Thomas, ma'am. The best tracker in northern Minnesota, if not the entire state."

Laura cringed at the awe in the officer's voice. "What's he tracking, Bigfoot?"

"No, a killer wolf that's been terrorizing this area for the past week." He leaned in closer and whispered, "His father was just buried today."

"The wolf's?"

"No, Thomas's. The wolf raided his father's place two days ago and caused his father to suffer a heart attack."

"Oh." Her reply seemed so inept, but she didn't know what else to say. Here she was pestering the man to find her brother, and his father had just died. The poor man. "I'm sorry, I didn't know."

"How about if we finish filling out some forms and then I'll take you back out to your brother's place and look around?"

Laura's gaze slid once more to the doors leading out into the night. The doors Delaney Thomas had just disappeared through. She wanted to go after him and apologize, but it would have to wait. Marcus needed her attention, and Delaney Thomas needed to track the wolf. "That would be helpful." She walked over to the desk Officer Bylic indicated and sat down.

Delaney sat in his Jeep and strung every curse he knew into one long sentence. He had almost helped the Kinkaid woman. *Laura. Laura Kinkaid.* Even her name sounded feminine, yet strong. When she'd first interrupted their meeting he couldn't believe her audacity or her beauty. Hair the color of pitch-darkness flowed halfway down her back. Her eyes were the vivid green of spring grass and her mouth was as ripe as summer raspberries. She was five feet six inches of pure dynamite and he wanted to watch her explode.

When she'd cracked that comment about the sheriff's brother-in-law, Randal, he had almost laughed out loud. He had to hand it to her; she had guts. He liked women with guts, who weren't afraid to stand up for what they believed in or protect someone they loved. Only problem was, women like that were hard to find. Laura Kinkaid had what his outfit in the marines had referred to as grit. If he didn't have the wolf to worry about he would have stuck around to see exactly how deep the grit went. It had been his experience with women that grit only went so deep. His immediate physical reaction to Ms. Kinkaid

told him one thing—it had been too long since he'd been
with a woman.

The tear-filled eyes that had pleaded with him reminded him of summer rain and broken promises.
They'd also ripped at his heart like a knife.

Delaney let out another string of curses and gripped
the steering wheel, until his knuckles turned white. It had
to be the exhaustion causing him to read anything into
Laura Kinkaid besides her being a concerned sister of
Marcus Kinkaid, whoever he was. The day had been pure
hell. It had started at five in the morning with his
searching the wooden acreage east of Pelican Falls. By
noon he had returned home, taken a quick shower and
made it to the cemetery, just in time to watch his father's
casket be lowered into the ground.

He had stood there alone except for the undertaker,
dry-eyed and unemotional. His father had never had grit.
He had been a weak man, a slave to the bottle and quick
with his fists when Delaney was young. He'd watched as
they'd lowered the casket so his father could rest in peace
next to his wife, Delaney's mother. Delaney could only
remember bits and pieces of her. The flowery scent of her
perfume, the smell of fresh baked bread and the soft
humming. He remembered her humming but not her
face. His father had destroyed all the faded photographs
years before in a drunken rage. Delaney had been too
small and young to stop him. His mother had died thirty
years ago, when he was only six. He couldn't remember
if Clair Thomas had had grit, but it didn't matter back
then. She'd had love.

Delaney left the cemetery before the first shovelful of
dirt hit the casket. He changed back into his camouflage
and started searching west of Pelican Falls. He was rewarded when he spotted some recent tracks of a large
wolf, but he was penalized with the approaching darkness. He stayed on the trail as long as the light allowed
and safety permitted. He didn't see the wolf, but he knew
where to begin come dawn.

He started the Jeep and headed home. He never should have barked that order to Ray Bennet when he left. Ray and he had been friends since high school, or as near as friends as Delaney would allow. They both respected each other, and to Delaney, that was all that mattered. It had been the sight of Laura sinking her teeth into her lower lip and drawing blood that had sent him into action. He'd wanted to kiss away the hurt so badly it had had him running scared. He had thrown Ray the order without a thought and headed for the door.

Delaney shook his head and jammed the Jeep into first. Imagine, Delaney Thomas running scared of some pint-size woman with tears in her eyes and more grit than some marines he knew. Lord save him from black-haired vixens. His ex-wife also had black hair, but she didn't have one ounce of grit. When the going got rough, Kathleen DuVal Thomas looked out for number one—herself. And she didn't care who got hurt in the process. Her selfishness had destroyed their marriage and almost his career.

Delaney wouldn't let any woman get that close to him again. No matter what her tear-filled eyes did to his heart or how much grit she might possess.

# Chapter 2

Laura closed and locked the door after Deputy Bylic left. She stood silently by the window and watched as the headlights of his car disappeared through the trees. She was alone. With a heavy sigh she turned and faced the room. Everything was still exactly as she had found it— a mess. And she was too damn tired to clean it up tonight. She had been on her feet since five o'clock, New York time, and it was already after ten. She needed a hot shower and a warm bed, but she needed Marcus home more.

Rick Bylic had been nice enough to secure the garage, check all the locks and windows and carry in her luggage. He also had been pretty insistent that she check into a hotel until her brother returned. She had firmly, but politely, refused. Marcus needed her here, and she wasn't budging. Officer Bylic had been first shocked, then quite impressed with her knowledge of and familiarity with Marcus's gun collection. When she'd selected a .270 Winchester and expertly snapped the magazine into place she had his undying attention and, if she wasn't mistaken, a hint of admiration.

Her grandfather had been an avid hunter and had taken her and Marcus out many times in their youth. Camping trips lasted from overnighters to a month-long trek through the province of Manitoba, Canada. While Grandfather and Marcus shot animals, Laura would only aim at a target. She was an excellent shot, knew how to handle a gun, but could never bring herself to pull the trigger at some animal in the name of sport. Grandfather had passed away years ago, but his teachings remained. Laura had no qualms about pulling the trigger to protect herself or Marcus. If whoever did this to Marcus's house returned, he wouldn't be leaving in one piece.

Laura slowly checked the front-door locks again. Deputy Bylic had come to the same conclusion she had. The entry hadn't been forced. None of the doors or windows showed signs of tampering. Whoever did this either walked right in—or was allowed in. After making sure the dead bolt was secure, she headed into the kitchen and cleaned the spilled coffee and the scattered grounds from the counter and washed the pot. The only thing that mattered in the morning was fresh, hot coffee and she wasn't about to wait for that first cup until she straightened up this mess. Besides, her nerves were so shot tonight it would be hours before sleep came, if it came at all.

For the next hour, Laura dumped everything from the refrigerator and cabinets that had been opened. The milk had expired four days ago and there wasn't a whole lot of other stuff. Marcus usually was fanatical about eating properly. Fresh vegetables and fruits could be found overflowing the shelves of any refrigerator he owned. Tonight the sick, acidy feeling in her stomach only increased as she dropped a moldy stalk of broccoli, two wrinkled oranges and a bunch of shriveled grapes into the green plastic trash bag. This couldn't have been all that her brother had been living on three days ago. Most of this stuff had to have been bad even then. The cabinets were just as depressingly bare.

She managed to find a can of coffee and set it by the maker. Her stomach rebelled at any thought of food. Breakfast had been cold eggs and soggy toast on the plane. She had eaten lunch—a greasy hamburger and greasier fries—while driving up to Moosehead Falls. What she needed now was sleep. With a clear mind, maybe tomorrow morning she could think of something concerning Marcus she had overlooked.

One glance at the bathroom convinced her a hot shower was out of the question for tonight. The powerful woodsy-musky scent of her brother's spilled aftershave made her gag. There was glass all over the floor and sink. And the knowledge that she wouldn't be able to hear if anyone arrived, Marcus or an intruder, while the shower was running sent the hair on the back of her neck tingling. She changed into an old baggy sweat suit and thick socks, brushed her teeth and hair and called it a night.

Sleeping in one of the bedrooms was out of the question. She grabbed the comforter off the spare-room floor, replaced the couch cushions and settled in for the remainder of the night. Even with the Winchester loaded and no more than a foot away from her hands, sleep was a long time coming. And when it did she was plagued with nightmares of Marcus calling her name, pleading for help, and her never finding him.

Laura jerked awake and instinctively grabbed the shotgun. Her heart was pounding, the palms of her hands were sweaty and Marcus's cries were still echoing through her dream-clouded mind. Another nightmare. The clock on the kitchen wall showed it was barely six in the morning. Dawn was just trying to break through. The skies weren't nearly as black as they had been at three, when she had finally drifted off. She knew it would be senseless to try to fall back to sleep. Mr. Sandman was miles away by now, and besides, she had too much to do.

First thing she needed was a cup of coffee. Then she would see about scrubbing the bathroom before taking a hot shower. In the daylight, a shower wouldn't seem so frightening.

Laura carried the shotgun into the kitchen and placed it on the table. Until Marcus returned, she wasn't going anywhere without the Winchester. The low-wattage hall light gave her enough illumination to see the coffeepot and dump in the water. Flooding the kitchen with two hundred watts from the overhead lights seemed about as appealing as burning her eyeballs with matches. Light could wait until after she downed her first cup of coffee.

She walked over to the kitchen window and stared out into the backyard. She could make out the garage, the grassy area and the edge of the woods. Morning had broken. She stood still and watched to see if any animals would wander into the yard as the fresh aroma of brewing coffee filled the kitchen.

With a sudden gasp she clutched the edge of the sink and stared harder into the shadows of the woods by the garage. She wasn't mistaken. A man was in the woods and he was carrying a gun! Laura glanced at the phone and groaned. There was no way to call for help. She quickly ran through her choices. She dismissed hiding as soon as it entered her mind. Making a dash for her car and driving to the sheriff's office sounded reasonable, cowardly and senseless. How was she to discover where Marcus was if she fled? Waiting for the gun-toting stranger to find her sounded stupid. That only left one option. She had to confront whoever was hiding in the woods and demand some answers of her own. He might know where Marcus was, or at least what had happened here.

She watched as the dark silhouette of the man bent to examine something on the ground. Whoever he was, he appeared to be big. Laura quickly grabbed her boots, laced them up, picked up the loaded shotgun and headed for the front door. Within minutes she had silently worked her way into the woods around the side of the house and come out by the front of the garage. She had caught only a glimpse of the man's shadowy profile. He was still at the back of the garage.

Laura took several deep breaths and forced her finger to relax on the trigger of the gun before it accidentally went off. What she needed to do was, as they said in dime-store novels, "get a drop on the guy" and force him to "spill his guts" before she turned him over to the sheriff's department. She inched her way around the side of the garage. The soft, dewy grass cushioned her every step. One of two things could give her away: the small cloud of vapor she released into the cold air with each breath she took, or the thunderous pounding of her heart.

She reached the end of the wall and listened. Nothing! She couldn't even tell if he was still there. For all she knew he could be sneaking around the front of the garage trying to "get the drop" on her. Laura glanced toward the front of the garage and held her breath. This was insane! All she had to do was step around to the back of the garage, barrel first, and demand to know why he was on Marcus's property at this hour. If she didn't like his answers, she had a hell of a lot more questions for him.

Laura sent a prayer heavenward just in case the early-morning hunter was some crazed lunatic, counted to three and stepped around the building. The barrel of her rifle jammed the man smack in the middle of his chest. Relief flooded through her as she recognized the camouflaged warrior from the sheriff's office, Delaney Thomas. "It's you!"

Delaney's gaze stayed riveted to the gun pointed at his chest. "Lady, you've got to the count of two to lower that rifle."

She took a step back, but didn't lower the gun. Laura didn't believe in coincidences. It struck her as odd that he was snooping around her brother's yard. "What are you doing out here? I thought you were tracking some wolf."

"Lady," growled Delaney softly, "point that thing at something else besides me." His golden brown eyes

gleamed with amber fury as he finally looked up, away
from the gun. "You don't even have the safety on!"

"Won't do me any good to have it on if I'm planning
on using it." But she did raise the barrel of the rifle so it
was now pointing at the top of the trees behind him.
"Now, would it?" She noticed the way his rigid muscles
relaxed, and for the first time she glanced down and saw
his right hand slowly lower the knife back into the sheath
strapped to his thigh. It was a bit disconcerting that she
had never seen him reach for it. "You were expecting a
wolf, perhaps?"

"No, I was expecting you to walk around the side of
the garage."

Laura flushed under his annoyed glare. She must look
a sight. Bulky hiking boots, an old faded-gray sweat suit
that should have been used to polish her car two years
ago and a tangled mass of black waves that were still
smashed and twisted from her restless sleep on the couch.
She wondered what had scared him more, the muzzle of
her rifle slamming into his chest or her appearance. "You
knew I was there?"

"Lady, you made enough noise coming through the
woods I thought it was an elephant at first." He glanced
meaningfully at her wrinkled gray sweat suit.

Laura flushed a deep shade of pink and honestly
thought about lowering the barrel of her rifle back to his
chest. *An elephant! Who in the hell did he think he was?*
"If you call me 'lady' one more time in that tone of voice
I'll shoot your toe off." It wasn't her first choice of ap-
pendages, but it would do. "You couldn't possibly have
known I was here." She had been so quiet her grandfather would have been proud of her. Logic must have told
him that since he didn't see her cross the yard, she had to
have come through the woods.

Delaney crossed his arms over his chest and glared.
"La—" He saw the rifle lower slightly and clamped his
mouth shut before the rest of the word came out. "Ms.
Kinkaid, you entered the woods at the front of the
house." His arm swung in the exact direction she had

been. "You tromped your way around this way and came out in front of the garage, where you proceeded—somewhat quietly, I admit—to make your way toward the rear."

"If you knew I was there, why didn't you say anything?"

"I was waiting for you to call out some type of greeting, since you were the one stalking me." His gaze seemed to search her face for some answers to unasked questions. "What took you so long?"

"I was getting up my nerve." She didn't like the idea that this man had known her every move.

One of his brows arched in astonishment or amusement, she couldn't tell which. "To say good morning?"

"No, to shoot you if I had to!" She didn't like being laughed at, especially first thing in the morning. Since she hadn't even had a chance to drink a cup of coffee yet, Delaney Thomas was managing to push every one of her buttons.

He cracked a smile. Granted, it was a tiny smile and it seemed to go against the natural formation of his face, but it was a smile. "Why would you want to shoot me?"

"I didn't know it was you snooping around my brother's woods. All I saw was a man with a gun, and after my brother's disappearance and his trashed house, I wasn't waiting until you came stalking me."

Delaney's smile vanished as quickly as it appeared. "You mean to tell me you came out here expecting to confront a stranger who might possibly have something to do with your brother's disappearance?" He thrust a hand through his hair. "Are you out of your mind?"

He didn't have to make it sound as though she were some idiot or something. She knew exactly what she was doing. Confronting a trespasser. "You are a stranger, and you still haven't told me why you are snooping around out here at such an ungodly hour."

"I'm doing the same thing I was doing all day yesterday until the light failed. I'm tracking a wolf." He glanced at the house and the surrounding yard. "This your brother's place?"

"Yeah. I thought wolves tended to stay far away from people." She followed his gaze around the yard and the back of the house. "There's nothing here for it to eat. No pets. Even the garbage cans are kept in the garage." She glanced toward the front of the building. "The garage door was open when I got here yesterday, but the garbage cans weren't disturbed." She returned her attention to the man standing before her scowling. "How do you know the wolf's even in the area?"

Delaney took a couple of steps back, closer to the woods. "Tracks." He knelt near a patch of mud and added, "Recent tracks."

Laura glanced over his shoulder and studied the prints in the mud. They looked like a thousand others she had seen over the years camping with her grandfather. She'd have to take his word that he knew what wolf tracks looked like. "How do you know it's the wolf you want?"

"It's the one." Delaney slowly straightened back up. "It has some unusual characteristics."

"Such as?" The few prints she could make out in the soft dirt appeared unimpressionable.

Delaney glanced down at her, seemed to think about it for a moment, before he answered. "The wolf I'm after is extremely large. Most males weigh from seventy-five to around a hundred and twenty pounds." He pointed at the print in the mud. "This fellow goes around one-forty, one-fifty."

"A fat wolf?"

"No, he's not fat. He's big." He glanced around the wooded area, which had lightened considerably since he'd arrived. "I've seen this one. He's pure black and doesn't scare easily."

Laura followed his gaze into the woods and shivered. The one thing she didn't need was some killer wolf stalking the woods surrounding the house. Didn't she have enough to worry about? The menacing trees encircling the house were beginning to unnerve her. Delaney

Thomas obviously had a very good reason to be trespassing through her brother's property and she was feeling kind of foolish for the way she'd jammed the muzzle of her rifle into his chest. "Would you accept a cup of freshly brewed coffee as an apology for the way I greeted you?" She saw him hesitate and managed a small smile as she clicked the safety on the rifle. "I promise not to shoot your toe off."

The corner of his mouth twitched for a second. "How could I refuse such a gracious invitation?"

Laura grinned and led the way around to the front of the house and into the living room. Neither of them noticed the large, black wolf concealed in the dense underbrush on the other side of the property, watching every move they made.

Delaney surveyed the room. He knew the house had been trashed from what she'd told Sheriff Bennet yesterday, so he wasn't surprised to see the shattered lamp or the broken clay pots. He had been expecting worse. The freshly brewed aroma of coffee filled the kitchen as he followed Laura into the room. If he spent half as much time examining the house instead of Laura's figure, he would have noticed the extent of the damage. As it was, Laura's concealed figure beneath the hideous sweat suit captured his attention. How in the hell had she managed to look so damn sexy in such a baggy, unflattering outfit? Next to his six-foot-two frame her five-foot-six height seemed petite. He guessed her weight was between one hundred and twenty and one-thirty. She wasn't all skin and bones the way his ex-wife had been. Laura Kinkaid had some meat on her bones, and it appeared all the meat was in the right places. When he made that crack about an elephant, he was referring to the wrinkled, gray sweat suit, not her size. If he hadn't been so attuned to the woods and every little sound, he never would have heard her coming. She obviously knew her way around woods.

He had stayed in back of the garage and waited to see what she would do. His assessment of her last night had

been right on the money. Laura had grit. Stupid, stubborn grit that could have gotten her killed had he been
some dangerous lunatic lurking in the woods. He didn't
like the idea of her staying here alone and confronting
strangers. Especially since her brother had obviously
disappeared.

Laura took down two coffee cups. "I hope you don't
use cream. All the milk in the refrigerator was spoiled and
I had to throw it out."

"Black, no sugar is fine." He noticed the large, green
plastic trash bag sitting in the corner and figured Laura
had spent part of last night cleaning up. "What did the
deputy say about your brother and the house?" He
walked over to the kitchen table and righted the two
chairs that were still knocked over, before accepting the
cup from Laura.

"He'll file a missing-person report on Marcus and notify the surrounding counties." She took a sip of coffee.
"As for the house, he said there's no sign of any forced
entry or even a struggle. The trashing appears to be
wanton destruction, so maybe some kids found the door
unlocked after Marcus left and wrecked the place. After
all, isn't this Crazy Kinkaid's house?"

Delaney stared at her for a moment over the brim of
his cup. The helplessness gleaming in the depths of her
eyes tugged at his heart. The desire to pull her into his
arms and comfort her was unbearable. He fought the
destructive urge. Laura Kinkaid was trouble and he didn't
need any more trouble in his life. He'd realized that fact
last night in the sheriff's office. Someone had played a
cruel joke on him this morning by leading him directly
into her backyard. That someone was the wolf. It was just
one more strike against the creature. He took a sip of
coffee and causally asked, "Is your brother crazy?"

"No."

He noticed the way her chin went up and the helpless
gleam in her eye turned to anger. The grit was back.
"Mind if I look around?"

"Be my guest." She waved her arm toward the hall. "Maybe you'll spot something the deputy and I overlooked."

Delaney lowered his rifle to the table and shrugged out of his backpack. He picked up his coffee cup and slowly made his way down the hall. He surveyed every detail of the spare bedroom, silently continued into the master bedroom and did a thorough exam of the room. He opened drawers, checked the closet, even under the bed. Without saying a word or disturbing anything, he left the room and walked into the bathroom.

The broken mirror on the medicine cabinet above the sink bothered him. The rest of the house looked like someone had purposely tried to mess up the place, sweeping contents off the top of bureaus, pulling sheets and blankets off the beds. Even the broken television in the bed appeared just to have been pushed off the cart. A kid with more energy than intelligence could have done the trashing. Robbery obviously wasn't the motive. An expensive stereo system, TV and VCR had been untouched in the living room. There had even been a handful of bills sitting on the dresser in the bedroom; now they were scattered on the rug with the rest of the stuff. Whoever had done the trashing had caused minimal damage to the house and contents.

He stepped closer and examined the jagged edges of the mirror and the sink below. "You clean up the glass?"

Laura stood in the doorway, watching his every move. "Just what was in the sink so I could brush my teeth and wash my face last night."

"Was there a lot of blood?" He noticed a trace of blood by one of the spigots, which she had missed, and there were a few traces of the stuff on the jagged edges of the mirror still connected to the cabinet door.

"Not much, only a couple of drops."

"Was it fresh?"

"No, it was dried and crusty." She wrinkled her nose at the overpowering scent from the two smashed aftershave bottles. The fragrances never should have been mixed. Pepe Le Pew would have smelled better. "Whoever smashed the mirror cut himself doing it."

"That bothers me. Anyone with half a brain in his head knows that if you smash glass, you're going to get cut. Why not pick up something and throw it at the mirror if you want it broken? Why risk cutting yourself?"

Laura worried her lower lip and gazed at the mirror. "You could be right."

Delaney raised one brow. "Could be?" He quickly glanced away from the enticing sight of her chewing on her lower lip. He wanted to be the one nibbling on that mouth. Instead, he downed the rest of the cold coffee sitting in the cup and gently pushed by her. He needed to put some room between them. Even with the horrible stench of after-shave penetrating the room he could still pick up Laura's scent. She used something containing coconut to shampoo her hair and there was just a hint left of the flowery-smelling perfume she had had on last night. The hunger clawing at his gut had nothing to do with the fact he had grabbed only a granola bar before leaving his home this morning and everything to do with the fact he wanted to pull Laura into his arms and drown in her scent.

Laura followed him back into the kitchen and refilled their cups. "So what do you think?"

"No sign of a struggle or forced entry."

"I knew that already."

Delaney nodded. Laura Kinkaid might be trouble, but she was smart trouble. She wanted answers, and she wanted them honestly. He never liked to mince words or paint pretty pictures, so he leaned a hip against the counter and gave her his honest opinion. "This isn't the house of a crazy person."

Laura nodded and waited.

"It could have happened the way the deputy said. Some kid or kids just walked in and trashed the place. But I don't think so. Kids might not have stolen the TV and VCR for fear it could be traced back to here, but there's money lying on the bedroom floor. They would have taken that without a thought.''

"True. So what do you think happened?"

"Is your brother known for throwing fits? Tantrums?"

"I saw him throw a tantrum once." She saluted him with her cup. "He was five years old and my parents wouldn't buy him the blue bicycle he wanted."

"What happened?"

"If I recall correctly, he got his bottom warmed and had to ride my old pink tricycle until Santa showed up with the one he wanted for Christmas."

"Anything more recent?"

"Not that I know of. Marcus is easygoing and one of the sweetest persons I know. The very idea that he ran through the house trashing the place is ludicrous."

"What's he do for a living?"

"He's a scientist."

"Where does he work? Have you tried reaching him there?"

"He's been doing all his work here, and I'm afraid I don't know what he has been working on recently." She nodded toward the basement door. "His lab's in the basement."

"Is it trashed, too?"

"Worse than the house." She moved around the counter and unlocked the basement door. "Under normal circumstances I never would allow you to search through his lab, but these aren't normal circumstances."

Delaney drained his coffee, placed the empty cup in the sink and followed her down the stairs. His head was telling him to distance himself from Laura and her problems. He should let the sheriff handle Laura and her brother; he had a wolf to kill. From what he had seen of the house, his educated guess was Marcus had thrown a fit about something and then probably gone off to sulk somewhere. But his gut was churning with curiosity. He wanted to see the basement.

The wooden steps were well lit. From her stiff and jittery movements, he could tell Laura wasn't comfortable coming down here. But who could blame her? Weren't the monsters always hiding in the basement of every horror film ever made?

He surveyed the room from the bottom of the steps. The scent of fear permeated the room. Not the musky pungency of human fear, but the stench of animal fear. Something wild had released the scent into the room. Delaney's gaze shot immediately to a large metal cage in the corner of the room. "What's that?"

Laura followed his gaze and shrugged. "It's some type of cage."

Delaney stepped around broken beakers and vials and slowly walked to the cage. The smashed lab equipment didn't bother him, the cage did. "What was it used for?" He didn't like cages of any type. He'd rather see an animal hunted down and killed than locked up in a cage. He tentatively touch the cold bars with the warm palm of his hand and could feel a cold sweat break out across his back.

Memories of being helpless, confused, scared and angry behind the cold metal bars of a military prison assaulted him. He had been locked up like some animal for seven months while the only two men he could honestly call friends dug up the information needed to prove his innocence. He had almost been convicted of treason. The trumped-up charges never would have made it into court if it hadn't been for his ex-wife. After two years of marriage to a military man, Kathleen had begun to realize it wasn't the bed of roses she had envisioned. Delaney's pay wasn't up to what she thought her standard of living should be. He was away a lot of the time, and the future children he kept mentioning weren't in her plans. She'd taken one look at the young prosecuting attorney for the military trying to pin the case against Delaney and jumped on his bandwagon. Being the wife of an attorney sounded a whole lot better than being the wife of some sergeant with a treason charge against him.

The last Delaney heard, the attorney had been drummed out of the military and disbarred for unethical practices. Kathleen had run through the little money she had managed to get from him in a divorce settlement and had been living with some shoe salesman in Fort Worth. Delaney had all records of the charges erased from his file and was reinstated, but he elected to take an early retirement from the military. Memories of his wife's and the military's betrayal were too painful. He had moved back home to northern Minnesota and started his own business. Delaney now ran a guide service for city slickers wanting to come to Minnesota and try their hand at fishing or hunting.

"Are you all right?" asked Laura.

Delaney shook his head to release the memories and looked at her. He didn't like the concerned expression that had softened her eyes. "What did your brother keep in here?" The cage had been occupied as recently as a week or two ago.

"I don't know." She started to chew on her lower lip, heard Delaney growl something, and immediately came to her brother's defense. "Marcus never used animals in any of his projects. I didn't know he was using any now."

"You have no idea what he was working on?" The dewy softness of her lower lip was driving him crazy.

"None. For some reason he never wanted to talk about it while we were on the phone." She frowned at the cage. "I can't imagine Marcus hurting an animal."

Delaney snapped, "Tell that to the poor creature that must have been inside there." He walked away from the empty cage and surveyed the rest of the room. It was the same as upstairs. Destructive vandalism. Someone had apparently swept the counters clean, smashing beakers, vials and Lord only knows what else onto the tiled floor. Papers, notebooks and books where scattered everywhere. A keyboard from the computer appeared to be damaged, but the main computer looked untouched. Another valuable piece of equipment left behind.

He tried to ignore Laura, who was leaning against the counter, watching his every move. He had no idea what she expected him to do. He was a tracker, not a magician. He couldn't pull her brother out of thin air for her. His boots crunched broken glass as he angrily thought about the empty cage, Laura's clear green eyes, midnight-black hair or the way her lower lip looked swollen and moist after she chewed on it. Why in the hell did she have to look so damn sexy in that baggy sweat suit? She wasn't his type at all. For the past five years he had purposely picked blondes who knew and accepted his rules, no commitment and no future. None of the women from his past would have been caught dead in some baggy sweat suit.

Delaney stopped in front of the unlocked gun cabinet. He had to stop thinking about Laura and her delectable mouth. "This where you got your friend upstairs?" There were a couple of very expensive hunting rifles inside.

"The Winchester is my brother's. The rest of the collection was my grandfather's. He left it to Marcus in his will. When we were kids, Grandpop Kinkaid took Marcus and me camping and hunting all the time."

"Why leave the guns to Marcus if you both hunt?"

"Grandpop and Marcus hunted. I camped and explored Mother Nature." She gave a slight shrug. "I could never see the sense in killing an animal I wasn't going to eat."

"Marcus a good hunter?"

"Average, I guess." She opened the cabinet door. "All the guns that I knew he had are here. Nothing's missing, and the only one he's added since the last time I saw the collection is this." She picked up a gray case from the bottom of the cabinet and handed it to Delaney.

He knew what it was before he opened it. He had three of them back at the lodge where all the city slickers stayed in relative comfort while paying a fortune to become sportsmen. Delaney flicked the latch and opened the case. A tranquilizer gun and an assortment of darts were cushioned in gray spongy foam. Two of the darts were missing—the ones already prepackaged to bring down an animal between one hundred and one hundred and thirty pounds. "Any idea what your brother might have been after?"

"None." She closed the case and returned it to the cabinet. "So now what do you think?"

Delaney glanced one last time around the lab. He didn't find any signs that anything drastic had happened to her brother. It didn't mean that nothing had; it just meant he couldn't see any signs of it. "I think whatever your brother was working on didn't turn out to his liking. He threw a hissy fit, decided he needed a break from it all and left."

"Without his car?"

"A friend." Delaney's gaze met hers for a minute. "It's not unusual that a man might have a female for a friend. Maybe he went off with some woman for a few days of—" a frown pulled at his forehead "—R and R." It wasn't the term he was going to use, but he couldn't bring himself to say to Laura what had crudely gone through his mind. Sometimes a man wanted nothing more than a soft bed and a willing woman. Delaney was afraid his "sometime" was now. Laura was presenting a host of problems, the least of which was her missing brother.

Laura seemed to give his suggestion some thought. "You could be right about the woman. Marcus is a normal red-blooded male. But I have to disagree about him throwing a fit and trashing the lab. This work—" she swept her hand to encompass the room "—is his life. He would never purposely destroy it, no matter how frustrated he became."

Delaney studied her face. She was telling the truth, at least the truth as far as she knew it. "Sometimes people change."

She slowly nodded, as if she would consider his words. Her shoulders, beneath yards of cloth, gave a slight shrug as she glanced around the lab. "What should I do now?"

The tears forming in her eyes pierced his heart, but he didn't comfort her. He couldn't comfort her. He'd lost that ability years ago. "I don't think you should stay here. Whoever did this could come back."

"What if Marcus returns?"

"Leave a note, stay at a motel and keep in touch with the sheriff. Let the law handle it now."

Laura slowly shook her head. "No can do."

"Why?"

She slowly shook her head again. "Do you have a brother, Mr. Thomas?"

"No." *I'm all alone in this world.* He knew what she was trying to do. What did it matter if he had a brother or not? He would never put himself in unnecessary personal jeopardy.

"My brother needs me here."

"Being here isn't going to make him return any sooner." He knew he shouldn't care one way or the other what she did, but he did, and that made him angry with himself, not her. Seeing the stubborn tilt of her chin, he snapped, "Suit yourself, lady."

Laura ground her teeth at his using the word *lady.* "I can take care of myself."

"Fine." Lord save him from mule-headed, opinionated women! Laura Kinkaid had grit all right. All the sandy mixture was packed between her ears. He marched up the steps and started to strap on his backpack. He needed to get away from there before he did something incredibly stupid, like plead with her to go to a motel.

She followed him up the stairs and watched as he positioned the pack and picked up his rifle. "Thanks for taking the time to look around."

Delaney shook his head. She refused to listen to his advice, yet she thanked him anyway. It made absolutely no sense to him. He walked to the front door, opened it and made the mistake of turning around to look at her. She appeared so lost and confused standing in the middle of the messy living room. Damn! "Listen . . ."

Her lips trembled slightly, shaking the foundation of his soul like an earthquake. Confused and distrustful of the effect she was having on his mind and body, he growled, ''If you go outside, beware of the wolf.''

# Chapter 3

Laura wrapped her brother's robe around her and tied the sash. The hot shower she had just taken felt like heaven and had relieved a lot of the soreness and tension the day had brought. About two hours after Delaney Thomas had left that morning she had been surprised, yet thankful, when a telephone repairman arrived. Deputy Bylic had pulled some strings to have the repairman's first stop be Marcus's house. After he'd gone, she had spent hours on the phone calling every hospital in northern Minnesota, looking for her brother. Nothing. Then she had driven into town to talk to the sheriff, thank the deputy and pick up some groceries. When she'd returned to Marcus's house she'd had a quick lunch, found Marcus's address book and proceeded to call just about everyone in it. Again, nothing. No one had heard from or seen Marcus. Feeling frustrated and disheartened, she'd then undertaken the job of straightening up the house. She'd run the vacuum, scrubbed the kitchen drawers, washed floors and cleaned up every room in the house, except the lab. Darkness had fallen while she'd finished up in the last room, changing the sheets and re-making the bed in the guest room.

She had meant to take a shower while there was still daylight, but she had been so caught up in the cleaning that the sun had set without her realizing it. The shower had been shorter than she'd wanted, but she didn't like the feeling of isolation the running water caused. If Marcus tried to call, she wouldn't be able to hear the phone. If people came she wouldn't hear their knock. Hell, she wouldn't even be able to hear if they broke down the front door. That was why the Winchester had been loaded and leaning against the bathroom wall. Never more than two feet away from her at all times.

Laura bent at the waist and vigorously rubbed her long black hair with a fluffy white towel. She had been in such a hurry to leave Saint Paul she had forgotten to pack a hair dryer and Marcus obviously didn't own one. With a fierce shake of her head, she stood up and gazed at her-self in the mirror connected to Marcus's bureau. She looked like the bride of Frankenstein with her pale com-plexion, faint shadows beneath her eyes and thick black hair sticking out in every direction. Her brother's pale-blue robe was four sizes too large for her and the hem practically reached her ankles.

When she had cleaned the bathroom she had removed the remaining shattered mirror from the cabinet door, leaving the room mirrorless. The huge mirror in the master bedroom was the only one in the house, except for the small round one in the lid of her compact, which was buried in her purse. The wild mass of damp hair sur-rounding her face needed a lot of extra attention to-night.

Laura picked up a comb just as someone pounded on the front door. Marcus! She had taken three steps down the hallway, before it dawned on her that Marcus wouldn't have to knock on his own door. Cold fear gripped her heart until she realized that burglars or van-dals wouldn't be knocking. She retraced her steps and grabbed the rifle before heading for the door.

The pounding sounded again just as she reached the door. The heavy drapes were drawn against the darkness, so whoever was out there couldn't see in. "Who is it?" she shouted.

The reply was muffled, yet authoritative. "Delaney Thomas."

Laura glanced at the door in surprise. She hadn't expected him to return after this morning. Maybe he had some news about Marcus. She undid the chain, released the dead bolt and opened the door with a quick jerk. "Did you hear anything?" She had her answer before he even spoke. She could read it in the fatigue beneath his eyes.

"Nothing, sorry." He stood there silently, running his gaze from her damp wild hair, down the ridiculously large robe and over her bare feet. He noticed that her toenails were painted a deep red and that she still clutched the Winchester in her hand. Contradictions. Laura Kinkaid was a mass of contradictions. Frumpy old sweat suit, but sexy as sin. Independent and full of grit, yet tears filled her eyes whenever she mentioned her brother. Maybe that was what fascinated him so intensely about her. Today he'd had a hard time concentrating on the wolf he was tracking. A deadly sin if ever there was one. The creature was abnormally large, intelligent and deadly, and should have had one hundred percent of his attention. It didn't. Laura had a chunk of his concern. He couldn't help but worry about her being alone out there in the middle of nowhere. "I just came from the sheriff's office. Nothing new to report." His mind had told him to keep going past White Birch Lane on his way home, but somehow his hands turned the wheel of his Jeep and he had ended up in her driveway.

"Want to come in? I was just about ready to eat."

"I don't want to disturb you." His gaze shot behind her to the kitchen. He could smell tomato sauce cooking from where he stood in the doorway.

"There's plenty for two." She shifted her bare feet. "I thought if I made Marcus's favorite he'd show up."

The corner of Delaney's mouth twitched. It made perfect sense to him. "What's his favorite?" He knew he would be accepting, no matter what it was. He was starving. The two peanut butter-and-jelly sandwiches and the apple he'd had around noon were long gone. He had been hoping to make the thirty-mile drive up to his place and catch dinner at the lodge. George Whitecloud, the lodge's cook, could make tree bark edible. The aroma pouring from Laura's kitchen smelled delicious.

"Spaghetti and meatballs. I had them cooking in the crockpot all afternoon." She opened the door wider and smiled invitingly.

Delaney glanced at his muddy boots. "Mind if I take these off?"

She glanced at the boots and grimaced. "I would prefer that you did."

He bent over and deftly undid the laces and stepped out of the mud-caked boots and into the clean living room. Laura apparently had been one busy lady. Roy Bennet had told him she'd stopped in earlier and had been driving him crazy. Delaney sympathized with the sheriff. Laura was driving him crazy, too, but in a different way. He closed the door behind him. Laura looked so warm and sweet in the robe that had to be her brother's. Fresh from a shower, she smelled of coconut shampoo and soap.

"I'll put the water on for the noodles and then change." Laura moved to the kitchen and filled a pot with water. "Make yourself at home. Dinner will be ready as soon as the noodles cook." She turned the burner on under the pot and disappeared down the hallway.

Delaney shook his head at her hasty retreat. It appeared she just realized that she had answered the door in her robe. A frown pulled at his mouth as he studied the empty hallway and wondered what she had on under the robe. Desire tightened his body into one agonizing ache. The only excuse he could give for his treacherous body was that it had been one hell of a week. How long had it

been since he'd last visited Jane Daniels over in Buyck?
A month? Two? He ran his hand through his hair and
silently promised himself to go pay the accommodating
Jane a visit as soon as the wolf was dead.

He took off his camouflage jacket and laid it across the
back of one of the chairs in the living room. He eyed the
couch for a moment. It looked comfortable as all hell. He
glanced into the kitchen at the pot of water, which hadn't
started to boil yet. What did noodles take to cook—ten
minutes? He sat on the couch and sighed. The days and
nights with only grabbing a couple of hours sleep here
and there were catching up with him fast. He lay down
and closed his eyes, telling himself he'd sit back up as
soon as he heard Laura leave the bedroom.

Laura slowly entered the living room four minutes later
and smiled. Delaney Thomas was asleep on the couch.
She stood by the chair where his jacket was and studied
him. Here she'd thought all men looked like little boys
when they slept. Her brother did and even her father had
that innocent expression while napping in his favorite
chair. Delaney didn't. She very much doubted if Delaney had looked like a little boy even when he had been a
little boy. And it wasn't just his height. There was something hard about him, as if he were afraid to relax, even
in sleep.

The dark shadow of his whiskers only seemed to
heighten the sharp plane of his jaw. His face was tanned,
as though he spent a lot of time outdoors. Being a
tracker, she had to assume he did. Tracker? What kind of
career was that? How often could a renegade wolf ter-
rorize this part of Minnesota? She scrutinized every detail of his face, searching for a softness that wasn't there.

His hair was medium brown, with traces of golden
blond, deep brown, even reddish hairs, and was cut rel-
atively short, considering some of today's styles. Longer
than a military cut, but nowhere near his collar. Disci-
pline—that was what it reminded her of. He would allow it to grow so long, and no more. The stubble covering
his jaw was the same medium brown. She guessed his age

to be between thirty-five and forty. Only a few years older than her thirty-one.

She knew his eyes were a light brown, which burned golden amber when he was angry. They were surrounded by thick black lashes she would have killed for. Why was it that men were blessed with long, lush lashes and women ended up with skimpy, pale ones that required tubes and tubes of mascara? His nose had a slight bump near the bridge, indicating it had at one time been broken, and his cheekbones were high. His upper lip was a thin, disapproving line, while his lower lip contradicted it with its fullness and seductiveness.

Laura frowned at the words *seductive* and *Delaney* in the same sentence. Why hadn't she realized it before now? Delaney Thomas was one very compelling man. She had picked up on his strength, power and dark side of danger that emanated from him, but never the seductiveness.

Her gaze caressed his chest, where his tight, long-sleeved, insulated shirt clung to every muscle. There were one hell of a lot of muscles to cling to. Even relaxed in sleep, not one inch of flab overhung his belt. His camouflage pants of muted greens and browns gripped his rock-hard thighs. Snowy white wool socks covered his feet. The man sleeping on her couch was breathtaking in his masculinity. She had to be either blind or dead not to have noticed his body before now. No, that wasn't true. She had been worried, anxious and scared for her brother. For the past twenty-four hours, while she had been in Moosehead Falls, she hadn't heard one word on Marcus. Frustration raged through her body.

Her glance immediately shot back to Delaney's mouth. Maybe all her frustration wasn't because of Marcus's disappearance. When was the last time she'd enjoyed the company of a man? Laura worried her lower lip and thought. It had been New Year's Eve, over ten months ago!

Quentin Richardson had been warm, caring and friendly. She would have been better off leaving him in the friendship category than the lover category; at least then she would still have a friend. It wasn't Quentin's fault that instead of fireworks there had only been a fizzle. Quentin was everything a woman would want—handsome, successful, intelligent and caring. She should have fallen head over heels in love with the man. By breakfast New Year's Day they both had known it wasn't going to work.

Laura shook her head at Delaney. She couldn't imagine him causing a fizzle in any woman. It was a good thing he wasn't her type at all, or she just might be tempted to see if she would fizzle or flare when they kissed. Delaney had all the key elements for Mr. Right. He seemed intelligent, handsome went without saying and he was probably a very successful tracker. He obviously was caring, or he wouldn't have bothered to take the time to stop by to give her the latest report on Marcus and to check up on her. But Delaney also had a few extra elements that didn't mesh with her idea of Mr. Right. He was dangerous. She picked that up the first time she ever laid eyes on him, and the notion that he had pulled his lethal-looking knife on her, without her noticing, clenched it. His idea of a nice relaxing evening probably consisted of killing some animal and roasting the carcass for dinner.

Laura gave a slight shudder and headed for the kitchen to finish cooking dinner. If meat didn't come in some nice foam-and-plastic container in a supermarket, she wasn't eating it. She dumped the noodles into the pot of boiling water and chuckled for the first time in days. She had to be more tired than she had thought. Imagining her and Mr. Commando in a relationship was about as absurd as her and Mel Gibson having an affair.

By the time dinner was ready, Delaney still wasn't awake. She checked on him twice and couldn't bring herself to rouse him. This morning when she'd confronted him by the garage he had looked tired and drawn. This evening when she'd opened the door he had looked beat.

She ate her dinner while reading the weekly paper she had picked up in town that morning. The article on the front page about a lone wolf terrorizing some local ranchers and killing some sheep gave her the chills. It had to be the same wolf Delaney was tracking, but it didn't mention him or his efforts. But then, the paper had been printed five days ago. By the time she was done loading the dishwasher and putting away the food it was nine o'clock and she was exhausted. She could either wake up Delaney and send him on his way, or she could let him sleep.

It took her exactly thirty seconds to make up her mind. As unrealistic as it seemed, she felt safer with Delaney in the house. Quietly she went into the spare bedroom and took the comforter—the same one she'd used last night—off the bed and covered Delaney. She locked the front door, attached the chain and clicked off the lights. Laura left the hall light burning as she, her trusty Winchester in hand, entered the master bedroom and closed the door.

The smell of coffee and bacon cooking penetrated Delaney's sleep. He slowly opened his eyes and looked around. It took a moment for his mind to clear. He was lying on Laura Kinkaid's sofa! By the faint light streaming through the kitchen windows, he would have to say it was morning and he had spent the entire night on Laura's couch. He pushed aside the flowery print comforter and sat up. Every muscle in his back screamed in agony from sleeping on the too-short couch.

The sound of sizzling bacon and someone moving around in the kitchen reached his ears. Laura. With a heavy groan he ran his hands down his face and flinched as the coarse whiskers scraped his palms. He must look like hell. He wanted a hot shower, craved the coffee, and if the insistent rumbling of his stomach was any indication, he needed the bacon. Why in the hell hadn't she woken his sorry butt up and thrown him out last night?

"Oh, good, you're up," said Laura from the archway to the kitchen. "I thought I heard you."

"What time is it?" Why in the hell did she have to look so fresh and sunny this morning? She was wearing a deep-green sweatshirt with huge yellow sunflowers printed on the front. Faded jeans, a yellow turtleneck under the sweatshirt and thick yellow socks completed the outfit. Even her midnight-black hair was pulled back with a thick yellow ribbon. Whatever happened to the gray wrinkled sweat suit? He could at least concentrate around her when she wore that.

"Nearly seven." She nodded toward the hall. "Bathroom's free if you want it."

He lifted one eyebrow in question. Since when did he need a woman to remind him about the bathroom? "I don't have to go."

A fiery blush swept up her cheeks. "I was referring to washing up for breakfast, not that."

Delaney forced himself not to color. *You have class, Thomas, real class.* "Breakfast?"

"Since you slept through dinner, I assume you must be hungry. It will be ready in about ten minutes." She turned around and walked back to the stove.

The mouth-watering aroma of the bacon propelled him from the couch and out the front door. Before Laura had finished flipping the bacon strips he had returned carrying his backpack and headed for the bathroom.

Laura called, "How do you like your eggs?" as he was about to close the bathroom door.

He stuck out his head and flashed his teeth. "Cooked!" He missed Laura's next question as he shut the door and turned on the shower.

Ten minutes later he joined Laura in the kitchen, dressed in wrinkled but clean jeans, a thermal long-sleeved undershirt and a red plaid flannel shirt. His motto of always being prepared had come in handy this morning. He could survive over a week in the wilderness with what he had in his backpack. His hair was still damp, but he had managed to shave in the shower without too much damage to his face. There was a nick under his chin.

"Smells delicious."

She placed a plate piled high with scrambled eggs, bacon and toast in front of him. "I hope you're hungry." A cup of coffee and a small glass of orange juice were by each plate and a bowl of fresh fruit sat in the middle of the table.

"Starved." He glanced at her plate, which contained two strips of bacon, one egg and a piece of toast. "Is that all you're having?"

"I, unlike some people I know, had dinner last night."

Delaney dug into his breakfast. "Sorry about that. Why didn't you wake me?"

She poked at her egg with her fork. "You looked so peaceful sleeping I didn't have the heart to disturb you."

His forkful of eggs halted in midair. "You're kidding, right?"

"Why would I kid about something like that?"

"You let a perfect stranger sleep on your couch all night long just because he looked peaceful?" He knew yesterday morning that she possessed more grit than brains when she confronted him with the rifle. But to allow a stranger to crash on her couch wasn't grit. It was insane. The lady had to have a death wish.

"You're not a perfect stranger. The sheriff trusts you, and Deputy Bylic thinks you're Superman of the north." She took a bite of bacon and smiled. "If you wanted to do me harm you would have done it yesterday morning while we were alone in the house."

"With that line of deductive reasoning you allowed me to sleep in the next room?"

"No, on instinct I allowed you stay."

'What instinct?" The woman was certifiable. Instinct made birds fly south for the winter, bears hibernate and raccoons wash their food. Women didn't have instinct.

"The gut feeling I had knowing that you would keep me safe."

Delaney felt his heart stop dead in his chest. The damn organ missed three whole beats before resuming its thunderous pounding. She felt safe with him! Was she crazy? Didn't she realize how much control he was asserting just to sit across this table from her and eat without giving in to his greater hunger? The need to kiss her was growing more powerful with each passing moment. If he had known she had been sleeping in the next room all night, he never would have drifted off. He had to have been more exhausted than even he had realized. For the past five days, ever since Nevil Thomas had died and his quest to kill the wolf had begun, he hadn't had more than a couple of hours' shut-eye each night. Maybe the fact that she was in the next room had allowed him to sleep for nearly ten hours straight. "Define *safe?*"

She nibbled on a piece of bacon and thought before answering. "I know you think Marcus probably trashed his own house, but I don't. Whoever did the vandalism could come back, and maybe just seeing my car parked out front won't stop him from trying something again. Having you camping out on the couch was my first line of defense."

That was a switch. For thirteen years of military service he had played on the offensive team. He was the guy they sent in to solve the problem before it became a defensive matter. Uncle Sam preferred to handle matters before they became of interest to national security and were brought to the public's attention. He didn't like being someone's first line of defense. Laura shouldn't need a defense. She should have been sleeping in some nice, safe motel room. "What was your second line?"

"The Winchester." She gave a small smile and took a sip of coffee. "It was never more than two feet away from me all night."

He raised one eyebrow. "I noticed your *friend* when you answered the door last night." He glanced around the kitchen and spotted the rifle leaning up against the wall.

"I'm not stupid. I know staying here might not be the smartest thing to do, but I don't take chances."

"You don't consider allowing a stranger to sleep on your sofa a chance?" Okay, so he admired the fact that she had at least had the rifle in the bedroom with her last night. She hadn't been as negligent as he had first thought. But if he'd really wanted to do her harm he still could have, rifle or not.

"In your case, no. The odds were in my favor."

"You always play the odds?"

"Scientists always take them into consideration." She finished off her breakfast and reached for an apple.

"You're a scientist, too?" He hadn't thought about what she might do for a living, but a scientist? Hell, she blew every one of his preconceived notions about nerdy scientists dressed in white lab coats and sporting thick glasses.

"Runs in the family. I work in the field of botany and our parents are currently collaborating overseas with other scientists on nuclear fusion."

Lord! A whole family of brain heads. They all had college degrees and a hell of a lot of letters to go after their names. It had to be in the genes. His mother was a high-school dropout who had had to get married, his father a drunk and he had barely graduated from high school. College wasn't an option. His grades weren't good enough for scholarships and his father drank every penny he ever earned. The military seemed like the perfect choice. The U.S. Marines were very happy to have him after they discovered his one-and-only claim to fame. Delaney Thomas was an excellent shot and could handle any firearm they threw at him. Within a year of enlisting, he was handpicked for an elite group of sharpshooters. Uncle Sam and the marines didn't care about college degrees and fancy initials; all they wanted was for him to hit whatever they told him to aim at. He had. The marines became his family and his home. For thirteen years they lived in harmony, respecting each other and mutually obtaining their goals. Until the day four military police knocked on his front door and arrested him for treason. Not only had his military family betrayed him, so had his wife.

"Is Marcus younger or older than you?" asked Delaney. Why brood about the past? There wasn't a thing he could do to change it.

"Younger by three years." She watched as he finished the rest of his meal. "I promised my parents I would take care of him while they were out of the country."

"How old is he? Twenty-six, twenty-seven?" Marcus Kinkaid had to be a full-grown man.

"Twenty-eight."

"So why does he need looking out for?"

"We're family." She stood up and started to clear off the table. "A family takes care of one another."

Delaney leaned back in his chair and released a harsh laugh. That was rich. *A family takes care of one another.* The only one who took care of Delaney Thomas was Delaney Thomas.

Laura frowned at his laughter and glanced at him. Compassion darkened her eyes as she set down the dirty plates and walked over to him. "I'm sorry. That was thoughtless of me to mention my family when you've just lost your father."

He pushed back his chair and stood up. He didn't need or want her pity. He'd lost his father when he was six, not five days ago. The body of the man had been the same, only older. But the man inside had died the same day Delaney's mother had. He detested pity. Pity and a quarter wouldn't get you a cup of coffee. "You've been busy, haven't you?" he sneered.

At the tone of his voice, her shoulders snapped back and her chin rose a fraction of an inch. "Deputy Bylic . . ."

"Deputy Bylic ought to mind his own business." He grabbed his backpack from the living-room floor and his jacket from the chair. Small towns! Lord save him from small towns and gossipy people. Laura probably knew every detail of his life by now, from the treason charge to his divorce. All his dishonor and failures had been spread before her. It was amazing that she'd allowed him into the house, let alone permitted him to sleep on the couch.

"Delaney, I..." Laura spread her hands and followed him into the living room. He continued to pull on his jacket without so much as glancing at her. Very softly she said, "I want to thank you for stopping by and checking on me last night. You don't have to bother anymore. I'll be fine."

He growled something deep in his throat and turned around. "Listen, lady, with your *instincts* you'll probably be dead within a week." He snapped the last snap on his jacket. "Never, and I mean never, allow a strange man to sleep on your sofa again."

"Why? Nothing happened."

The obstinate gleam in her eyes burned a hole in his gut. She would probably go out and invite every strange man she could find to spend the night on her coach just to prove to him she could do as she pleased. He needed to show her the dangers in trusting people and he had just the way.

"This could have happened." In a flash he hauled her into his arms and captured her mouth in a punishing kiss. He wasn't going to be nice. He wasn't going to be gentle. He wanted to show her some men just took what they wanted without asking. And he had wanted to kiss her from the moment he'd spotted the small cut on her lower lip in the police station and watched her worry it with her teeth. His mouth crushed hers beneath his as he buried his fingers in her hair and held her head still.

Laura stiffened in protest as his mouth ground against hers. Her hands pushed against his chest as she tried twisting her head away from his assault.

Delaney felt her struggle and gentled his assault. His hunger was to kiss Laura, not frighten her. He'd figure out another way to show her the error of her ways later. For now he wanted to savor the sweetness he suspected was behind her lips. His tongue slowly traced her lower lip, seductively pleading for entrance. He was rewarded with a gentle moan and the slight parting of her lips. He swept into her mouth and tasted heaven.

Laura's hands ceased their pushing and wrapped around his neck. Her tongue met his every stroke as she opened wider to deepen the kiss. Wave after wave of hot desire crashed through her body, causing her breasts to swell and her nipples to harden. She closed her eyes and welcomed the storm Delaney was generating.

A heavy moan of need vibrated deep within his chest as he clutched Laura's hip and pulled her closer. The gentle curves of her breasts were crushed against his chest and her greedy fingers were pulling him closer. Hot, heavy desire, unlike anything he had ever experienced before, rushed to his groin. His hard arousal bulged against his zipper. He instinctively flexed his hips and rubbed against the softness of her abdomen. His shaft hardened further as she melted against him in a bundle of soft, womanly curves.

He broke the kiss and strung wet, urgent kisses to her ear. His teeth nipped at her ear lobe as he inhaled the seductive fragrance of coconut shampoo and soap.

She jerked her hips into his, silently answering his demand. Laura tilted her head, granting him better access to wherever he wanted to go, and groaned his name. "Delaney."

The sound of his name, whispered with such gripping desire, broke the spell she had woven. What in the hell was he doing? He commanded his body to take a step back. Despair, desire and need tore at his gut when Laura opened her eyes and gazed at him. He could see the need burning deep in her eyes. Green fire flickered and danced within their depths. He wanted that fire more than his next breath, but he couldn't have it. Laura Kinkaid wanted more than a satisfying roll in the bed. She deserved more than he was capable or willing to give.

He never should have kissed her. His punishment had only been self-inflicted. He feared the taste of Laura would haunt him for a long time coming, perhaps for the rest of his life. Delaney took another step back as she moved closer. He needed space, and he needed it now. Huge, mind-numbing space. Laura Kinkaid living in the same state would be too great a temptation. He didn't have a lot left in life except his guide business and his honor. If he gave Laura what her eyes were pleading for, he wouldn't have his honor left. The military hadn't destroyed his honor, but Laura could.

Delaney slowly wiped his hand across his mouth in distaste. "See what could happen when you invite a stranger into your home?" His heart cringed as the green fire in her eyes turned to confusion, then embarrassment. He quickly turned and opened the door. "Remember that. Next time you might not get off so easily."

Laura slowly raised her fingers to her swollen, moist lips as the door slammed behind Delaney. He was lying. She had seen the fire that had burned in his eyes when he'd kissed her. Felt his thick desire behind the barrier of his jeans as it had rubbed up against her. No man could have faked those responses. So why did he stop and pretend the whole experience had been an act to show her how foolish she had been by allowing him to spend the night on the sofa?

Her fingertips could still feel the heat of his kiss. Lord help her, she had never been kissed like that before. Only one word could do Delaney Thomas's kisses justice, and that word she whispered into the now-empty room. "Fireworks."

# Chapter 4

Laura gasped in shock after reading the first entry in Marcus's journal. She had spent the entire morning cleaning up the lab, and had just located the thin leather-bound journal under his desk. It went against her principles of privacy, but she opened the book anyway and started to read. The first entry, written in her brother's scribbly hand, had caused her to reach behind her and grab hold of the chair. Her rear hit the soft pad of the chair as she shook her head in disbelief and reread the entry.

> The dream has been with me since I was seven. Laura, with mischievously sister intent, gave me the dream. I'm sure she only meant to scare the beejee-bees out of me, as older sisters have been doing to younger brothers for centuries. Instead she piqued my curiosity with her hair-raising tales of sharp fangs, hairy faces, full moons and the thirst for blood. Werewolves! Creatures of the night who were neither man nor beast. Could such creatures exist?

Legends about werewolves have been recorded since ancient Rome. Could something that has been recorded through time and in every country be true? There has to be some basis behind the legend. After twenty-two years of dreams, I, Marcus Kinkaid, will try to unlock the door and discover the truth behind the legends. The following pages contain my personal and professional observations.

The sun had been set for hours by the time Laura read the last page and closed the journal. For months her brother had been silently crying out for help, and she had never even heard him. She had been so caught up in her own affairs that she had never even realized Marcus's pain and frustration. For a fleeting moment she wondered if her brother might not have slipped over the edge of reality, but she quickly pushed that thought out of her mind. Marcus was as sane as the next man. He was a man of science, and men of science were known for their passion when it came to their work. Her brother had converted his passion into an obsession. An obsession with werewolves.

Her gaze shot over to the empty cage in the corner of the lab. A shudder slid down her spine as she thought about the wolf her brother had captured and had been using for his experiments. The wolf, whom Marcus had nicknamed XYZ due to its unknown qualities and his dislike for algebra, had become the catalyst of her brother's slip from reality. Five days before Marcus had left the message on her answering machine, XYZ had escaped. For three days her brother had gone without sleep while hunting for the wolf. Without XYZ most of her brother's work was useless. It meant he would have to start all over again, and he wasn't willing to do that.

Marcus had felt he was inches away from a breakthrough. By the time he had called her, the lack of sleep and the frustration had taken their toll. In an irrational act of stupidity, Marcus had compiled all his known data and injected himself with a serum consisting of part

plasma, taken from his own blood, and an enzyme he had
separated from the wolf's red blood cells. The serum
sounded dangerous, if not deadly, to Laura. Whoever
heard of injecting oneself with a component of wolf's
blood?

Laura glanced around the clean lab and pictured how
it was when she'd first walked into it the other night.
Broken glass and vials, counters swept clean and papers
scattered everywhere. Had Marcus caused all the damage? If so, what had happened to her brother? Where was
he? There wasn't any mention in the journal of an assis-
tant or even another colleague knowing about his experiments. Marcus's car was still parked in the garage. So
what had taken place after he injected himself?

With a sense of dread, Laura opened the journal to the
last entry:

It's done! As I write this, the serum is flowing
through my veins. No effects yet, but I'm not expecting instant results. Full moon is scheduled for
tomorrow night. I should know something by then,
maybe sooner. The changes shouldn't be drastic—
the enzyme level was low—but since I'm charting
unknown territory, nothing is black or white. Everything is gray. Who knows, maybe tomorrow night
I'll give Lon Chaney, Jr. a run for his money.

Laura shivered and briskly rubbed her arms through
her thick sweatshirt. Was it possible? Could it be possible? Enzymes, red blood cells and the effects of gravitational pull on the blood system, caused by the full moon,
were out of her league. Her field of specialty was botany
and the wonders Mother Nature grew in her backyard
called the Earth. What could she possibly know about
blood enzymes and werewolves?

The unpainted tip of her fingernail tapped the deep-
brown leather cover of the journal. She now knew what
Marcus had been working on and part of what happened after he had left the message on her machine. So

where was he? She had skimmed the remaining blank pages of the journal, hoping to find a clue. All that greeted her were more empty pages. Marcus hadn't made another journal entry after his sick little joke about Lon Chaney, Jr.

Laura worried her lower lip and increased the rhythm of her tapping. What had the serum done to her brother? He'd obviously gone a little crazy; Marcus would never have trashed his own lab otherwise. But were there any other side effects? Was he ill? Was he lying somewhere dead or near death? Tears filled her eyes and her fingers started to tremble. She forced herself to calm down and to think logically. What was the worst-case scenario? Marcus was lying somewhere dead.

The chair slid backward and banged into the wall behind her as she jumped to her feet. Marcus being dead wasn't the worst-case scenario—achieving what he had been after was. What if he had succeeded? What if the serum actually had changed him into a werewolf? Her thick midnight-black ponytail swished forcefully as Laura shook her head. Impossible! There weren't such things as werewolves!

Laura walked over to the cage, gripped the cold metal bars and stared at the empty space inside. How could Marcus lock up some poor wolf and use it the way he had? Hadn't their grandfather taught them to respect nature and all that was in it? Sure, their grandfather had shown Marcus the thrill of the hunt, but he'd also preached about cruelty and waste. Hunters should kill for only two reasons: food and self-protection. She wearily closed her eyes and leaned her forehead against a bar. The poor wolf!

Her eyes flew open as she spun around. Wolf! Why didn't she see the connection before? Delaney was hunting a wolf, but it couldn't be XYZ. By Marcus's description, XYZ was a young adult male who hadn't reached his full weight. And by Delaney's description, the wolf he was after was black and extremely large, abnormally large.

For a fleeting moment an absurd thought streaked through her mind. Marcus had black hair and would make an extremely large wolf. Impossible! Or was it? The thought of Marcus actually turning into a wolf was insane, but what if the serum he'd injected had affected his mind and he thought he was a wolf? That would explain about the trashed lab and why his car was still in the garage. Marcus was running through the woods, thinking he was a wolf, and Delaney was out to kill him!

Laura's feet flew up the stairs. Without bothering with the lights, she picked up her purse and coat and sprinted for her car. She needed to find Delaney and stop him.

Laura slowly pulled her car up behind Delaney's Jeep and killed the engine. Half an hour ago she had reached the main street of Moosehead Falls, before realizing she didn't know how to contact Delaney. She had stopped in the sheriff's office and caught Sheriff Bennet on his way home. He had told her that Delaney was staking out Fred Zimmerman's sheep ranch, a few miles from town. It had taken her an additional five minutes to wheedle the directions to the ranch out of the sheriff.

She sat in the car and silently studied the farm spread out before her. The neat two-and-a-half-story house was a good distance away. A single porch light was left burning. It was barely ten o'clock at night, but there weren't any lights glowing from within the house. Obviously the Zimmermans were the early-to-bed, early-to-rise type of people. She glanced at the crowded pens surrounding the barn. It appeared Fred Zimmerman had moved his sheep from the pastures into the cramped pens. Probably for their own protection. From what the sheriff had told her, the Zimmermans' sheep had been the victims of quite a few attacks by the wolf. It was understandable why Delaney had chosen this ranch to stake out.

Her glance slid over the pens. Where would she hide if she was on a stakeout for a hungry wolf? The dense woods, a good quarter mile from the barn, were out of the question. The wolf would be coming from there. Being too close to the sheep could alert the wolf to human presence. She scanned the barn. The open hayloft door had the perfect view of the surrounding pens. Delaney couldn't have asked for a better spot. A wolf couldn't get within a hundred yards of the sheep without him noticing. And if Delaney was an expert shot, as the sheriff seemed to think he was, he could shoot and kill the wolf before Zimmerman lost any more sheep. Laura's gut churned with that thought.

With trembling fingers, she reached for the bag of goodies she had stopped to purchase on the way out of town. The small convenience store had been just closing for the night when she had rushed in and procured the last two cups of coffee. She'd also added a couple of donuts and a few chocolate candy bars. The knowledge that she was trying to "sweeten" Delaney up didn't escape her. She knew it was going to take more than a few gooey donuts for her to talk Delaney out of shooting the wolf. At least until she had some more information.

As silently as possible, she got out of the car, closed the door and headed for the barn. Her heart slammed against her chest as she cautiously made her way through the barn. What little light the moon gave was barely enough to outline the equipment scattered throughout the barn. She found the ladder to the hayloft by slamming her shin into it. Suppressing a curse, she gingerly climbed the ladder with one hand, while clutching the bag of goodies with the other. She utterly refused to think about the kiss she and Delaney had shared this morning.

Laura cautiously peeked over the edge of the hayloft and picked out the silhouette of a man sitting by the open loft door. "Delaney?" she whispered into the dark. She was going to feel mighty foolish if the man turned out to be Fred Zimmerman.

"Who else were you expecting?" came rumbling back.

How could the man's voice rumble and still be considered a whisper? Delaney didn't sound none too pleased that she was crashing his stakeout. Taking a deep breath, she asked, "May I come up?" After a moment of thick

silence, she added, "I brought you a hot cup of coffee."
It was only a minor lie. The coffee wasn't hot, at best she
would consider it warm.

"You might as well. Any wolf within a mile would have
heard your car." He turned back toward the opening and
gazed at the pens below. Most of his bulk was hidden
behind a couple of bales of hay so he wouldn't have to
worry about his movements.

Laura made her way into the loft, dodged a couple of
stacks of baled hay and sat near him. She frowned as the
brown paper bag she opened seemed to be making an
unusual amount of noise. Antagonizing Delaney further
wasn't on her agenda. As quietly as possible she pulled
out the two coffees, and handed Delaney one. "Better
drink it up. It's not too hot."

"Why?" He peeled off the white plastic lid and took
a sip.

"Because I bought it in town and by the time I drove
all the way out here, it cooled off some."

"I wasn't asking why it cooled down. I'm asking why
the coffee." He took another sip after searching the
ground below.

"It seemed like the neighborly thing to do, since I was
coming out here anyway. A nice cup of coffee on a nippy
fall night seemed like a good idea to me." She kept her
voice so low that if they hadn't been sitting so close, he
would never have heard her.

Delaney turned away from the door and appeared to
study her in the darkness. "Why the visit?"

Laura quickly dug back into the bag and pulled out the
donuts. "Are you hungry?"

"Laura?" There was a threatening ring to his throaty
whisper.

"All right." She slapped a powdery donut and a napkin into his hand. "If you must know, I'm trying to
sweeten you up."

"Why?"

"Because I have a favor to ask." Her chin rose an inch,
and with the moon sliding out from behind a cloud, she

could make out the thoughtful expression hardening Delaney's jaw. It was going to take more than a fierce scowl to intimidate her. Her brother needed her strength now more than ever. For Marcus she would ask Lucifer himself for a favor.

His gaze bore into hers. Laura was positive he was trying to read her soul. After a moment, he asked, "What's the favor?"

"Don't shoot the wolf." Seeing him jerk back in surprise, she uttered one heartfelt word. "Please."

Delaney turned away from the silent pleading that was in her eyes. The damn moon should have stayed behind the clouds. That way he wouldn't be able to see her eyes. Beautiful, pleading eyes. *Don't shoot the wolf!* He couldn't believed she had asked him that. Of all the favors he could think of for her to ask, that wasn't one of them. It was the one favor he could never grant.

Ten minutes ago when he'd seen her car pull up behind his Jeep he had silently cursed a blue streak. Not only because she had invaded his stakeout, but mainly because of the joy that had sparked through his body at the sight of her. Laura Kinkaid was a complication he didn't need. The kiss they had shared this morning had been a mistake. A big, haunting mistake. It never should have happened, and he never should have allowed one simple kiss to haunt his day.

Curious, despite himself, about why she would request such an outrageous favor, he asked, "Why don't you want me to shoot the wolf?" He didn't turn around to face her. Instead he kept a close eye on the pens below. When she didn't respond he forced himself to glance over his shoulder. A rough moan escaped his throat when he saw her chewing on her lower lip. Visions of what he would like to be doing to that lip tumbled through his mind and desire tightened his gut into one large mass of need. "Laura?"

A film of tears sparkled in her eyes. "I can't tell you why."

That hurt. Laura couldn't tell him why. He turned back toward the night. "Then you can understand why I have to turn down such a request."

Ten minutes went by in strained silence. Delaney stared out into the night. His gaze might be on the sheep pens below, but his mind was on the woman sitting beside him. He could feel her frustration, but he refused to ask her again why she didn't want the wolf killed. As far as he was concerned, once was enough. He was dying of curiosity about why she would request such a favor. Wasn't she in Moosehead Falls to search for her brother? How could the wolf possibly figure in with her purpose? As far as he knew, the only connection between the wolf and the absent brother were the tracks he had found outside of Marcus's house.

Laura was the first to break the silence with a tentative whisper. "Have you ever heard of lycanthropy?"

"Lycan-what?"

"Lycanthropy. It's the ability to assume the form and the characteristics of a wolf." Her fingers nervously folded and refolded a paper napkin.

Delaney finally turned away from the opening and stared at her. *To assume the form of a wolf?* "What in the hell are you talking about?" The moon had slid behind a cloud again and he couldn't read the expression on her face.

"You might know it better if I used the word *werewolf.*"

He felt his jaw drop open in astonishment. Why hadn't he picked up on the fact that Laura was obviously marching to a different drummer, one on another planet? "You think the wolf I'm after is a werewolf?"

"I think the *presumed* wolf might be my brother."

She had the face of an angel, a body constructed for sin and a mind like Swiss cheese, full of holes. He sadly shook his head at the waste. "I'm sorry, Laura, there is no *presumed* wolf. I saw it. The wolf is real and a danger."

The fragile napkin ripped within her fingers. He could see that her shoulders had slumped and her head leaned wearily against the bale of hay behind her. For some reason the wolf seemed awfully important to her. "I arrived at my father's cabin just in time to watch him suffer a heart attack and die. He was outside by a small pen where he kept a couple of sheep. He was shouting and firing his shotgun into the surrounding woods. By the time I reached him he was on the ground, losing his battle with death and muttering something about a wolf and his sheep."

"I'm sorry, Delaney." Her hand came out and covered his tight fist, which rested on his thigh.

He could feel the warmth of her fingers against his hand. For some reason, that simple gesture gave him comfort. "When I looked up the wolf was standing at the edge of the woods with a dead sheep at its feet. I picked up my father's shotgun and fired. If the gun hadn't been so neglected through the years I would have killed the wolf then, but the shot went wide and the wolf escaped into the woods." He pulled his hand away from her warmth. "I have to kill the wolf, Laura. I promised my father I would." He turned back toward the opening and slowly shook his head. He couldn't understand why he had told Laura about the day his father had died. The only one he had related the story to was Doc Wyman in Moosehead Falls.

"Tell me more about what the wolf looks like. Was there anything different or strange about it—besides its size?"

"He's *unusually* large." Delaney gave a quiet sigh as he surveyed the moonlit pens below. Everything looked peaceful. "He's also a loner. Most wolves travel in packs."

"I've heard of 'lone wolves' before."

"Lone wolves are wolves that have left the pack, either because they are no longer the dominant male or they never were. A lone wolf will travel alone until he finds a mate, and if they have pups they will start a new pack of their own." Delaney shook his head. "Believe me, this fellow would have been the dominant male."

"Maybe you missed seeing the signs of the rest of the pack?"

Delaney looked over at her as if she had lost her mind, which he was afraid she had. "I make my living by tracking and hunting game. If there was a pack of wolves roaming this area I would have seen the signs."

"Did you see any unusual signs?"

"What do you mean by 'unusual'?" If she mentioned a werewolf again he was afraid he would have to drive her into town and drop her off at either Doc Wyman's or the sheriff's office.

"Human signs. Like someone was out in the woods."

"I don't think there's a place left in America where there aren't any signs of human existence. Everywhere you look you can spot litter, old campsites or the destruction of the forest by greedy lumber companies who don't realize that it takes them five minutes to cut down what it took Mother Nature a hundred years to grow."

"I have to agree with you there." She gave him a sad little smile. "But I was wondering if you'd noticed any signs of one particular human who might be a little confused? Disoriented?"

"Marcus?"

"Yes."

Delaney stared at her for a long time before turning back to the pens below. She didn't seem deranged or even halfway demented. She looked like a sister who was very concerned about her brother's welfare. "Want to tell me why you think your brother would be running through the woods confused?" A harsh chuckle rumbled in his chest. "And what in the hell gave you the idea that your brother could be a werewolf?" That was one explanation he was dying to hear. The way his life was going lately, he could use a good joke. Werewolves in Minnesota! Next thing he knew there would be hunting parties tramping through the woods searching for Bigfoot.

Laura took the two candy bars from the bag and re-filled it with the empty coffee cups and napkins. She handed one of the bars to Delaney. "I was cleaning up the lab today and found his journal." She broke off a piece of chocolate from her bar and popped it into her mouth. "I'm a firm believer in privacy, but with what happened at his house and his disappearance, I needed to know what he had been working on."

"Which was?"

"Lycanthropy. My brother was trying to prove scien-tifically that lycanthropy is possible."

Delaney dropped all pretenses of looking out at the sheep. "You're kidding." If the wolf got anywhere near them they would cause a ruckus. He needn't be watch-ing over them constantly.

"I wish I were." Laura toyed with her candy-bar wrapper. "It's all my fault."

"What is?"

"The fact that Marcus was studying werewolves."

"You believe in werewolves?"

"No, of course not," snapped Laura, barely keeping her voice low.

"Now I'm the one confused." Delaney shifted his po-sition to a more comfortable one. It looked as though it would be a long night. "First you think your brother is a werewolf, or running around the woods confused. Next you tell me you don't believe in werewolves. Now you say it's all your fault." He stretched his legs out in front of him. "Care to explain?"

"When we were little I used to try to scare Marcus with tales of ghosts, vampires and, yes, werewolves. It was just some sisterly prank. Marcus was a quiet, studious little guy. He was always bringing home straight *A*s on his re-port card, had his nose buried in some book or conduct-ing some experiment. I had been hoping to loosen him up a little bit. Instead he seemed to love the tales, so I con-tinued to indulge him by reading everything I could find on the 'strange and unusual' and proceeded to make up scarier stories for him."

"Did you believe the tales you were telling?"

"No. I don't believe in ghosts, vampires or even were-wolves. They are childish tales and that was where I left them, in our childhood." Laura rewrapped her candy bar and sat it on the bale of hay next to her. "At least I thought we had."

"Marcus obviously had other ideas."

"When he moved here he had enough saved up to live on for over a year. He decided to explore and experiment on one of his secret dreams—proving the existence of werewolves. Over the years he had read everything he could find on the subject and knew where to start."

"How does one prove a myth?" Visions of the empty once-used cage in the corner of Marcus's lab filled his mind. His gut was telling him what animal had been locked up behind those cold metal bars—a wolf.

"A lot of what Marcus had written was too technical for me to fully understand, but I got the gist of what he was doing. Have you ever heard about the connection between the full moon and human behavior?"

"If you are referring to popular belief that if it's a full moon the loonies will be out, then yes."

"I wouldn't put it quite that way, but yes. It's a documented fact that there are more accidents, births and sick human behavior during a full moon. Marcus believed he could explain these phenomenons. He theorized that the moon's gravitational pull affects our flow of blood. Fifty-five to sixty percent of our blood is plasma, which carries our red and white blood cells along with platelets. Plasma is made up mostly of water and the gravitational pull from the moon affects the flow by slowing it down. This, he theorized, slows down and reduces the number of red blood cells, which in turn reduces not only the amount of oxygen delivered, but decreases the amount of carbon dioxide removed from the body's tissues. Hence, the strange phenomena in human behavior during a full moon."

Delaney sat there for a moment and thought. "Sounds reasonable to me." He took a bite out of his candy bar. "What's all this got to do with werewolves?"

"Most legends have it that werewolves appear during a full moon."

"And can only be killed with a silver bullet."

"I'll ignore that comment." Laura stretched out her legs and rubbed the cramping in her calves. "Marcus theorized that werewolves, or people suffering from lycanthropy, actually have an unknown blood disease. I'm not certain of the technical end, but it centers around a certain enzyme found in wolf's blood and not human. One of the beliefs is that you can only become a werewolf if you are bitten by a werewolf. This could explain the rare transference of the disease from animal to human. It has to be a blood-to-blood contact. Anyway, when the gravitational pull slows the plasma flow, this enzyme reacts, causing the person to feel that he is going through a metamorphosis of some kind—most likely that of a wolf or large canine. This explains why the person takes on the characteristics and mannerisms of a wolf."

"I'm sorry, Laura, but the animal I saw was a real wolf, not some person thinking he was one." The light from the moon bathed her face. He could see the concern and fatigue etched around her sparkling green eyes. Eyes a man could drown in if he wasn't careful. He glanced away from her face and ended up swallowing a groan as he encountered her long, shapely legs, which were spread out before her. "Was your brother ever bitten by a wolf?"

"Not that I'm aware of."

"Then why would you think he was running around the woods acting like a wolf?" All of Marcus's theories sounded reasonable to him, except he didn't believe that people who had blood-to-blood contact with a wolf would take on the manners of the animal. People who made contact might contract a disease, but not lycanthropy. Not for one minute did he believe in werewolves or any other monster that went bump in the night.

Laura entwined her fingers and started to twist them into knots. "Marcus had captured a young male wolf and was holding him in the cage in the lab. He used the animal to run some experiments on."

"Nice guy," Delaney muttered in disgust.

"I don't approve of what he did to the wolf, either, so let's leave it at that." She crossed her ankles and shifted her bottom on the straw-covered floor. "Five days before Marcus tried to reach me, the wolf escaped. He did try to recapture the animal, but failed. By the time he called me he was severely depressed and was contemplating doing something irrational. I didn't know what until I read his journal this morning."

Delaney's gut was telling him he wasn't going to like the answer to his next question. "What did your brother do, Laura?"

"He took some of his own plasma and mixed it with the enzyme he'd extracted from the wolf's red blood cells and injected it into his arm."

"Sweet Mary! You're *not* kidding, are you."

"Do you honestly believe I would be here if I wasn't so concerned for my brother's well-being?"

She didn't have to make it sound as though he were the last person on earth she would go to for help. After this morning's incident he could see her point. Hell, he wouldn't want to come to him, either. But he was the one man who might be able to help her locate her brother. "I'm sorry, Laura, but there weren't any signs surrounding your brother's house or anywhere else to indicate that a man was wandering the woods lost, confused or totally deranged."

"Nothing?"

"Nothing."

"And the wolf you are after?"

"Is just a wolf, Laura. Nothing more." A strange, huge, terrifying wolf, but a wolf just the same. "I suggest you call the nearest hospitals to see if Marcus has been admitted." He didn't know what effect injecting oneself with a wolf's enzyme would have, but it didn't sound too healthy to him.

"I've already done that. I also called every colleague in his phone book I could reach. No one has seen or heard from him in months." She brushed away a tear that had escaped the pool clouding her vision and gave a delicate sniffle.

"I hate to be the one to break this to you, but I think you already know it, Laura. It sounds like your brother has a serious mental problem."

She shook her head and wiped the back of her hand across her eyes. "I don't believe that. I can't believe that."

Delaney was about to answer, when the hysterical sounds of baaing erupted in the farthest pen. He immediately swung around and aimed his rifle in one fluid motion. The only movement he could detect was the panicky shifting of the sheep in the pens. By now the sheep in the other pens were all fussing and the moon had slipped behind another cloud, leaving the pens in total darkness. Delaney cursed his luck and ignored Laura, who had risen to her knees beside him.

As the moon slipped out from behind the cloud the animals calmed back down. He couldn't detect anything wrong or out of place. Everything looked peaceful and quiet. Whatever had frightened the sheep was now gone. Maybe it was nothing.

"Is it the wolf?" whispered Laura a few inches from his ear. Her gaze was skimming the area below.

The warm breath of her words sent a shiver down his spine. She was so close he could feel her warmth and smell the elusive scent that was hers and hers alone. "Whatever it was, it's gone now."

"Didn't you see anything?"

"Nothing." He continued to watch below as Laura moved away. He had noticed the way her fingers had trembled against the hay. The night had gone from being chilly to downright cold. "There's a sleeping bag and a blanket over there." He nodded to his right. "Why don't you wrap up and get warm? Unless you're ready to leave now."

"I'm not leaving." She found the rolled-up sleeping bag and unzipped it.

He really should insist that she leave now, but he couldn't. The idea of her going back to Marcus's house alone and in the dead of night disturbed him. She was probably staying so that in case the wolf did show up she could scare it off before he had a chance to shoot the animal. It had nothing to do with him personally. "Why don't you roll up in the sleeping bag and I'll take the blanket?"

Laura handed him the thick blanket before kicking off her boots and sliding into the sleeping bag. "Why so nice?"

"Last night you let me sleep on your couch and gave me a nice blanket to keep warm. Tonight I'll return the favor."

"A hard barn floor, the aroma of manure and hay sticking me in places I'm too much of a lady to mention?"

Delaney softly chuckled. "At least the sleeping bag is insulated and guaranteed to thirty below." He didn't turn around to watch her slip in between the soft thickness of his sleeping bag. He had had the bag for the past five years. It went everywhere with him. He had spent almost as many nights sleeping in it as in his own bed. There was something extremely personal about Laura using it. He wrapped the blanket around his shoulders and continued to watch below. The sheep were once again silent and the night was nothing more than the night.

Ten minutes later Laura softly asked, "Delaney, what if he did it?"

He didn't have to ask who or what. He had been thinking along the same lines. What if Marcus had found a way to become a werewolf? Not a physical wolf, but real live human being thinking he was a wolf. "Go to sleep, Laura." He couldn't answer her, because to answer was to admit there might be some truth behind her fears.

Half an hour later he turned around and leaned against the bales of hay. His legs were killing him and the sheep would alert him to any danger. He stretched out his legs and studied the woman sleeping not four feet away. Laura. The faint moonlight streaking its way in through the open hayloft door highlighted her pale face and her midnight-black hair, which spread out across his sleeping bag. The delicate sweep of her jaw and the seductive pout pulling at her lower lip warmed his body better than the thick blanket wrapped around his shoulders. He could tell that her lower lip was darker than the top, caused by her habit of chewing on it when worried—and Marcus had given her a lot to worry about these past couple of days. Delaney knew that endearing habit of hers was going to be his downfall. The more she worried, the more he wanted to kiss the hurt away.

He shook his head and forced himself to look away from Laura. She and her unseen, certifiable brother were trouble, and he didn't need any more misery in his life. He had had enough trouble to last a lifetime. What he needed now was to fulfill his promise to his father and kill the wolf. He should have sent Laura packing hours ago. It wasn't his problem that she would have to return to an empty house. He hadn't invited her. He didn't want her here. Her presence only reminded him more clearly of the kiss they had shared that morning. A kiss that should never have happened.

With a quick shove he moved two bales of hay a couple of inches away from the doorway. He now had a halfway decent view of the pens below without squatting all night. He let his eyes slowly lower as he listened to the night sounds. Peaceful, tranquil sounds of the night. Sounds he had been listening to all his life.

Delaney gently shook Laura's shoulder. "Time to get up, sleepyhead." He refused to examine the tender feelings that had washed over him when he'd come awake five minutes ago and spotted her sleeping next to his legs. What he needed to do was to send her on her way home and get back to tracking the wolf.

"Hmm . . ." She buried her nose deeper into the sleeping bag.

"Come on, Laura, time to get up." The sun hadn't risen yet, but the skies were turning a dull gray. Within minutes the farm would be waking, and he wanted to be gone by then. Explaining to Fred Zimmerman how Laura had come to spend the night with him in the barn wasn't in his plans.

"What time is it?" Laura stretched her arms above her head and yawned.

"Time for you to head home." He folded his blanket and started to gather up the rest of his stuff.

Laura unzipped the bag and shivered. "Lord, it's cold." She jammed her feet into her boots and started to roll up the bag. "What I wouldn't do for a cup of hot coffee."

For one split second Delaney was tempted to see exactly what she would do for a cup of hot coffee but caught himself in time. He was supposed to be sending her home and away from him, not fantasizing about caffeine and silky skin. He picked up the sleeping bag and headed for the loft ladder. "Sorry, no time this morning."

She followed him down the ladder and out of the barn. The skies were turning from a dark gray to a lighter gray, even as she watched. Her gaze turned eastward as she searched for the sun.

He turned around and saw that she had stopped and was staring off into the distance. "Let's get moving, Laura." The temptation to run his fingers through her hair or to kiss her awake was growing stronger every instant.

Laura continued to walk. Right on past him. She headed for her car but came to a sudden stop by the front of his Jeep. Her hand flew up to her mouth as she whirled around toward Delaney.

He saw her reaction and came sprinting up to the front of the Jeep. He'd seen what she had seen and instinctively pulled her into his arms and buried her face in the front of his coat. There on the ground not two feet in front of his Jeep was a sheep. A dead sheep. A river of blood coated the thick, woolly, once-white fleece. It was a sick, horrendous killing, and it wasn't done by a human. He was experienced enough to see that from where he was standing.

The sheep had been killed by an animal, and his guess was a wolf. A big wolf. Delaney's gut burned. The wolf had been here last night and was crafty enough to have pulled this off right under his nose. He silently upgraded the wolf's intelligence. But it left another disturbing problem.

The wolf hadn't killed for food. That could only mean one thing. It had killed for the pleasure. That was unheard of. Wolves didn't kill for pleasure; they killed to eat or to protect themselves or their young. And the sheep obviously wasn't any threat to the wolf or to its young.

The burning in his gut turned into a fiery inferno. No normal wolf would have killed for the pleasure. Something wasn't right. Something was very, very wrong. "Come on, Laura, we'll use your car." He opened the passenger door to her vehicle and gently pushed her in.

Without thinking, she handed him her keys. "Where are we going?"

"To Marcus's house. I want to read that journal."

# Chapter 5

Cooking breakfast for Delaney was beginning to feel like a habit. For the second day in a row she was standing over the stove, cooking the man breakfast. This morning she'd decided on pancakes instead of bacon and eggs. Werewolves might not be real, but cholesterol was. She glanced over her shoulder into the living room. Delaney hadn't moved from the chair since he had sat down over half an hour ago with Marcus's journal.

She gave the three fluffy pancakes in the pan a quick turn. While he had been busily reading she had made a pot of coffee, downed two cups and taken a shower. She knew exactly what Delaney was reading and what he must be feeling—total disbelief. The only difference in Delaney's doubt and hers was that they disbelieved two separate things. Delaney was probably having a difficult time with the actual process her brother had been experimenting with. To the layman, a lot of what Marcus had been doing seemed impossible. To her, it was the fact that it was her baby brother doing the experimenting that had caused the disbelief. Sweet, lovable Marcus injecting himself with wolf enzymes was a lot to swallow. Especially with the guilt hanging over her head. She was the reason her baby brother had become fascinated with the subject of lycanthropy in the first place, and that lay heavy on her mind as well as her heart.

She willed the tears not to fall. Crying wouldn't help Marcus. Right now her best chance at helping her brother was the man in the other room. Delaney knew about wolves. She knew about Marcus. Hopefully between the two of them they could unravel the mystery and find her brother. All she needed was Delaney's cooperation. If cooking the man breakfast until Marcus was found was Delaney's price, then she would do it.

She had just finished setting the table, when Delaney walked into the room and dropped the journal onto his plate. The loud thud threatened to splash the orange juice, which she had just poured, over the top of his glass. She watched as the juice swished from side to side before settling back down. Not one drop was spilled.

"Is all that stuff true?" Delaney frowned at the perfectly set table before sitting down and helping himself to the stack of pancakes piled in the center of the table.

"I really don't know." Laura placed two pancakes on her plate and poured strawberry sauce over them. "Marcus is a very competent scientist. He has the ability and apparently the equipment to separate certain enzymes from red blood cells."

"So it is possible?"

Laura almost chuckled at the look of horror spreading over Delaney's face. Someone would think he had just learned Dr. Frankenstein had been experimenting in the lab below them. If it wasn't for the fact that it was her brother's health, if not life, at stake, she would have laughed. "Scientists have been isolating enzymes since 1926 and have been creating synthetic ones since the late sixties. All enzymes are protein molecules that speed up chemical reactions in all plants and animals. Without enzymes these reactions would occur too slowly or not at all and life wouldn't be possible. Doctors use the enzymes in our blood and other body fluids to diagnose diseases. Without enzymes we wouldn't be here. They are part of our bodies.''

''And the wolf?''

She chewed a mouthful of pancakes before answering. ''I would guess the same would hold true for any animal or living thing.''

''So it's possible that your brother did separate a certain enzyme from the wolf's red blood cells?''

''I believe Marcus separated *something* from the red blood cells. If it was the enzyme that causes a chemical reaction that could make a human think he was a wolf, I don't know.''

Delaney ate his breakfast in silence for a moment. ''Wouldn't this enzyme harm Marcus?''

Laura worried her lower lip and pushed a hunk of pancake around her plate. She'd just lost her appetite. Talking about enzymes and cells was one thing; talking about Marcus injecting himself was another. ''I don't know.'' She shook her head and continued to stare at her plate. She didn't want Delaney to see the tears that had resurfaced. Emotion would only be considered a sign of weakness in Delaney's eyes. ''First, I'm not positive it *was* an enzyme Marcus managed to separate—we only have his word on that. The second question I must ask myself is, if it *was* an enzyme, what was its function? Each enzyme performs one specific job—what this particular enzyme does, I don't know.''

''Who would?''

''Marcus.'' She got up and scraped the remaining breakfast off her plate into the garbage. ''I didn't find anything in the lab that I could take to another biochemist and have analyzed. Whoever trashed the lab destroyed all the samples.''

''So we only have Marcus's word that he injected himself with wolf enzymes?''

''No, you have my word Marcus injected himself with what *he believed* was a wolf enzyme.'' She placed her plate in the dishwasher and started to load in the frying pan and mixing bowl with more force than was necessary. "If Marcus said he injected himself, then he injected himself. This isn't some type of hoax."

"I didn't say it was." Delaney got up and placed his empty plate in the dishwasher. He closed the door of the machine and leaned his hip against the counter. "Listen, Laura, you have to see it from my point of view."

She jammed her hands on her hips and glared. "And that is?"

"Marcus's journal reads like a Bram Stroker or a Mary Shelley novel."

"That's it, Delaney, make fun of what you don't understand. People have been doing it since the beginning of time. I'm sure people reading about the first organ transplant compared the doctors with Frankenstein. Now it's hailed almost as a common operation."

"Do you honestly believe what your brother has written?"

Laura's chest heaved with indignity. How dared Delaney judge and convict her brother on his own ignorance? "Most of what Marcus has written is theory. Don't you understand the difference between theory and fact?"

"And you agree with this theory?" Delaney's voice rose a decibel in disbelief.

"A theory is an assumption based on accepted principles and rules," Laura shouted. She walked over to the bay window overlooking the backyard and forced herself to take deep calming breaths. Arguing with Delaney wasn't going to find Marcus. After a moment she turned around and faced Delaney. He appeared to be thoughtful and somewhat regretful that their discussion had become a shouting match. In a composed voice she said, "Marcus stated his assumptions and all the rules and principles that supported his theory in a logical and scientific manner."

"So you believe him?"

Laura's trembling fingers gripped the back of one of the wooden kitchen chairs. Delaney had just asked the question that had been burning a hole in her stomach since she'd read the journal. *Did she believe Marcus?* How could she not? He was her brother. "If you are asking me if I can disprove his theory, then no, I cannot. Everything he has written supports his theory and is based on scientific fact. As far as I know, Marcus's theory is correct."

Delaney tilted his head and studied the woman halfway across the room. "You honestly believe your brother has turned himself into a werewolf?"

She didn't want to answer that. How could she without appearing as crazy as Marcus? "Do you have a younger brother?"

"No."

"An older one?" At the shake of his head she asked, "Any siblings at all?"

"No, I was an only child. What does my having brothers and sisters have to do with this?"

Flat, to-the-point answers without a hint as to how he felt about it. Laura sighed. How was she going to appeal to sibling love, when he was an only child? "Marcus is my brother, Delaney. Do you understand the closeness between us, the bond, the love?"

"I understand about the responsibilities that come with a family."

"I'm not talking about responsibilities, Delaney. I'm talking about love, unconditional love." At his look of disgust, she dropped the subject. Obviously her and Delaney's upbringing were worlds apart. "There's only one person who could prove or disprove Marcus's theory, and he's missing." Turbulent tears filled her eyes. "The enzymes are flowing through his blood, causing Lord knows what kind of chemical reactions."

"He caused it all himself, Laura."

"That doesn't mean he doesn't need my help." She blinked rapidly and forced the tears to retreat. "So what's our next step?"

*"Our?"*

"Yes, our, as in you and me, *we.*" She gave Delaney a smile that would have spoken volumes if he had paid attention. There was no way she was letting him walk out that door without her. Delaney knew how to track that wolf, and she wanted that wolf. "We're a team now."

"Since when?"

"Since we have a common goal—the wolf."

"No, no and double no. You are not coming with me and that's final."

"Why not?"

Delaney paced to the end of the hallway and back again. The idea of Laura trekking through the woods with him, hunting the wolf, was ridiculous. If the thought of her returning last night to an empty house had sent chills down his spine, what would he do if she was face-to-face with a wolf? "It's too dangerous."

"I'm willing to take the risk."

"Well, I'm not." He turned away from the delight-fully stubborn tilt of her chin. Laura was showing her gumption again. Just once he would love to see her confront someone else besides him.

"If you don't allow me to come with you, I promise I'll follow you through the entire state of Minnesota." She crossed her arms and tapped her foot. "And I promise that every animal within a mile of me will know I'm there."

Exasperated, he ran his fingers through his hair. "I thought you didn't want me to hunt the wolf."

"To hunt the wolf is one thing, to kill it is another." She jerked her head toward the basement door. "There's a tranquilizer rifle in the lab."

"You want me to tranquilize it?"

"No, I can handle the rifle. I want you to track it for me."

"Listen, Laura, I admire your gumption and your sis-terly concern for your brother, but the wolf is just a wolf. A dangerous, livestock-killing wolf."

"Are you sure?" She tilted up her chin and glared. "Are you one hundred percent absolutely positive that there is nothing unusual about this wolf? Are you certain there are no *what ifs* playing in the back of your mind? Can you take that chance?''

Delaney frowned and walked to the windows overlooking the backyard. The morning sun had broken through the clouds and another beautiful crisp fall day had arrived. The day was at complete opposites with his mood. How could he not have questions about the wolf's uniqueness? The cunning the animal had displayed last night alone should give him pause. The wolf had crept right under his nose, killed a sheep and then deposited it directly in front of his Jeep, raising only a few hysterical baas from the surrounding sheep. Cries he had dismissed as unimportant. That quality alone set the wolf in a category all its own. The fact that the wolf had killed for the sheer pleasure was terrifying. It the wolf killed a sheep just for the enjoyment, what would he do to a man? Contrary to what most people believe, wolves avoided people as much as possible. At least healthy ones did. This one appeared physically healthy; it was the wolf's mental health that had him concerned. The sooner he located the animal, the better.

Delaney studied Laura's reflection in the glass without turning around. If body language could talk, hers was shouting. Laura was not going to let him go wandering off into the woods after the wolf alone, at least not without a fight. She had the right to be worried about Marcus. If he had a brother who'd pulled such a stupid stunt, he'd be worried, too. But that didn't mean there was a connection between the wolf he was hunting and Laura's brother. The *what if* game wasn't clouding his judgment. He had seen the uncertainty in Laura's eyes when he'd asked if she believed in werewolves. There was a part of Laura who believed, no matter if she wanted to or not.

He couldn't chance Laura following him into the woods and possibly confronting the wolf alone. He trusted her and her ability to use a rifle—it was the wolf he didn't trust. The animal was unpredictable, and that made him deadly. He sighed heavily and continued to stare at her reflection. "There are a couple of conditions."

"Such as?"

"I'm the boss. When I say stop, you stop. If I say jump, you ask how high."

Laura glared at the back of his head. "What else?"

"You complain or slow me down, I'll drop you off at the nearest ranch or house." He turned around and locked gazes with her. "If for whatever reason I deem it necessary to shoot the wolf, instead of you using the tranquilizer gun, I will."

"Couldn't we discuss it?"

"Out there—" he jerked his head to the woods outside "—when the situation warrants an animal's death, there usually isn't any time for a discussion. My judgment is final. Take it, or track the wolf yourself."

He hadn't realized how anxious he was about her answer until she slowly nodded and said, "Deal."

"You go put together a backpack while I take a shower." He walked into the living room and picked up his pack before heading for the bathroom. "Make sure you include some food, warm clothes and a sleeping bag." He opened the bathroom door. "There's a good chance we won't make it back tonight."

He closed the door behind him, leaving Laura to wonder what exactly she had gotten herself into.

Hours later Laura didn't have to wonder any longer what she had gotten herself into; she knew. Pure hell. Her shoulders and back were killing her from the unaccustomed weight of the pack. Her thighs burned and her feet ached with every step she took. Years of sitting around in the lab had taken their toll. The specimens her work required didn't take a lot of physical energy to obtain. She usually parked her car off the nearest road, then took a gentle stroll through the woods until she spotted the specimens she needed. There was nothing gentle or stroll-like in Delaney's pace.

The man moved with grace and silence. His bulky hiking boots looked about as elegant as hers, yet when he walked, barely a crisp fall leaf crumbled beneath him. She tried to follow in his footsteps, yet when she walked it sounded as if an eight-headed Hydra were strolling through the woods while munching on potato chips.

Lunch had been a quiet affair. Delaney didn't seem to be in the mood for talking, and she wasn't going to annoy him with a bunch of chitchat. They weren't that far from their starting point, the Zimmermans' ranch. The wolf seemed to be playing games with them. Delaney had picked the trail up immediately. First the wolf led them around the entire ranch, then north and then south. By the time Delaney had called a break for lunch they had been approximately a mile from where they'd parked her car, but they had managed to walk a good twelve miles.

Now the wolf was leading them in a northeasterly direction, and all uphill. How could hills just have an up side? Didn't they come equipped with a down side any longer? The Zimmerman ranch was miles behind them, and so was the memory of lunch. Laura shifted the strap of the Winchester, which was digging into her left shoulder. Delaney had insisted that she take the rifle along with the tranquilizer gun. Be Prepared was not only the Boy Scouts' motto; it was also Delaney's. He had inspected her sleeping bag, her clothes, even the food she had packed. When he had taken the canned goods from her pack and replaced them with soft packaged food from his pack, she had started to complain. He very bluntly pointed out that since it was her idea to tranquilize the wolf, she had the honor of carrying two rifles.

Laura brushed wispy damp curls away from her face and tried to tug them behind her ear. The temperature was somewhere around the low fifties, but it felt like summer in Florida. The sun was starting to set. Within half an hour it was going to be dark and she hadn't any idea where they were. This part of Minnesota was as foreign to her as the Amazon, and for the first time she started to realize just how isolated she and Delaney were.

At that thought, she was momentarily distracted from concentrating on where she was going, and she stepped on a dry twig. The sharp crack of the twig breaking sounded like a gunshot echoing through the woods. Laura held her breath and waited for Delaney to lecture her.

He didn't. Instead he knelt and studied a partial imprint of a wolf's paw in the dirt. She watched as he stood up to assess the wolf's path deeper into the woods with his gaze. A moment later he surprised her by heading off in an entirely different direction. She shifted her backpack, suppressed a groan as the straps dug deeper into her shoulders and as silently as possible followed Delaney into the gathering dusk.

Ten minutes later her feet hit a dirt road that apparently Delaney had been heading for. He continued down the road for a few yards before realizing she had stopped in the middle of the road behind him. "We're almost there," he called.

Laura stared at the road in disbelief. Only one thought flashed through her numb mind: *if there was a road, they could have driven here instead of hiking the twenty miles.* The sound of Delaney's voice brought her out of her daze. He talked to her; the great hunter had spoken. It was a hell of a shame that she had missed what he'd said. "What did you say?"

"I said, we're almost there."

She didn't like the way he was staring at her. It looked as if he were expecting her to fall flat on her face in the middle of the road. She frowned at the ruts and rocks scattered throughout the road. She'd take that back, it was a path at best, but a four-wheel-drive Jeep could have made it to where they were standing with no problems. At his concerned expression, she straightened her shoulders and raised her chin an extra inch. "May I ask what *there* is?" Laura cringed as her little-used voice contained a rough quality, but she forced her feet to start walking again. She didn't care where they were headed, as long as she could finally sit down, it sounded like heaven to her.

"Around the next bend in the road is a small one-room cabin."

If he had told her a hotel was around the bend, she wouldn't have been happier. A one-room cabin sounded like luxury to her. "Does anyone live there?"

"Not any longer."

"Will the owner object if we use it for the night?" She caught up to Delaney and matched him stride for stride.

"No, I won't object."

Laura's feet faulted, only for a second. She quickly resumed her pace. "You own the cabin?"

"I guess." He didn't meet her searching look. "It was my father's, so I guess now it's mine."

"I'm sorry."

"You just might be," Delaney said with a grin, "after you see it. There's no running water, the outhouse out back is minus the door and the roof leaks."

Maybe she'd been a tad hasty in comparing it to a hotel. "What about heat?"

"The potbelly stove's in decent shape and there's a good supply of firewood already cut. Plus there's a shortwave radio so we can check in with the sheriff to see if he has any word on your brother."

Laura rounded the bend in the so-called road, and stifled her groan. It looked worse than Delaney had described it.

"Oh, I forgot. It leans to the right."

Leans to the right! The leaning tower of Pisa would be green with envy if it ever saw this cabin. She cautiously eyed the tilting structure. Maybe it was the approaching darkness that made the little cabin appear so dilapidated. "Is it safe?"

Delaney walked up to the front door, turned the knob and gave it a mighty shove. "The front door sticks just a little, but besides that it's safe."

Laura peered into the semidark room. The notion that one-room cabins were quaint evaporated with her glance. With a weary sigh she shrugged out of her pack and entered the cabin. She counted five metal pots sitting around the room, filled with rainwater from the other night. A small twin bed was positioned crookedly against the back wall, so when it rained the leaks missed the mattress by mere inches. A scarred oak bureau stood near the bed. The potbelly stove was against the far wall and an oak rocker, with a quilt thrown over its back, sat directly in front of it. A small wooden table with only one chair was in front of the only window overlooking what should have been the front yard, instead the area was taken up with an empty pen. Two cabinets and some shelves were nailed haphazardly to the wall. An assortment of cups, plates and canned goods vied for space.

The cabin wasn't filthy. There were no spider webs, rodents or even dirty dishes lying around. But it didn't conjure up any picture of a home she'd ever seen. How could Delaney allow his father to live in such a place? She watched as Delaney lit a kerosene lamp and started a blazing fire in the stove. He obviously knew his way around the cabin. By the time the fire was burning merrily there were only a few sticks of wood left in the box near the stove. "Want me to go bring in some more wood?" Near the cabin had been a huge pile of firewood already stacked and split for winter.

Delaney glanced out the window and frowned at the darkness. "No, I'll get it." He closed the stove door, brushed his palms on his jeans and stood up. "Why don't you see what we have to heat up for dinner?" He reached up on the shelf and pulled down an old, dented coffeepot. "I'll bring in some water. There's a pump on the other side of the cabin."

A chill slid down her spine as he picked up his rifle and left the cabin. Delaney didn't trust the wolf. That was why he didn't want her going back outside, not because he wanted someone to cook his meals. He was trying to protect her. Laura didn't quite know what to do with the feelings that assaulted her. On the one hand she was aggravated that he'd pulled such a macho number. She knew how to protect herself and didn't need any hairy-chested man to do it for her. On the other hand she thought it was sweet of Delaney to be concerned. Of course it was going to prove to be interesting when she had to pay a visit to the "little girl's room" out back later.

Laura reached down for Delaney's backpack and nearly pulled a hernia lifting it to the table in front of the window. How did the man manage to hike all day with that strapped to his back? She had been lucky to lift it the three feet off the ground and onto the table. If someone had strapped it to her back she would have fallen over backward and never gotten up. She would have lain on the floor with her legs and arms wildly kicking in the air like some heavy-shelled bug. Her mouth turned upward at the mental picture that thought created, as she undid the tie and opened Delaney's pack. She pulled out the two heaviest cans, read the identical labels and went searching for a pot. They were having chili tonight.

Delaney came in, placed two metal buckets filled with clean water by the stove and set the coffeepot on top of the stove. He glanced at the pot of chili Laura had just started to heat and without saying a word went back outside. Three minutes later he returned with his arms filled with firewood and dumped it into the box.

While Laura busied herself preparing dinner, Delaney emptied the filled rainwater pots and carefully positioned the now-empty pots in the exact location from which he had taken them. After glancing around the cabin to make sure everything was in order, he went over to the shortwave radio and called the sheriff's office. Sheriff Bennet had gone home for the night, but he managed to have a static-filled conversation with Deputy Bylic. No word on Marcus Kinkaid. The sheriff had gone out to Marcus's house twice during the day. No one was there and it was still locked up tight. There were no reports of any wolf incidents since this morning out at the Zimmermans'. Everything appeared quiet. Delaney signed off after telling the deputy where he or Laura could be reached for the remainder of the night.

Delaney sat on the kitchen chair and watched Laura as she put together a decent meal from various ingredients in their packs. She had surprised him more than once today. If he was honest with himself, he would have to say she did more than surprise him—she astonished him. Not one complaint tumbled from her seductive mouth. From the pace he had set, she had every right to complain. He told himself he needed to set the killer pace so he could capture or kill the wolf. The sooner the animal was disposed of, the safer the area would be. But he was afraid the pace had been set to test Laura. He needed to know exactly how far her gumption went. His bet with himself had been that she wouldn't last till lunch. By the time the sun had started to set, he had been beyond surprised and into admiration. That was why, instead of following the wolf until it became too dark to see and then set up camp, he'd headed for the cabin. He had expected Laura would start to crumble as soon as she saw the dilapidated cabin; instead she pushed up the sleeves of what had to be her brother's flannel shirt and started cooking a meal. The scene before him could have been taken straight out of "Little House on the Prairie" if not for her jeans and baggy shirt.

The golden glow from the kerosene lamps illuminated the cabin with soft light, giving everything a gentler, muted appearance. What was he to do now? He had expected Laura to be ranting and raving about the hike, the cabin, the food and especially the outhouse. He would have been able to handle the bitching. He preferred it over this capable, efficient, likable woman who was preparing his dinner. There wasn't a woman he knew who would have gone through what Laura had endured today and not gripe. His ex-wife wouldn't have made it around the Zimmerman ranch, let alone the other eighteen miles. Kathleen's idea of hiking had been having to park more than three parking spaces away from the doors of a mall.

The fatigue etched around Laura's eyes and mouth pulled at his conscience. "What can I do to help?"

"Nothing, it's ready." Laura took the pot of bubbling chili and poured some into two mismatched bowls she had found. A package of crackers, from her pack, was already sitting on the table, along with two cans of fruit juice. The pot of coffee was still brewing on the stove. She handed Delaney his bowl before sitting down in the rocking chair she had pulled up to the table.

Delaney took a mouthful of chili before saying, "Sorry, there's no word on your brother yet." She looked as if something were bothering her.

"I heard." She stirred her dinner around in the bowl for a minute. "What did the sheriff say this morning when you told him I was accompanying you on the hunt?"

*Ahhh, so that's what was bothering her.* This morning before they'd left Marcus's house, he had called the sheriff and reported the incident at the Zimmerman ranch. He had also told the sheriff that Laura would be joining the hunt and to please check on the house during the day. "Don't worry, your reputation is intact. The sheriff doesn't gossip."

"I wasn't worried about my reputation," Laura said with a sigh. "I'm more interested in what you may have told him concerning Marcus's theories."

"If you mean whether I told him about your brother's aspiration of becoming a werewolf, then no. I didn't tell the sheriff anything other than you would be joining me." She was more concerned about her brother's standing as a scientist than her own reputation. Here she was in the middle of nowhere, spending the night with a virtual stranger, and all she could worry about was what people would think if they learned her precious brother had more than a few screws loose. He shook his head at the seeming absurdity of the situation and went back to eating his dinner.

An hour later Laura glanced around the cabin in search of something that could be used as another bed. There wasn't anything. The dinner dishes were washed and put away. They had split a can of peaches for dessert and re-

the perfect position and reflected Delaney's magnificent naked upper body directly back at her. She told herself to do the decent thing and look away from the mirror, but she couldn't.

Never had she seen such grace, such strength, in a male body. His shoulders were wider than she'd suspected, and the way the muscles flexed with his every movement caused a slow burning of desire deep within her body. She watched, entranced, as the beige washcloth rubbed and scrubbed a film of small white bubbles across his golden skin. He abruptly disappeared from view, only to return to wipe the bubbles away.

She couldn't see him give the same sensual treatment to his lower body, but she could imagine, and visualize she did. By the time Delaney was dressed and his bathwater had joined hers, she was hot, flustered and excited. She was also appalled at her own behavior. She was a mature woman of thirty-one, not some nineteen-year-old drooling after a rock star. What she needed was some perspective and a good night's sleep.

Ten minutes later she allowed Delaney to win their argument out of shear exhaustion. She would take the bed, and he would sleep on the floor. The man had a stubborn streak wider than the Mississippi. She turned off the kerosene lamp on top of the bureau, dropped her jeans onto the end of the bed and crawled into her soft, warm sleeping bag. Laura tried to ignore the sounds of Delaney undressing and crawling into his sleeping bag after he had turned off the other kerosene lamp. The only light illuminating the cabin came from the open grate of the potbelly stove. A warm red light burned within.

Laura curled up on her side and felt her muscles finally relax. With a sleepy yawn, she called, "'Night, Delaney."

"'Night" came floating out of the darkness. Within minutes she was sound asleep.

Laura battled her way out of the dream as her blood chilled in her veins. With a strangled cry she tried to sit up, but her sleeping bag was twisted around her like a knot. She fought desperately against the material. At first she thought it was a dream that had awakened her from such a sound sleep; then she realized it wasn't. Her nightmare was on the other side of the cabin door and it was trying to get in.

Delaney's arms closed around her protectively just as a wolf's haunting cry split the night again.

# Chapter 6

Delaney whispered a soft "Shhh . . . it's me" in her ear before helping her by unzipping the sleeping bag. His arms came back around her trembling shoulders. The downy flannel of the shirt she had worn to bed felt warm against his palms and the silky length of her hair brushed against the back of his hands. It was too dark to see her face. "You're safe." When the wolf's unearthly howls had awoken him a moment ago, his first thought had been for Laura. She had barely started to struggle with her sleeping bag, when he'd reached her side.

"He's outside the door!" Laura cried as her gaze frantically searched the dark cabin.

"No, he's not, Laura." He let his hands fall away from her slender shoulders. "Out here in the woods sounds carry, especially at night."

She pulled her legs out of the sleeping bag and stood up. "Where's the tranquilizer gun?" She squinted into the darkness and headed for the area next to the front door where she had last seen the weapon.

Delaney's gaze followed the pale silhouette of her long bare legs as she moved across the cabin. A groan rum-

bled in his throat, a man could climb those limbs and find
heaven. He was pulled from his fanciful wandering by
another eerie howl. Damn! This gaze shot to the front
window. It did sound as if the damn wolf were sitting
under the window. In all his years of growing up in Minnesota, living at his lodge or traveling the world wherever Uncle Sam sent him, he had never heard such a wail.
The hair on the back of his neck was standing straight up
and chills slipped up his spine, causing his hands to
tremble.

Laura came to a dead stop in the middle of the cabin
as the howl penetrated the building's thin walls. She instinctively wrapped her arms around herself, and started
to rock. "Is he in pain?"

"I don't know," murmured Delaney as he got up and
joined her. "I've heard nearly a hundred wolves howl in
my life—one had even been caught in a leg trap—and
none of them ever sounded like that." He picked up the
quilt off the back of the rocker and draped it around her
shoulders.

"Shouldn't we go out and see if he's caught in a trap
or something?" Her hands went up to cover her ears as
another cry split the night.

"Too dangerous." He pulled the rocker closer to the
stove and gently pushed Laura into it. Without saying a
word, he opened the stove's door and started to pile on
more wood. The red embers burst into a glowing light as
the new wood caught. The cabin lit sufficiently for him
to see.

He moved away from Laura and pulled on his shirt and
boots. He had only managed to yank on a pair jeans
when the wolf had awoken him earlier. Now he finished
dressing and reached for his coat.

"Where are you going?" Laura demanded.

"I'm just going to check around the cabin." He rum-
maged through his backpack and pulled out a flashlight.

"I thought you said it was too dangerous."

"It's too risky to go tracking the wolf at night, even if
I could find a trail to follow. A wolf's senses are far su-

perior to man's. I'm just going out front to see if there's anything out of the ordinary.'' There were a hell of a lot of things out of the ordinary where this wolf was concerned. The beam of the flashlight played along his rifle as he made sure it was loaded and ready.

"Take the tranquilizer gun."

"No, Laura." He stood up and walked to the door. "We agreed to use the tranquilizer if the circumstances allowed. The middle of the night isn't one of those times." He gripped the doorknob as he glanced over his shoulder at her. He could see the stubborn tilt of her chin, and fire from the stove reflected in her gaze. She looked mad as hell, yet so soft and appealing with the patchwork quilt wrapped around her. Her black cloud of hair was tousled from sleep, and the pair of white socks covering her feet looked warm. It was the shapely calves peeking out from under the quilt that made his voice rougher than he had intended. "Whatever happens, don't come outside." He opened the door and stepped out into the night.

Laura sat there and rocked. Who in the hell did he think he was, tossing orders around? *Whatever happens, don't come outside.* What was he expecting to happen? Wasn't he the one who said that sounds carry out here, and that the wolf wasn't near the cabin? If that was true, why did he need to go outside to investigate? She jumped to her feet and raced over to her pack. After locating her flashlight, she made sure both her rifle and the tranquilizer gun were loaded. If Delaney got himself into trouble or ran into something bigger than he could handle alone, she was ready.

She cautiously made her way over to the window, and keeping her body from view, she peered out into the night. It took a minute to locate Delaney's flashlight playing along the ground. He seemed to be searching for tracks. Occasionally the powerful beam shot off into the surrounding woods as he made his way back toward the cabin. She couldn't detect anything out of the ordinary, but she'd noticed the wolf had stopped howling as soon as Delaney had stepped outside. Was that a good sign or bad?

Delaney opened the cabin door and stepped inside. The beam from his flashlight shot to the empty rocker in front of the stove. "Laura?"

"Over here." She continued to stare out into the darkness. The moon was waning, but there still should be enough light to pick up any movement across the yard. "See anything?"

He closed the door and lowered his rifle. The beam from his flashlight cut a streak of light through the dark room. "Nothing." He slipped out of his coat and hung it on the peg on back of the door. "No tracks or any other signs."

"Did you notice how he stopped howling as soon as you left the cabin?" She left the window and ignored Delaney's scowl when she placed the rifles back where she had had them.

"What were you planning to do with them?" The beam of light shone directly on the rifles, leaving her in no doubt about what he was referring to.

"Back you up in case you needed help." She shivered and wrapped the quilt tighter around her. He didn't have to sound so upset about it. Maybe what she should have done was spend the last heart-pounding minutes pulling on a pair of jeans and boots, possibly brushing her hair, instead of looking out for him. Imagine the scandal that would have caused. *Notorious tracker saved from savage wolf by female botanist wearing nothing other than a borrowed flannel shirt and thick cotton socks!* Laura was positive he would rather have the headline read *Notorious tracker gnawed to death by savage wolf while obedient, immaculately dressed female stands helplessly by.*

"I thought I told you to stay in the cabin."

"Did you see me outside?" She dropped the quilt back over the rocker and stomped over to the bed. Men! How in God's name could they be so thickheaded at times?

"Don't get smart."

"Don't get stupid." She pulled back the top of her sleeping bag and climbed inside.

Delaney growled her name in exasperation. "Laura..."

"Listen, Delaney. I didn't disobey your order." She gave the zipper a forceful yank and lay down. "All I did was make sure I was ready in case you needed me. Partners do that for each other." She brushed her hair out of her face and stared up at the ceiling.

"We're not partners," Delaney replied with a sigh as he clicked off the flashlight and started to undress.

"What are we then?" They weren't friends. They weren't lovers. All they were, were two different people in search of one answer—the wolf. To her way of thinking, that made them partners.

"I'm a tracker hunting a wolf. You are being allowed to tag along as long as you obey my rules." He settled down into his sleeping bag and gave a deep sigh. "That in no way makes us partners."

Laura smiled and snuggled deeper into the warmth of her sleeping bag. A "tag along," was she? Who did Delaney think he was fooling? She had heard the horror in his voice when she'd suggested they were partners. Delaney was a loner. If it made him feel safer being the one in charge, then fine, she'd allow him to think that until the wolf was caught. She would just have to be more careful on how she backed him up in the future. Delaney was her only chance at finding the wolf. "'Night."

"Try to get some sleep." Delaney gave a huge yawn. "Tomorrow is going to be another long day."

The crackle of the burning wood inside the stove was the only sound she could detect. Delaney's presence must have scared the wolf off, or he had gotten tired of baying at the moon. How could she even consider that horrible howling had been her brother? She just didn't know anymore. This morning she had been positive that Marcus was connected to the wolf; now, after hearing it for herself, she didn't know what to think. Her only hope was to capture the wolf alive. And Delaney was her best chance. Who better to catch a lone wolf than another lone wolf?

Delaney sat on the wooden fence that had once held his father's half a dozen or so sheep and slowly drank his coffee. The sun was just starting to rise, but everything was still bathed in twilight. It was his favorite time of the day. His rifle leaned against the toe of his boot as he surveyed the surrounding woods. How could this morning be so peaceful, when only hours before, in the dead of the night, it had been so eerie and quiet. He had never heard quiet like that before in his life. It had seemed as though the entire forest had been holding its breath and waiting. Waiting for what he wasn't sure, but his gut instinct was telling him it had had something to do with the wolf.

Last night when he'd returned to the cabin, he hadn't told Laura the entire truth. It was true that he hadn't seen anything outside the cabin—no animals and no tracks. But he had felt it. The wolf had been watching him. He would have bet the lodge on it. For one crazy moment last night he wondered, who had been tracking whom? The wolf seemed to be playing a game with him. He knew it was impossible; wolves didn't have the intelligence to mentally play games with mankind. Their existence was based on survival. They hunted, they mated; their social structure was formed around the pack, and they avoided humans. So why was this one particular wolf different? Was this wolf connected in any way to Marcus Kinkaid and his weird experiments? At first he had thought the wolf might be the escaped XYZ, but Marcus had described him as a young gray male, possibly not fully grown. The wolf he was hunting was large, black and probably a male, due to his size.

Delaney wished he had had the foresight to bring along Marcus's journal. When he had read it at Laura's he had only taken the time to skim through it and get the general idea. Most of the technical data had been completely over his head. But he wanted to review it again. Laura seemed convinced there was a connection. At first he had scoffed at the very idea of a werewolf, but after last night, Laura may have been on the right track. Not that there were any such things as werewolves, but the wolf might be connected to Marcus's work. It seemed like too big a coincidence that this ferocious, intelligent wolf had appeared in the area at the same time Kinkaid was playing Dr. Frankenstein in his lab. He didn't believe in coincidence. He also didn't believe in partners.

Delaney downed the rest of his coffee and took a last look around. The morning sounds of the forest turned his scowl into a small, fleeting smile. He could hear a couple of birds and the faint rustling of dried leaves as squirrels and chipmunks did some last-minute hoarding of food for the long winter to come. Time was a-wasting. It was turning light enough to follow any trail the wolf might have left and Laura wasn't even up yet.

He picked up his rifle and headed for the cabin. He had hoped the smell of freshly brewed coffee would have awakened her earlier. Yesterday's hike had been grueling, and with the wolf rousing them in the middle of the night, he hadn't had the heart to disturb her sleep. Besides, she had looked like an angel all curled up in her dark-green sleeping bag. So he had taken the first cup of coffee outside to greet the day in solitude. Just as he had done every day since returning to Minnesota. Just as he would do for the rest of his life. Alone, just him and the sunrise.

Delaney closed the cabin door with a bang and then suppressed a chuckle when Laura didn't even flinch. He slammed an empty pot onto the stove and started to pour in water for oatmeal. "Come on, sleepyhead. It's rise-and-shine time." He turned his back on Laura and grinned as she told him exactly what he could do with his rise and shine. So, she wasn't totally an angel in the morning.

"Coffee's ready when you are." He poured himself his second cup and continued to fix breakfast. Oatmeal, canned grapefruit sections and hot coffee. It wasn't as fancy as the meals Laura had cooked for them, but it was nutritious and filling.

Laura grumbled something incoherent, pulled on her jeans and jammed her feet into her boots. Without saying a word, she yanked her towel off a nail in the wall and left the cabin.

Delaney stood at the window and watched as she headed for the outhouse and pump out back. His glance slid to the rifles propped against the wall near the door. She had left without her gun. His glance shot to something else she had forgotten—her coat, hanging on the back of the door. With the brisk wind blowing and the temperature well into the low thirties, she wouldn't be long. His instincts told him the danger from last night had passed. The wolf had moved on, and so had the danger.

Last night when he'd returned to the cabin he had been shaken by the silence and the scent of evil that had penetrated the forest. When he'd spotted Laura, armed and ready to jump to his defense, he had momentarily lost his composure, something he had been doing regularly around her. The thought of Laura walking outside and confronting that evil had scared the hell out of him and he had taken it out on her. He owed her an apology, but if he did that, she would probably get it into her stubborn head that she could disobey his orders anytime she pleased. He couldn't risk her safety on a simple apology.

He had just finished pouring her a cup of coffee, when she came in through the door and hurried to the stove. "Lord, it's cold out there." Laura held her hands out toward the warmth radiating from the stove.

Delaney noticed the wet sheen to her face and hands. She must have stopped at the pump and splashed water onto her face. "I had warm water in here, if you wanted to wash up."

"I wanted to wake up, not wash up." She reached for the hot cup he was holding out to her, as if it contained life. "Thanks." A smile broke across her flushed face.

"You're welcome." He quickly turned away from her beautiful smile and nodded toward the table. "Breakfast, such as it is, is ready." Without waiting for her, he sat down and started in on his oatmeal.

Forty minutes later they were standing on top of a distant hill. Delaney knelt and closely examined the imprints in the dirt. "He was here last night." His fingers carefully removed a couple of brown leaves that had blown onto a track.

Laura tried not to step on anything that appeared to be a track, but it was nearly impossible. There were too many. The entire top of the barren hill was covered in tracks. They headed one way, then another. Most appeared to go in circles. "There's a pack, isn't there?"

"No, these are all made by the same wolf. The wolf we've been tracking." He stood up and scrutinized the tracks. "He was alone."

"He was pacing?" She frowned at the number of imprints. Even with four legs, it had to have taken him hours to make this many tracks. "Was this where he was when he was howling?"

"Probably. I didn't see any signs of him near the cabin." He glanced down, over the trees, to the sheltered valley below. His father's cabin was in clear view for anyone, or anything, standing here. If the wolf had been sitting on this hill when he'd emerged from the cabin last night, it couldn't have failed to spot him. With the light from his flashlight highlighting him, the wolf could have watched his every move. It was a chilling thought. So he hadn't imagined being watched last night. In all likelihood, he had been.

"I wonder why he didn't go down to the cabin."

"He most likely knew there wasn't any livestock down there to eat." The day after his father had died, Delaney had given away the few sheep his father had.

"He didn't eat the sheep he killed at the Zimmermans'."

Delaney scowled at that innocent statement. Laura had
no idea how much that killing worried him. It was un-
natural for a wolf to kill in that manner. "No, he didn't,
did he." He flexed his shoulders as the weight of his
backpack shifted, and headed down the far side of the
hill. "Come on," he growled, "we're wasting daylight."

If Laura felt tired yesterday, it was nothing compared
with how she was feeling now. It was only midafter-
noon, with a couple of hours of daylight left, and she was
ready to drop. She didn't know who was worse, Delaney
or the wolf. Delaney had barely taken a break for lunch.
That is, if someone could call sitting on an insect-infested
log, munching on granola bars and downing a can of
warm apple juice, lunch. His pace through the woods
after the hastily eaten meal should have broken world
records. She wouldn't be surprised to learn they had
crossed over into Wisconsin. The wolf was just as bad.
Didn't the animal sleep?

She leaned against a tree and silently watched as Delaney examined the ground. Was the man part blood-
hound? How could he spot the occasional imprint, let
alone track the creature, mile after mile? If Delaney
hadn't stopped once in a while or casually pointed to an
imprint, she never would have known they were still on
the trail. She followed as he stood up and finished
climbing the hill they had been going up the past twenty
minutes. She was so busy placing one foot in front of the
other as quietly as possible that she failed to notice when
Delaney halted directly in front of her. She walked right
into his backpack.

Delaney grunted, then muttered a curse that sent a
flood of red up her cheeks.

"Well, I'm sorry I bumped into you," Laura hissed,
"but you don't have to be so nasty about it."

He turned around and smiled sheepishly. "That wasn't
directed toward you, Laura." He pointed down the other
side of the hill at a peaceful-looking log cabin nestled in
a serene valley. He picked out a few enclosed pastures for

livestock, a barn and a sparkling creek. "The tracks head in that direction."

"Oh . . ." She shielded her eyes against the lowering sun, but couldn't detect any movement from below. "Do you think he stopped for lunch?"

"Let's hope not." He headed down the hill, with Laura hot on his heels.

Ten minutes later, their question was answered. As they cleared the woods they spotted a man and a woman in one of the pastures. The woman was obviously pregnant and upset. She was leaning against a post, crying her eyes out. The man was walking from sheep carcass to bloody sheep carcass, ranting and raving and waving his rifle in the air.

"It looks like we're too late," whispered Laura as the two people finally saw them crossing a field. The man stopped shouting, walked over to the woman and put his arm around her shoulders. Laura noticed that he didn't put down the gun. Her gaze swept the enclosed pasture. A dozen once-white sheep lay bloodied and dead. Not a one had been left alive. What name of wolf was this that had slaughtered an entire flock of helpless sheep? Laura glanced away from the horror and concentrated on the couple. Both appeared to be in their mid to late twenties.

Delaney walked to within a couple of yards of the couple and stared at the shotgun the man was holding. "We didn't hear any shots."

"Good God, man! Do you think I did this to my own sheep?"

"No, I was hoping you got off a couple rounds at the wolf."

"A wolf!" cried the woman. "Was that what did this?"

"You didn't see anything? Hear anything?" Delaney stepped into the pasture and slowly walked from sheep to sheep.

"We just got back from town. My wife had a doctor's appointment this morning and we made a day of it." The man stared at Delaney. "How do you know it was a wolf?"

"I've been tracking it for almost a week now." Delaney nodded to the hill they had just descended. "We've been following its trail all morning and it led directly here." He rubbed the back of his neck and surveyed the picturesque valley. "Any other animals killed?"

"No, we only had the sheep," sobbed the woman. "I'm a weaver and I use their wool in most of my work." She brushed the back of her hand across her eyes and then held it out. "I'm Melinda Spelling, and this is my husband, Frank."

Laura took the trembling hand and gave it a slight squeeze. "I'm Laura Kinkaid, and that's Delaney Thomas." She nodded in the direction he had just turned. "I wish we could have met under more pleasant circumstances." Melinda Spelling looked pale and ready to faint. Laura shot a glance at her huge stomach and cringed. This excitement couldn't be good for her or the baby.

"You two hunters?" asked Frank.

"No, Delaney's a tracker who's working closely with the sheriff's department in Moosehead Falls. I'm a 'tag along.'" She felt Delaney's gaze but ignored him. After all, he was the one who'd given her that name. She glanced at Melinda's large stomach again and then gave Frank a meaningful look. "How about if I take Melinda inside and fix her a nice cup of tea?"

Frank turned around and looked at his wife as if for the first time. "Oh, I'm sorry, honey." His arms went around her and pulled her against his chest. "You should be inside resting." He took her hand and started to lead her out of the pasture. "Come on . . ."

Laura stepped in front of him. "I'll take care of Melinda. Why don't you stay here." She nodded to Delaney, who was still examining the sheep. "I'm sure you and Delaney have a lot to discuss."

Frank frowned, clearly torn between his wife and the horrible scene behind him.

"Go on, Frank, I'll be fine," Melinda assured her husband. "We'll have coffee made when you're ready to come in." She gave the terrible scene before her one last glance before turning and slowly making her way to the log cabin.

Laura silently walked beside her, not knowing quite what to say. The standard "I'm sorry" seemed inadequate after the horrible slaughter that had taken place. She stepped up onto the porch and eyed the two rocking chairs and an old wooden wheelbarrow filled with hay, pumpkins and an assortment of gourds. It was a homey sight, so unlike the sterile entrance into her own apartment. A wooden door complete with a peephole and a brass number twelve, a long beige hallway with brown carpeting showing its wear, greeted any visitor who came to call. It was depressing. Now that she had a couple of bucks to rub together she should consider buying her own house. Someplace she could sit and watch Mother Nature and the sunset. Someplace like this peaceful little valley. Laura glanced over at the pasture one last time and watched as Delaney and Frank Spelling examined one of the sheep. Maybe "peaceful" was the wrong word to describe the valley today. The wolf had taken that adjective away.

"Make yourself at home while I put on some water," Melinda said as she stepped into the house.

Laura dropped her backpack on the porch before following her into the kitchen. "How about you sit down and tell me where everything is?" Laura looked around the beautifully decorated room. Pine floors and cabinets, white appliances and countertops, and a splash of cobalt blue everywhere.

Melinda slowly lowered her bulk onto a chair. "Thanks, my stomach is too queasy for me to think about being hospitable."

Laura filled the tea kettle and set it on a burner. "That's completely understandable." She eyed the coffee maker for a moment before turning to Melinda. "When's the little one due?"

Melinda's hand protectively caressed her abdomen. "In four weeks." She glanced out the window at the empty barn. "We heard about the wolf on the radio a couple of days ago, but he was reported to be north of Moosehead Falls. We're a good twenty miles east."

"Wolves can cover a large territory in a short amount of time." Laura located the filters and a can of coffee and started the machine. Most of Melinda's color seemed to have returned to her face. She took that as a good sign. "This wolf in particular likes to move around."

"Have you been tracking wolves a long time?"

"This is my first." She set out two cups and dropped a tea bag in each.

Melinda stood up and took a couple of bags of fancy cookies from a cabinet. She reached for a plate and started to arrange the cookies neatly. "If you don't mind me saying so, you don't look like any tracker I've ever seen. Mr. Thomas does, but not you."

"I'm not a tracker. As Delaney has pointed out to me, I'm only a 'tag along.'" Laura poured the boiling water into the cups and carried them over to the table.

Melinda placed the cookies on the table and sat back down. "What in the world would make you want to tag along on a wolf hunt?"

Laura frowned as she located the sugar bowl and some teaspoons. "Let's just say I'm very interested in this particular wolf."

"Has it killed like this before?"

Melinda's gaze went to the window again and Laura was glad to see the pasture wasn't in view. She didn't know what Delaney and Frank were going to do with the dead sheep, but she knew they couldn't be allowed to just lie there. "He's killed a sheep here, a sheep there, but never an entire flock before."

"Why did he kill them like that?" Melinda's eyes filled with tears. "They weren't any threat to him."

Laura shrugged and reached around for a tissue sitting in the box behind her. She handed Melinda the tissue. It was definitely time for a change in conversation.

Not only wasn't the talk about the wolf and what had just happened good for Melinda, but she herself was reluctant to discuss the creature. Having a theory about a werewolf was one thing; openly discussing it was another. Laura wasn't ready for the men in the white coats to come for her yet. Delaney was the only person who might—and it was a very big might—understand the connection between the wolf and her brother. "How long have you and Frank lived here?" The cabin appeared to be brand-new.

"We bought the land about two years back, but we only moved in about fourteen months ago." She glanced around the room with pride and love shining in her eyes. "We designed it ourselves and did most of the interior work. We wanted to start our family out here with nature." She idly fingered the spoon next to her tea. "I guess we didn't realize how cruel nature could be at times."

"There are a lot of concerns you have to face when living way out here." Laura noticed the look of despair clouding Melinda's face and hastily added, "Everyone has to deal with the problems of living, Melinda. People in large cities have problems, too. They're just a set of different problems—that's all." She picked up a cookie and smiled. "You just have to decide which problems you're willing to cope with and live with them." She took a bite out of the cookie. "For what it's worth, I think you and Frank made a very good choice."

"You do?"

"Absolutely. Don't let what has happened today ruin what you have. It's as unfortunate as it is unusual. Delaney will know more on the subject, but from what I've learned about wolves, they try to avoid humans as much as possible. They sometimes do kill livestock, but it's always for food."

"But this wolf didn't eat the sheep."

"I know. That's why Delaney is tracking this particular creature. It's dangerous and unpredictable."

"Will it come back?"

"I don't think so." She patted the other woman's hand. "You don't have any livestock left and I'm sure Delaney will capture it soon. From now on, though, listen to the radio, and when they have reports of threatening animals in the area, take extra precautions until the danger has passed."

Melinda gave her a watery smile. "Thanks for understanding so well."

"You're welcome. Now, drink your tea before it gets cold."

An hour later Delaney and Frank walked into the kitchen. Both looked filthy and exhausted. The stench of smoke and burned wool followed them into the room. Laura knew what they had done with the dead sheep without even asking. By the look of sadness on Melinda's face, she knew, too.

Frank bent and brushed a light kiss on Melinda's cheek. "You feeling better?"

"I'm fine, honey." She smiled at Delaney. "There's coffee made, and—" she pushed the cookie plate toward the men "—some cookies." A frowned pulled at her forehead as she glanced at the clock on the kitchen wall. "It's going to be dark soon. Why don't you stay for dinner?"

"Thanks for the invitation, but we have to be getting back to town," Delaney said. "Your husband has agreed to give us a ride to where we left our car, ma'am."

"Don't worry, hon, I'm not leaving you here." Frank gave her shoulder a light squeeze. "I figured tonight would be a perfect time to stop in at Blanche's and get that spaghetti dinner you've been craving."

"Would you two like to join us?" Melinda asked. "Blanche's has the best Italian food in northern Minnesota."

"I'm sorry, we can't," Delaney answered.

"I'll go clean up," Frank said. "Help yourself to some coffee, Delaney." He smiled gently at his wife. "See if you can find him something a little more filling than those fancy cookies you like so much."

Melinda gave her husband a silly smirk as he left the room and headed for the shower.

Delaney opened the back hatch of Frank's Bronco and hauled out his and Laura's backpacks. "Thanks again for the ride, Frank." He watched as Laura thanked Melinda before getting out of the vehicle. "If you're looking to replace those sheep, check with Zimmerman here." He nodded to the farmhouse on the other side of the barn. His and Laura's cars were still parked where they had picked up the wolf's trail the other day. Night had fallen and once again Zimmerman had crammed all his sheep in the two pens closest to the barn.

"Are you sure you can't join us? I would like to repay you for all your help this afternoon. I'm afraid I was a little lost when it came to handling a situation like that."

"You did just fine." Delaney handed Laura her pack as she joined him. "Remember, if you do replace the flock, keep them in the barn at night and when you're not around, until you hear the wolf has been taken care of."

Frank gave both Delaney and Laura his thanks again before driving off.

Laura tossed her pack into the back seat of her car. "Where do you want me to meet you tomorrow morning?"

"I'll be leaving from my place at first light. If you want to tag along you'll have to spend the night up at my place. I'm not waiting around for you to show up."

"Where's your place?"

"About thirty miles northeast of Pelican Lake, on Crane Lake." For the first time he realized how little Laura knew about him. "I own a hunting and fishing lodge."

"You do?"

"Why so surprised?" He was amused by the look on her face. "What did you think I do for a living, track wolves?"

"No, I don't think anyone tracks wolves for a living. They happen to be an endangered species."

"In Minnesota, they are only classed as an threatened species. But no one could make a living out of it. There aren't many left."

"What do you hunt?"

"I usually don't do any of the hunting. I'm a guide for rich city slickers who want to try their hand at deer, black bear and moose."

"And you can make a living at this?"

"You'd be surprised what some men will pay to have a set of moose antlers hanging on their wall." He tossed his pack into the back of his Jeep. "If you want to come, fine. I'm sure there's an extra room and plenty of hot water, and George Whitecloud could make dirt edible."

"You have a cook?"

"The lodge has a cook, two other full-time guides, housekeeping staff, a pilot and plane and, as of today, around seven guests."

Laura climbed in her car. "It sounds like you have more people there than the entire town of Moosehead Falls." She turned the key in the ignition. "If there's someplace I could do a load of laundry, count me in."

"Just follow me." Delaney got into his Jeep and started to drive away without glancing back to see if Laura was following. Why in the hell had he told her about the staff? He didn't want to impress her or anyone else for that matter, but it had rankled a little when she had thought all he did with his days was track wolves through the forest. For one fleeting instant, vanity had reared its ugly head and he'd wanted to prove to Laura he was a man of some means. That instant never should have happened.

## Chapter 7

Laura fought with the steering wheel of her car as she tried to keep up with the red taillights ahead. *Just follow me!* It was easier said than done. Delaney was driving a four-wheel-drive Jeep built for these pothole-encrusted roads and hills, while her nice American-made little compact seemed to be engineered for short hauls to the corner grocery store for milk. Following Delaney through the forests, into the valleys and over the hills of northern Minnesota should be an Olympic sport. She deserved a medal for just keeping his taillights in view. A scenic drive it wasn't. Everything was pitch-black and her headlights barely pierced the darkness in front of her. Once in a while she did catch a twinkling of light off in a distance. It was just enough to let her know she and the red taillights in front of her weren't alone in the world. Moosehead Falls was a thriving metropolis compared with this section of the state. This was where Delaney lived?

He had surprised her when he had announced that he owned a hunting and fishing lodge. But now that she had had time to reflect on his choice of vocations, it made perfect sense to her. Delaney blended in with nature. It wasn't just his rugged clothes or his physical strength that gave him this appearance of merging with nature. It had to do more with the way he moved. The stillness that encircled him even while hiking mile after mile. Not for the first time did she wonder if Delaney had Indian blood flowing through his veins. He moved with the grace and agility of a jungle cat on the prowl, even with a sixty-pound pack strapped to his back. He seemed perfectly at home in the middle of nowhere, surrounded by miles of forest and hundreds of animals, including one very dangerous wolf.

Laura frowned as she momentarily lost the taillights in front of her when Delaney disappeared around a curve in the road. She didn't know what to think about the wolf any longer. The very idea that her sweet, lovable younger brother and this vicious, senseless killer were one and the same was appalling. At first, when the theory of werewolves had come to light, it had been a monstrous idea. After reviewing the facts, she had no recourse but to swallow Marcus's theories. They had been presented extremely well, and there were tons of medical and scientific data to back them up. Theories were one thing, actual facts were another.

She believed Marcus had injected himself with this wolf enzyme; if her brother had written it in his journal, then he had done it. She could even entertain the idea that some type of physical change in Marcus had occurred. How much of one, she wasn't sure. Delaney swore that when he had seen the wolf, it was a standard, everyday wolf, except for its size. But Delaney had been standing over his father's body at the time. To her way of thinking, Delaney's mind hadn't been in the best of shape to judge the wolf or anything else at that time. The very idea of losing her father brought tears to her eyes and this horrid lump to her throat. She couldn't conceive what Delaney must have felt watching his father suffer a heart attack, knowing there was nothing he could do to save him. If it had been she, dancing pink elephants could have been preforming a ballet in front of her, and she probably would have sworn they were flamingos drinking tea.

Delaney's visual contact with the wolf was questionable. The haunting cries from last night had been real. They both had heard them, and it had sounded like a wolf baying at the moon. But men had been known to imitate animal cries before. Her own grandfather could cup his hands together and sound remarkably like a moose. As a small boy, Marcus used to practice making all kinds of animal calls with their grandfather. He could probably make a convincing wolf howl if given the chance and motivation. Believing himself to be wolf classified as a lot of motivation to her.

The paw prints were another story. She had seen the imprints with her own eyes. She might not be an expert on tracking, but they looked like wolf prints to her. There was no possible way Marcus could be leaving those imprints. They came from an animal, not a man. So if Marcus was the one making them, he was not a man pretending to be a wolf—he was a wolf. A wolf who went around viciously killing baby-faced woolly sheep. That was the hardest thing to accept.

Laura followed Delaney off the main road and onto a paved drive leading straight up the side of a hill. A mile later she pulled in behind Delaney and glanced out the windshield at what he had referred to as a "lodge." The Crane Lake Lodge was a sprawling log building. It sat proudly on top of a hill and combined rustic charm with modern grace. She followed Delaney's lead and got out of the car and reached for her backpack. A groan escaped her as she slung the pack over one shoulder. At least tonight there was the promise of a hot shower and a comfortable bed. Delaney reached past her and picked up both her Winchester and the tranquilizer gun. She closed the car door and glanced past the man beside her, silently surveying the area and the lodge. "You own all this?"

"Yeah, just me and the bank." Without turning around to see if she was following, he walked to the front of the lodge and climbed the four wooden steps to the porch that ran the entire length of the building. A balcony was on top of the porch, with a dozen or so French doors opening onto it.

Laura glanced up and down the porch. A couple of rockers and a handful of small tables dotted the eight-foot-wide area. Twin brass lights illuminated the wide double front doors and the scent of burning wood penetrated the air. She followed Delaney into the lodge and realized immediately she had stepped into a male domain. A chandelier made out of antlers dominated the reception area. Two dark-green couches and a couple of brick-colored chairs were clustered around a thick wool rug woven in a Native American design. A humongous moose head hung on the far wall. Not one flower arrangement or cute painting of scurrying chipmunks brightened the room.

Delaney walked behind the reception desk to the right of the door and picked up the phone. Laura watched as he spoke into the phone for a couple of minutes before hanging up and reaching behind him for a key. He tossed it to her and said, "You're in room number one." He nodded toward a set of thick wooden steps leading to the second floor. "Hang a right and it's the last door on the right. George is fixing us something to eat. We'll be eating in my office in about forty-five minutes." He turned and picked up his pack and the rifles. "George's wife, Lucy, will be coming up to your room in about five minutes. I asked her to find you something to wear for the night, and she'll take care of whatever laundry you have."

Laura palmed the key and shifted her pack. "Thanks." She walked toward the steps. "I'll see you in forty-five minutes." The heat from Delaney's gaze followed her up the steps and down the hall until she was out of his sight. She had to be mistaken about the intensity of Delaney's gaze. Why would there be heat? For the past two days he hadn't done one thing to cross the line of propriety—and there had been one hell of a lot of opportunities, too.

Hell, he'd barely even talked to her, and when he had it was usually short crisp sentences that were anything but sweet. Delaney was a man of few words, and obviously fewer actions. If there was heat in his eyes, then it was probably there because of irritation, not desire.

Laura inserted the key and opened the door to room number one. She reached for the light switch and gasped. Either this was a five-star hotel, or Delaney had given her the best room in the lodge. It wasn't even a room; it was a suite. A manly decorated suite, but a suite no less. One entire wall was done in stone, complete with a fireplace, stacked and ready to go. All she needed was a match. A comfortable-looking couch and recliner, upholstered in rich burgundy leather, faced the fireplace. A bar, constructed of knotty pine, with burgundy leather stools, stood in the corner, and a set of French doors led onto a balcony.

She stepped into the bedroom and almost drooled at the king-size bed that took up practically the entire room. The decor was once again manly, but it felt comfortable. She opened the dark-green drapes and stared out another set of French doors. Dark skies and shadowy silhouettes of trees were all she could see. Not a light anywhere burned below. Delaney's lodge was indeed in the middle of nowhere. With a weary sigh she lowered the pack to a chair positioned by a small table and started to remove the clothes she had worn yesterday, and the used towel and washcloth.

A loud knock on the sitting-room door interrupted her. She hurried over and opened it. A small woman around fifty stood there grinning. "Hello, you must be Lucy." She stood back and allowed the woman to enter.

"Yes, and you must be Thomas's woman."

"Thomas? Oh, you mean Delaney." It took her a moment to realize that Lucy was referring to him by his last name. "No, I'm not Delaney's woman. My name is Laura Kinkaid."

Lucy clucked her tongue twice and kept on grinning. "I brought you a skirt with a drawstring, one of George's sweaters he never wears and a pair of thick socks." She glanced at Laura's feet. "I could run back to my house and get you a pair of shoes if you wish. They should be about your size."

"No, no, this is fine, Lucy. I was only going to grab something to eat before hitting the bed." She took the flowing multicolored skirt, the thick off-white cable-knit sweater and the socks. "Thank you very much."

"Thomas said he didn't know your size." Lucy shook her head and chuckled.

"Why should he?" Laura felt as if she had missed some joke. The way Lucy was grinning at her and the knowing twinkle in her deep, dark eyes were beginning to make her uneasy.

"Thomas knows everything, sees everything." Lucy looked around the room. "Thomas said you have some laundry that needs to be done."

"It's in the other room. I'll get it." Laura walked into the bedroom and picked up the pile of clothes. She handed the garments to Lucy, who had followed. "What does Delaney knowing everything have to do with me and my size?"

"He knows your size."

"If he knew what size I was, why didn't he just tell you?"

"That—" she glanced at Laura's left hand "—Miss Laura, is the real question." Lucy wrinkled her nose at Laura's dirty flannel shirt, jeans and boots. "There's a robe in the closet. Put it on and give me the rest of your clothes. By the look of things I would say you've been tracking with Thomas."

"Two days now." Laura reached for the lush hunter-green terry-cloth robe in the closet. "The man doesn't know the meaning of the word *rest.*"

Lucy clucked her tongue again and headed for the bathroom. After flipping on the light switch, she walked over to huge whirlpool bathtub and started to fill it with steaming water. "Thomas won't rest until he has what he wants."

Laura glanced around the huge bathroom and nearly groaned with ecstasy. Toilets that worked, and hot running water. Heaven should be this luxurious. She started to unlace her boots. "What does he want?"

"When he left here, days ago, he wanted to kill a wolf."

Laura cringed but kept on unlacing. "He still wants that."

"So why did he return?" Lucy checked the counter surrounding the double sinks and made sure everything was in place.

"If I had all this to return to, I'd come back, too." Laura unbuttoned the flannel shirt and dropped it on the tiled floor.

"Ah...." Lucy sighed as she headed for the door. "But he hasn't killed the wolf yet, has he?"

"No, but everyone deserves a break." She removed her belt.

"No one deserves a break more than Thomas." Lucy gave Laura a thoughtful look before adding, "But he never stops before he has obtained what he went after."

"We're heading back out in the morning." Laura didn't understand Lucy's look. She seemed to be measuring something, measuring her.

"Maybe Thomas has changed what he wanted." Lucy smiled knowingly and closed the door behind her.

Laura frowned at the door as she removed her remaining clothes. What was that supposed to mean? Delaney still wanted the wolf. He might be willing to allow her to try to take it alive, but he still wanted the wolf. He hadn't changed his mind. She wrapped a towel around her, scooped up the pile of clothes and opened the bathroom door. Lucy was waiting patiently by the French doors with that silly grin still plastered on her face.

"Give me your boots and I'll make sure they get clean, too."

"You don't have to do this, Lucy. If you tell me where a washer and dryer are, I'll do them after I eat."

"Nonsense. Thomas pays me very well and very rarely asks for any favors. George and I owe him a lot, and it will give me pleasure to repay him any way I can."

"But this is my laundry, not Delaney's."

Lucy continued to smile. "Ah, but Thomas was the one to request this favor, not you. So it is Thomas whom I will please."

Laura followed Lucy to the suite's door. She wondered what Delaney had done to inspire such loyalty. "Where's Delaney's office? I'm supposed to meet him there in about forty minutes."

"Go down the stairs, turn left. At the end of the hall is a door marked Private. It leads to Thomas's private rooms." Lucy gave Laura one last knowing look and disappeared down the hall, softly singing.

Forty-five minutes later Laura hurried down the stairs. She was running late and it was all because of the whirlpool tub. She couldn't bear to get out of it. The gentle jets of hot water had pounded her aching muscles into jelly. When Lucy had left Laura had taken a shower and washed her hair before climbing into the tub. It was only after she had reluctantly emerged from the tub that she realized she had given all her undergarments to Lucy to be cleaned. After searching through her backpack, she had discovered an old T-shirt of her brother's and a pair of white silk panties she had packed in case she needed a pair of pajamas. She didn't have that much luck when it came to a bra. She had hurriedly dressed and then had a good laugh looking at herself in the massive mirrors in the bathroom.

George was roughly the size of Paul Bunyan, and if not for the drawstring on the skirt the garment would have landed at her feet. As it was, the multicolored skirt done in golds, browns and creams was full and flowing, and hit her below midcalf. The gold socks, while neatly cuffed, still looked ridiculous with the skirt and no shoes. George's sweater was big enough that three of her could have fit into it. The sleeves touched her fingertips, the hem bagged around midthigh and there was absolutely no shape to it—or to her, for that matter. She had taken precious moments fastening her brown leather belt around her waist, then turning it so that the buckle was in the back. The blow-dryer on the bathroom wall had only been used long enough to bring her wet hair to damp hair. There hadn't been time to root through the pack again for a rubber band, so she had left her hair loose. She had managed time for brushing her teeth, rubbing in moisturizer to her face and hands and applying a lip gloss she had packed away for protection against the elements.

She felt human again, but not feminine or pretty. Her clothes were not her colors at all. They were too "earthy," while she considered herself in need of a more colorful wardrobe. With very dark hair and a naturally light complexion she always tried to soften the contrast with colors. Why she was worried about how she looked was beyond her. All she was going to do was eat dinner with Delaney, return to her room and see if that king-size bed was as comfortable as it looked. With any luck she would be able to haul her aching body out of bed before first light and meet Delaney downstairs for another marathon hike through the forest. Appearances had nothing to do with their relationship; stamina did.

Laura looked at the oak door and the brass name plate that read Private and took a deep breath. Who was she kidding? She knew exactly why she was concerned with her appearance. She was attracted to Delaney, and the feminine core deep inside her wanted to look drop-dead gorgeous when she joined him for dinner in his office. Hiking over hills, following a dangerous animal, wasn't the time or place to show Delaney her more womanly side. Now was the time, except she didn't have the equipment. No pretty clothes, no makeup, no jewelry, not even a drop of seductive fragrance guaranteed to drive a man wild. She was joining Delaney for dinner wearing baggy clothes, no shoes, hair that smelled like hotel shampoo and not even her cleavage-enhancing bra to loan her support. The only nice thing she could say about herself was, at least she was clean and neat. She took another deep breath, raised her hand and knocked on the door.

Delaney's voice came from within. "Come in."

The rich woodsy scent of a burning fire was the second thing she noticed as she walked into the room. The first was Delaney sitting at a huge desk, poring over maps and talking to someone on the phone. He glanced up for a second, raked her from head to toe with one look and went back to his conversation. Laura softly closed the door behind her and idly surveyed the room. It appeared to be a combination of office, library and living room.

The section of the room Delaney was sitting in contained the massive oak desk, three oak file cabinets and a table directly behind his desk, holding a computer and a fax machine. In another section of the sizable room was a stone fireplace, identical to the one up in her suite. A cheery fire blazed brightly and the couch sitting in front of it was upholstered in a deep-blue plaid instead of rich leather. Delaney's couch looked more inviting than the one upstairs. A wall entertainment system separated the office from the living-room area. She walked over to the French doors leading to the porch and surveyed the view. It was identical to the one she had from her suite. Delaney had given her a suite directly above his private rooms.

She listened to Delaney's end of the conversation and concluded that he was talking to Ray Bennet, the sheriff, about the hunt. He commented on the killings at Frank and Melinda's place and muttered his disgust about not finding the wolf. Laura moved away from the French doors and past the small, round table set between the cozy living room and the bar on the opposite wall. Dinner was waiting for them under two silver domes, and the delicious aroma was driving her crazy.

A short hallway gave her a glimpse of a microscopic kitchen barely big enough to make a cup of coffee in, doors most likely leading to closets, and Delaney's bedroom. She quickly turned away and walked to the section of the room that fascinated her the most—the library.

Massive floor-to-ceiling shelves not only separated this portion of the room but were crammed with books. She scanned the titles and her fingers itched to explore the wonderful treasures before her. In this modern day of computers, videos and satellite hookups, books were becoming extinct. If people needed information, they booted up their computers and within minutes were swamped with more data on any given subject than they could possibly use. Is someone wanted to relax and sink into a fictional world, he slapped in a videotape and was whisked away for two hours into the magical land of Hollywood. Why read the book, when the movie would be out soon? Lord help most of the population if they had to rely on their own minds or imaginations. She had noticed Delaney's healthy video collection next to the television, but by the look of things she would have to guess Delaney never waited for the movie.

Hardbacks, paperbacks and expensive leather-bound collector's editions all jostled for shelf space. Latest bestsellers, aged classics and books worn from countless readings were all squeezed side by side. Books on hunting, fishing, game preservation and the environment were mixed in with science fiction, detective novels, westerns and mysteries. Nonfiction books with subjects ranging from American Indians to veterinary medicine filled the area.

Many of his books duplicated the equally impressive collection she had at home. The only difference was, hers were in neat subject-matter order, while his were jammed into the shelves with no particular arrangement. She did notice one other thing about Delaney's collection; not one ever-popular self-help book was among them. Delaney obviously didn't believe in reading a book to figure out how to fix what was wrong with his life. She couldn't imagine him buying a book to solve a personal problem, correct a bad habit or improve his image. Delaney was the type of man who was what he was, and if you had a problem with that, it was your problem, not his.

Her gaze caught a couple of old, dog-eared children's books hidden on a bottom shelf. She pulled out one of them and smiled. It was an old nursery-rhyme book. She opened it, and inside, printed neatly, but fading, was Delaney's name. *This book belongs to: Delaney William Thomas.* He had saved his first books. She closed the book and grinned at the cover. A cow was jumping over a moon, a little girl was sitting next to a spider and an old shoe with over a dozen kids were brightly illustrated.

"Dinner's getting cold," Delaney said.

Laura nearly dropped the book. She had been so intent on discovering what kind of books he read that she failed to notice he had finished his call and was standing directly behind her. She did notice, however, that he was frowning at the book in her hands. "Sorry." She carefully slid the book back in where she had gotten it.

"I thought you were starving." He walked away from the bookshelves and over to the table, already set with their dinner.

"I am, but I decided to wait for you anyway." She sat down and was momentarily thrown off-balance when he pushed in her chair and then took his own seat. Such a gentlemanly act from a man who made his living hunting animals. The two qualities seemed at odds with each other, yet Delaney exhibited them with ease. "Something smells delicious." Her nose had been telling her roast beef since she'd entered the room. She followed Delaney's lead and removed the silver dome over her plate.

"Roast beef and mashed potatoes," confirmed Delaney. He picked up a bottle of red wine and poured them each a glass.

Laura's stomach growled as a fresh wave of aroma assaulted her senses. Her plate was overloaded with perfectly cooked roast beef, a mound of creamy mashed potatoes, complete with gravy, and fresh string beans. A wicker basket overflowing with warm rolls and a plate of butter patties sat in the middle of the table. A rolling cart stood by the wall, with a coffeepot and cups. She didn't know what to dig into first. Had it only been six and a half hours since lunch? It felt more like twenty-four, and the twelve-mile hike since then hadn't helped. Tea at the Spellings' had done nothing more than quench her thirst. "Everything looks delicious." Laura picked up her fork and dug in.

"George said to tell you to save room for dessert."

Her fork stopped in midair and her eyes glazed over with all the possibilities. "Dessert?"

He chuckled at the expression on her face. "Strawberry shortcake, made with fresh strawberries."

"Fresh strawberries, this time of year?"

"I don't ask how George manages to obtain such quality food, and he doesn't ask me how to track a moose." He took a mouthful of dinner and thought. "I guess we're both better off not knowing."

Laura ate for a couple of minutes to ease the hunger. "I take it George isn't a hunter?"

"George wouldn't step on an ant if he could prevent it."

She reached for a roll and buttered it. "And he works for you?" It seemed like a strange combination to her— a hunter and a pacifist.

"It's in his job description that he doesn't have to go out and kill dinner."

She noticed a twinkling in Delaney's eyes. He was either secretly amused by the thought of George shooting their dinner or a very lustful idea had just occurred to him. She'd wager it was George getting a moose within his cross hairs. "Lucy seemed like a very nice woman."

"She is." He went back to eating.

Simple and to the point. The fine art of casual conversation had obviously been left out of Delaney's education. "Do they live here?"

"Not in the lodge. They have a cabin a couple hundred yards into the woods, but they manage to spend a lot of time around here."

She could tell by the softening of his voice that George and Lucy meant a lot to him. Underneath his rough veneer there actually beat a heart. One that obviously had a soft spot or two. "You live here, don't you?" She glanced around the room and noticed very few personal items. No framed family photos, no mementos, no knickknacks. The most personal things in the room were his video collections and his choice of books. If you took them away, anyone could be living in this room. She wondered if his bureau in the bedroom or the nightstand held a picture of a loved one. For some unknown reason, she doubted it. If Delaney's heart was taken, she doubted if he would wear it on his sleeve.

"When I bought the place five years ago, there were only three small hunting cabins on the property. It took over nine months for the lodge to be completed. I've been living here ever since."

"Who lives in the other two cabins? The guides?"

"I almost forgot I told you about the guides." He gave a small laugh, directed mostly at himself, not her. "George and Lucy live in the larger of the cabins. Their son, Clint, who is a guide, lives in one, and Jake Stoner, the other guide, has the remaining one."

"What about the rest of the staff?"

"They mostly live in the town of Crane Lake."

"I didn't notice any town." She'd finished off the beef and the potatoes and was working on the roll and beans.

"At night it's very difficult to see from the road." He shot her an amused grin, allowing her a small glimpse of his sense of humor. "Even if you drive through it by day it's hard to see. Blink twice and you're through."

"Was that where you were raised?" She couldn't imagine anyone raising a little boy who cherished a nursery-rhyme book, in the cabin where his father had been living.

Delaney studied her face for a long time before answering. "No, we lived about a mile out of Moosehead Falls."

"Who's the 'we'?"

"Mostly just me and my father." He gave her a look that clearly stated the discussion was at an end.

She ignored his glare. "What about your mother?"

"Are you writing a book?"

"No, I'm just trying to be friendly." She carefully placed her fork on her plate. So much for any glimpses of humor. Only a few stray beans were left, but her appetite had fled. Did the man have to bristle at everything? If it wasn't for the fact that she knew firsthand he cared about George and Lucy, she would swear he was inhuman. Here she had been trekking through half the state of Minnesota with the man, and he was reluctant to answer if he even had a mother. She ignored the half-filled wineglass in front of her and stood up. "I'm getting a cup of coffee. Would you like one?"

She was at the cart, pouring herself a cup before he answered. "Yes, please."

"Black, no sugar, right?" She placed a cup in front of him and sat back down with her cup.

Delaney took a sip of coffee and replaced the cup on the saucer. "My mother died when I was six, I don't have any sisters or brothers and my father was an alcoholic on his last downhill slide when he suffered the heart attack. Any more questions?"

Laura felt like a heel. No wonder he didn't want to talk about his family. There was none! Delaney Thomas was alone in the world. That explained a lot about him. The quietness that surrounded him, the seriousness with which he undertook everything and the sad solitary look that darkened his eyes all reflected his lack of family. Had there ever been any laughter or happiness in his life? Somehow she doubted it. "Sounds like a rough life for a little boy."

"The little boy survived." Delaney downed the rest of his coffee and stood up. He walked across the room and studied the map spread out across his desk. "I came to the conclusion that I can't track this particular wolf."

Laura frowned. Casual dinner conversation was officially over; now on to the business at hand—the wolf.

"Why not?" She picked up her coffee and joined him at the desk. She was familiar enough with the area now to recognize some of the landmarks on the map. The detailed map encompassed Saint Louis, Lake and Cook counties. So far the wolf had stayed within Saint Louis County.

"He's moving too much. He's not heeding any territorial boundaries."

"Am I slowing you down?" She hated to ask that question, but she had to know. Was she the reason the wolf was still out there terrorizing the area? Was the concern she had for her brother jeopardizing other people's lives?

Delaney glanced up from the map, obviously surprised by her question. His gaze hungrily devoured her mouth for a moment before dropping back to the map. "No." He cleared the roughness from his voice. "He's moving too fast for any man to catch him. If he's stopping to rest, it's only for short periods. He's not hunting for food. If he comes across any animals, he kills but doesn't eat."

"Like the Spellings' sheep?" The heat from his gaze had produced a raging inferno within her body. He had wanted to kiss her. It had been in his eyes. She unconsciously ran her tongue over her dry lower lip and squirmed as her nipples beaded against the rough knit of the sweater. Desire tightened her breasts as she watched his trembling fingers clutch a pencil. She wasn't imagining it. Delaney was feeling the same sexual pull she was.

His gaze climbed as high as the front of her sweater. "Yeah, the Spellings' sheep."

Laura had no idea what they were talking about. She could only feel the heat of his gaze and the excitement her sensitive nipples were exploding with as they brushed against the coarse knit. Heat warmed her cheeks and her fingers gripped the desk as he raised his gaze to hers. His golden brown eyes were dark, turbulent pools of need. She wanted to drown within that need. She wanted to experience his kiss again. No man had ever made her want him with just a look. His name, "Delaney," tumbled from her lips in a soft whisper, half inviting, half pleading.

The yellow pencil snapped between his fingers as a loud knock on the door shattered the strain. Delaney glared at the door and bellowed, "Come in."

Laura studied the map on the desk as if her life depended upon it. Whoever it was couldn't fail to notice the flush sweeping up her face or the tension so thick in the room a person would need a chain saw to cut it. She allowed a wave of black hair to sweep forward and obscure the side of her face.

"Who are you yelling at? I ain't deaf." A large man came strolling into the room, carrying a tray loaded with two giant slices of strawberry shortcake smothered under a mountain of whipped cream and a bowl of fresh fruit.

"Sorry, George," Delaney said.

Laura shot a quick look at Delaney. He had actually sounded sheepish. There was a hint of pink creeping up his cheeks under his natural sun-darkened bronze complexion. Delaney was embarrassed! She wasn't sure which embarrassed him more—what could have been going on if George hadn't knocked or the fact that he had lost his control and snapped at the intruder. In an uncharacteristic move, she did something she never thought she would do; she chuckled. Her amusement was mostly directed at herself and the situation she found herself in. Imagine, at her age being flustered by a knock on the door.

Delaney glared at Laura. "George Whitecloud, this is Laura Kinkaid."

George set down the tray and shook her hand. His gaze traveled down her body before lingering on her top. "The sweater looks familiar."

"It should. It's yours." Laura grinned and continued to shake the man's hand. First impressions counted for a lot in her book, and George was passing with flying colors. First because he'd barked right back at Delaney and second because of the friendship sparkling in his eyes. The man towered over her by a good foot, but he reminded her of a big soft teddy bear. George Whitecloud would indeed step over an ant if he saw one.

"Lucy bought it for me a couple of Christmases ago, but I never wear it." He gave a shrug of his massive shoulders and began to clean up the dinner dishes. "Something about the way it rubbed against my skin that bothered me."

Laura bit the inside of her cheek and willed the tide of embarrassment not to flood her face. If only he knew! She refused to meet Delaney's questioning glance. "Thank you for loaning it to me."

"My pleasure." George put the two plates with desserts on the table and piled all the dinner dishes onto the tray. He turned to Delaney and grinned. "Anything else, boss?"

"Everything was delicious, as usual." Delaney glanced at Laura. "Do you need anything else for the night?"

"No, I'm fine."

"That's it, George. You and Lucy can go on home. Doug's handling the bar and anything else that comes up for the night."

"What time are you two heading out in the morning?"

"First light."

George nodded once at Delaney and gave Laura a huge grin. The grin told Laura he had been conversing with Lucy and had agreed with her conclusion that she was Delaney's woman. She gently shook her head. The reasoning behind their conclusion still escaped her, but by Delaney's glare he was picking up on the secret message passing between George and her. George released a full-bellied laugh, picked up the tray of dirty dishes and left the room.

"What was all that about?" Delaney demanded.

"What?" Laura tried to look innocent. There wasn't enough money in the world to make her explain to him how his staff had labeled her "his woman."

"That look?"

"What look?" She headed for the strawberry short-cake and ignored his scowl. A change in subject was definitely called for. If George hadn't knocked on the door, heaven knows what kind of dessert she would be enjoying right now. "If we can't catch the wolf by trailing him, how do you suggest we go about it?"

He tossed the two halves of the broken pencil into the garbage can under his desk and joined her at the table. "We have to outthink it."

She allowed a forkful of whipped cream to melt in her mouth. "How do we do that?"

Delaney only had a one-word answer to her question. "Luck."

# Chapter 8

Laura pushed back the covers with a violent shove and got out of bed. She couldn't believe how warm it was. After thirty minutes of lying in a heavenly, comfortable bed, all clean, her stomach filled with George's delicious cooking, sleep still wouldn't come. She was exhausted and every bone in her body ached from the past two days of strenuous exercise. But every time she closed her eyes she pictured Delaney as he had been downstairs earlier.

Delaney had been all rough barks and seriousness after George left. His barks hadn't bothered her as much as they'd used to. Who could be in awe of a man who had saved his nursery-rhyme book? He had purposely put as much distance between Laura and him as possible and never once met her gaze. The only discussion they'd had was about the wolf and some ideas on how to find it. There hadn't been any more sightings or livestock killings since the Spellings' place. Sheriff Bennet also had told Delaney that he periodically checked Marcus's house. The good news was there hadn't been any more vandalism; the bad news was Marcus still hadn't returned home. Laura refused to allow the bad news to bring her down.

Marcus couldn't have disappeared off the face of the earth, and the only lead she had was the wolf. She had to find the wolf. To see the animal for herself. Then she would know one way or another. Either Marcus's experiment had succeeded even beyond his wildest expectations, or the wolf was a very unusual, highly improbable, vicious animal that just happened to be in the right area at the right time. Laura didn't believe in coincidences.

To achieve her goal of locating the wolf, she needed Delaney, and that brought on a whole new set of problems. She not only needed Delaney, she wanted him. The physical attraction between them was so tangible that even George had picked up on it. Delaney had felt it— hell, he generated it. He also ignored it. For some reason he wasn't willing to explore this attraction, and she couldn't blame him. Just thinking about the complications a physical relationship would produce was enough to kill any desire. How could two people conduct an affair while tramping through the forest? What would happen when they finally located the wolf? Delaney would still like to kill it first and asks questions second, while she wanted carefully to tranquilize it and bring it back to Marcus's lab for an examination. What would happen when Marcus was returned safe and sound to his house? She had a career and life to get back to in Saint Paul, while Delaney had the lodge to run up here. It could never work; there were just too many complications. They were two different people, heading in two different directions. Delaney had the right idea after all— ignore the attraction.

Laura flipped on the small lamp in the corner of the room and headed for the closet. She pulled on the thick deep-green robe and tied the sash. She was hot. The room was hot. She pulled the cord and opened the drapes across the French doors. The balcony was in darkness, except where the light in the room spilled out through the doors, and the night sky twinkled with a thousand stars.

The glass of the doors felt cool and inviting against her fingers. She needed some fresh air to clear her head and a cool breeze to bathe her feverish skin. Maybe then she could finally get some sleep. She flipped the lock and opened the door. A thirty-eight-degree wind whipped into the room and plastered the robe against her body as she stepped out onto the balcony.

Delaney lay in bed and listened to the patio doors of Laura's bedroom open. Sleeping with the windows cracked not only let in some fresh air, it also allowed him to hear what was happening outside. There were two small squeaks as she stepped out onto the balcony. After four years he knew every squeak, every sound the lodge made, and if he didn't recognize the noise, he went investigating. Laura was having as much trouble as he was trying to fall asleep. He knew the reason. They both were fighting the same devil—lust.

Every muscle in his body was tight and hard with the desire he felt for Laura. Desire he was powerless to control, and that scared the hell out of him. Imagine being scared of a woman who barely reached his chin, had hair the color of midnight and whose eyes reminded him of springtime grass. When she walked into the same room, his body ached and his mind drifted. If she accidentally brushed up against him, he ceased thinking altogether and became rock hard. Tonight in his office, he had wanted to kiss her so badly that his hands had trembled, and he'd literally yelled at George. He hadn't known it was George at the time, but if his mind had been functioning properly he would have. He was the one who had told George, when he had been setting the table with dinner, to come back with the dessert in about forty minutes.

Laura had him so tied up in knots that he was shouting at his employees, snapping pencils in half and not knowing if he was hurrying through the woods to capture a wolf or to outrun her. This had to stop. The only way he knew how to put an end to this foolishness was to allow the desire to run its course. Laura wanted him; that wasn't the problem. When he'd kissed her the other day she had melted into his arms like a lover. The problem was Laura. She wasn't like any other woman he knew. The only thing Laura had in common with his ex-wife, Kathleen, was that their hair was about the same color. Kathleen's had come from a bottle at a fancy salon and had cost more to maintain than his Jeep, while he'd bet next year's profits that Laura's was natural.

He had been hoping that by not telling Lucy Laura's size, she would deliver something hideous for her to wear. His prayers hadn't been answered, and when Laura had walked into his office earlier, he'd felt the familiar desire slam into his gut like a freight train. How could a woman look so damn appealing wearing one of George's sweaters, Lucy's skirt and a pair of socks? Laura's hair had still been damp, not one drop of makeup had enhanced her features, and she still had the longest, thickest eyelashes he had ever seen. The part that really drove him crazy was, she didn't have on a bra. He could tell. She was too generously endowed for him not to notice. All through dinner he'd had to avoid looking at the front of her, or he never would have been able to swallow. When she had stood beside him at the desk and whispered his name, in such a sweet plea, he knew he had lost the battle with his control. He would have taken her on the spot if George hadn't chosen that particular instant to knock.

He should have told whoever was knocking to go away, then dragged Laura down onto the floor or up onto the desk top and made sweet love to her until this horrible ache had gone. He never would have made it to the couch ten feet away or even to his bedroom down the hall. Now he still ached, and Laura obviously wasn't in any better shape. Ignoring the problem wasn't the answer. The desire wasn't going away. It was only growing stronger.

With a violent oath, he kicked off the covers and got out of bed. What he should do was ignore the fact that Laura was standing all alone on the balcony upstairs and head for the shower. A freezing-cold shower. Delaney yanked his navy blue velour robe off the bathroom door and put it over his naked body. He glanced between the bathroom and the doors leading to his private patio directly under where Laura was standing. There wasn't any decision to make. It had already been made days ago. The instant she'd stepped around the garage and jammed the barrel of her rifle into his chest he had known they would become lovers.

A woman like that only came along once in a man's lifetime, if at all. For thirty-six years he had been waiting for someone like her. It was a real shame she had happened along too late to change anything. They could become lovers, but nothing more. He had nothing more to give. Whatever spark of loyalty, hope for the future or whatever you wanted to call it, even love, was gone. It had died a slow, painful death behind the cold metal bars of a military prison. Between his drunken father, Kathleen's deceit and the betrayal the military had shown him, whatever spark a man carried around within his soul had been extinguished. If Laura could accept him as he was, then fine, they would become lovers for however long the hunt lasted. When it was over and the wolf caught, they could go their separate ways and nobody would be hurt. If she needed useless promises and lies, then it was going to be a very long, agonizing hunt for them both. He couldn't give her promises of a tomorrow.

Delaney opened his patio doors and stepped out into the chilly night air. Within five steps he was climbing the outside wooden stairs to Laura's balcony. His bare feet hardly made a sound, but he could tell by the way her shoulders stiffened that she had heard him.

Laura didn't turn around. She knew who it was—Delaney. She had heard his patio door open and then close. For the past five minutes she had been contemplating the night and what she would do if Delaney joined her. She had just come to the conclusion that she was tired of living with regrets. In high school boys never interested her, she had been too busy worrying about SAT scores and getting into the college of her choice. All through college she had concentrated on grades, not on the male population roaming the campus. She'd dated occasionally, but nothing serious. Then, when she'd finally graduated, her time and energy had gone into her career, not building relationships. Now at the age of thirty-one she was wondering how much of life had passed her by while she'd concentrated on her career.

She'd never experienced the kind of desire Delaney's kiss had generated. The hot, intense flames that implored a person to step into their heat and discover heaven. She wanted to touch those flames. She wanted to burn. Delaney was the only man she had ever met who could ignite that fire.

Her hands were buried deep within the pockets of the robe. A moment ago she had been freezing; now the wind didn't seem to blow as hard and the boards beneath her bare feet weren't so cold. Her gaze stayed riveted to the forest and sky beyond the balcony railing. Was it possible for the stars to be bigger, closer to the earth in northern Minnesota than Saint Paul? She knew it wasn't scientifically possible; they just seemed that way. "It's beautiful up here."

"You should see it in the winter." He joined her at the railing and followed her gaze. "The snow is so thick and bright the slightest moonlight lights up the sky."

"I imagine you get a lot of snow up here."

"Tons of it. As long as you prepare for it, it's not too bad." He looked out over the land. "A good hard winter makes you appreciate spring that much more."

Laura chuckled. She had never heard that logic before. Most everyone she knew complained about Minnesota's winters and the snow, and the snow, and the snow. "I take it you like the snow."

"Not necessarily. Business is slow. Not many city slickers relish the idea of strapping on snowshoes to bag a moose."

"So what do you do all winter when you're snowed in?"

"Play poker with George, read, watch television. We're in the modern age of the superhighway. Crane Lake, Minnesota, isn't as isolated as it once was. If all else fails, go ice fishing." He captured a wave of her hair that was blowing across her face and slowly wrapped it around his finger. "What do you do down in Saint Paul?"

"Work, read and work some more." He was so close she could see the fire kindle in his eyes. His big body was blocking the wind and she could feel his warmth.

His hungry gaze caressed her mouth. "I'm going to kiss you."

Laura forgot how to breathe. How could such a simple statement cause her knees to tremble and her toes to curl? A smile tugged at the corners of her mouth. "Good." She wanted that kiss. Hell, she wanted a lot more than just a kiss.

His work-roughened finger caressed her lower lip. It trembled beneath his touch.

"I want to do more than just kiss you."

"Good."

His hot gaze shot up to lock with hers. He seemed to be searching her soul.

"I can't offer you any promises."

"I don't remember asking for any."

Delaney's mouth covered hers with the speed of a highway pileup. Any doubts she might have harbored were incinerated in the crash. She felt herself being crushed against his chest and welcomed the fervor. This was where she wanted to be, in Delaney's arms. Her arms encircled his neck and her fingers wove their way through his hair. When his tongue swept over her lips, demanding entrance, she received him with a moan.

In one swift movement he picked her up and carried her back inside her bedroom. Without releasing her mouth, he closed the door behind them and yanked the drapes closed.

Laura slowly caressed the side of his jaw and the strong column of his throat with her fingertips. They provocatively teased their way lower over his heated flesh as her tongue danced against his. Her fingers stroked the soft velour of the lapel on his robe before sliding inside to weave their way into the thick hair covering his chest. This was what she had been missing from her life—the desire, the excitement, Delaney.

With a tug of the sash and a gentle brush against her shoulder, Delaney sent her robe cascading to the floor. He lifted his head and gazed at the white T-shirt she wore. It covered her from her neck to the top of her creamy thighs. Twin nipples jutted out beneath the fabric, begging for his attention. His hands trembled as they encircled her waist, and he slowly raised them upward to cradle her breasts. His thumbs brushed over the rigid peaks and a harsh groan escaped his throat as they beaded more. His voice was filled with wonder as he whispered, "So responsive."

Laura clung to him as he lowered his head and captured a pleading nub between his lips. Through the light cotton material of the T-shirt she could feel the movement of his tongue and the warmth of his breath. If she let go of him, she would shatter into a million pieces of need. He was the only thing holding her together. That and the knowledge there was more to come. She had experienced the mechanics before, but never this emotion. This fire. It heightened the desire and fine-tuned the need to the breaking point. She reached for the sash belted around his waist and gave a yank.

Delaney's robe hit the floor the same instant he grabbed the hem of her T-shirt and tugged it over her head. She reached out and stroked her fingertips over the dark nipples buried beneath the soft curls covering his chest. A gentle smile curved her mouth as they sprang into tight little beads. She glanced up and met his gaze "So responsive."

A groan rumbled in the room as he swung her up into his arms and then dropped her onto the bed. "I'll give you responsive."

Her gaze dropped to his waist and below. The light burning next to the bed cast him in a golden glow as he stood there in pure male glory. He was hard. He was ready. "So I see."

Delaney captured a trim ankle in each of his hands. "You haven't even begun to *see* what you do to me." He inched his fingers higher.

Laura felt his heated gaze singe her flesh, and melted into the mattress. The intensity and concentration he had shown on the hunt were directed solely at her. He wanted her. She could tell by the way his hands trembled against her knees as they skimmed higher. The hunt was on, and she was his quarry. A very willing prey, if the moisture dampening her white silk panties was any judge.

His fingers slid teasingly over the sensitive skin of her inner thighs. Laura arched her hips and tried to bring his hands closer to her need. He smiled and she closed her eyes and whispered, "Please." A whole lifetime of fiery desires was evident in that one word.

Coarse fingertips rubbed the tiny lace edging of the only material separating him from her womanhood. Delaney seemed mesmerized by the contrast of his dark work-roughened fingers and the luxurious silk of her panties. Moist heat greeted his finger as he pushed aside the silken barrier and caressed the silkier woman beneath.

Laura moved her thighs wider apart and nearly shattered as he slowly inserted a finger, testing for her readiness. Her hips bucked. A kiss landed on the slight curve of her abdomen.

"Easy, love," murmured Delaney as he eased his finger out and tugged the silken barrier down her legs. "What were you saying about responsive?" Within a heartbeat he was positioned between her thighs.

Her arms encircled his back as her thighs wrapped themselves around his hips. "For a man who never talks much—" she rubbed the moist opening against his shaft "—you seem mighty chatty all of a sudden."

Delaney entered her in one quick thrust and stopped. She gasped in surprise and held her breath as her body adjusted itself to his size. Heat turned into a raging inferno as he lowered his head and gently nipped her nipples. This time when she bucked her hips, he didn't try to stop her. He was with her all the way. After a few uncontrollable bucks, he held her hips and slowed the rhythm to a seductive dance. She matched him thrust for thrust, and as the dance increased in tempo, so did the desire.

She was reaching for the peak of some unknown destination. It was directly in front of her; she could almost touch it. All she had to do was stay with Delaney and it would be hers. She wanted it, almost as much as she feared it.

Delaney felt her fight as she trembled beneath him. He held her tighter and whispered in her ear, "Go for it, Laura. I've got you."

The blaze that was in his gaze gave her the confidence to let go and allow the sensations to carry her over the top. With his next plunge she gave a low yell as she went free-falling over the edge.

Delaney captured her cry with his mouth and roared his own release as he followed her over the edge.

Ten minutes later, Laura lifted her head off of Delaney's chest and stared down at her foot. Something had been disturbing her satisfied daze. There, wrapped around her right ankle, was the pair of white silk panties. In his haste, Delaney never managed to get them all the way off. She raised her leg. The panties dangled from her ankle. "Oh, my." She had no idea if she was referring to the panties or to what they represented. Her wanton behavior was inexcusable. She had never done anything like this in her entire life. And to do it with Delaney! A man she barely knew.

Delaney gazed down at the white scrap of silk holding Laura's attention. He was waiting for hysterics after the way they had just gone at it. Where were the tears, embarrassment and, most of all, regrets? Hell, he was surprised she didn't scream in terror after the way he'd treated her. He had been afraid of losing his control, and he had. He might not be able to give her promises, but he could have at least shown some restraint. "Is that all you can say?"

Laura glanced away from her leg and slowly slid her gaze up his gorgeous body. Delaney was all male, and she was all satisfied. How could she possibly regret one moment of their lovemaking? Granted, it had been wild and frenzied and totally out of character for her, but he had been the one to set the pace. She had only followed his lead. The thick, quilted bedspread and two of the pillows had been knocked off the bed during the melee. The blanket and sheets were a twisted mess beneath them. They couldn't have gotten under the covers if they'd tried. She wanted to laugh. "Well, what do you have to say for yourself?"

He noticed the smile tugging at the corners of her mouth and the laughter sparkling in her eyes. Darn her, she wanted to laugh. He glanced at the twisted sheets under their moist, naked bodies and saw the humor in the situation for the first time. Laura wasn't embarrassed or regretful. She had been with him every step of the way. The little minx. He raised one eyebrow. "I've never been called 'chatty' before."

She kicked her ankle and sent the pair of panties flying. Her fingers lightly walked down his chest, to circle his navel and beyond. "Remind me to do it more often."

With a deep groan of desire, Delaney reached for her wandering fingers. Heat pounded through his veins as he took her over the edge for the second time. The control he so desired never materialized.

Delaney heard the outer door to Laura's suite open. He lay perfectly still as light, graceful footsteps sounded in the outer room. Lucy. He recognized her step. There was a slight noise, as if she were setting something down, and then she left. He turned his head and glanced at the bedside clock. Dawn was breaking, and he wasn't even out of bed, never mind ready to leave.

He stilled as Laura shifted sleepily in his arms. All midnight hair and pale, smooth skin nestled against him. Lord, she was beautiful, and he was in trouble. He hadn't expected the emotions that assaulted him during the night. It was supposed to have been a mutual understanding and the releasing of the tension between them. Instead of lying here deeply satisfied, he was troubled. The physical aspects of their lovemaking had left him fulfilled. A deep, mind-numbing satisfaction left him drained. Laura's thigh moved between his legs and rubbed against his groin. Blood pounded and heat stirred once again. Maybe he wasn't as satisfied as he thought he was. Laura had this amazing ability to move him the way no other woman had. And that was what troubled him.

The desire to spend the rest of the day—hell, the week—in bed with Laura pulled at his gut. She was so responsive to his every touch. She had burned hotter than the sun and his body still carried the scorch marks. Laura was a sweet temptation he couldn't afford to indulge in right now. He had a wolf to hunt, and if anything, the animal was going to tear them apart. He didn't want to examine all the reasons he was letting Laura tag along on the hunt. He was afraid he wouldn't like the answers.

The idea that the wolf and Marcus were one and the same was ridiculous. Nothing on this earth could make him accept the theory of werewolves. He didn't care how much data and how many facts Marcus had written in his journal. Werewolves didn't exist. They were products of folklore and scary tales passed from generation to generation to scare misbehaving children. Werewolves belonged in the same category as vampires and the bogeyman.

His theory concerning the wolf he was hunting was simple. The wolf deserved to be killed. He was a menace to mankind. He killed for the pleasure of killing, and that was dangerous. There had already been three failed manhunts for the animal before he joined the hunt. The ranchers were upset and a couple of radicals, fearing for their livestock, had already tried to assemble mass hunts against all wolves.

Delaney had no conflict with other wolves. As far as he was concerned they had as much right to the forests of northern Minnesota as he did. They were an intricate part of the food chain. Without them, diseased and weak animals would contaminate entire herds of healthy animals. Many animals would starve to death in the cruel winter while weaker, older animals took food needed to feed the young. It was a harsh reality, but one Delaney accepted.

If he didn't capture this wolf soon, he wasn't sure how much longer Sheriff Bennet could contain the ranchers. Soon there would be so many hunters out in the forests, shooting at anything that moved, it would be impossible not to trip over each other. Never mind the inexperienced hunters who'd pull the trigger first and find out what they were shooting at later. Many a good hunter had been mistaken for game and it only took one bullet to kill a man or a woman. Delaney brushed a black curl away from his nose. Once the ranchers got into the hunt, Laura would have to stay out of the forests. He couldn't chance some yahoo mistaking her for a wolf. She wasn't going to like it, but she'd understand.

She would also understand why this particular wolf had to be killed. Once a creature started on a path of destruction, there was no turning back. You couldn't change the wolf's behavior. Even if you released it into the wild, far away from human occupation, it would be merciless to the other animals of the region. This wolf didn't kill for survival or food; it killed for the pleasure.

He had agreed with Laura to try to tranquilize the wolf for the purpose of testing the animal. To see if there was an explanation for the bizarre behavior. Hopefully it didn't have a contagious disease. He couldn't imagine an entire pack of ten or twenty wolves viciously roaming the territory, killing everything in their path.

The other reason he wanted the wolf dead was more emotional and less rational. The wolf had caused his father to have a heart attack and die. It was a tangible thing he could vent his anger and frustration on. He knew deep down that his father's heart had been weak and dying long before the wolf had shown up at his place. Nevil Thomas had been slowly killing himself with whiskey for thirty years. Delaney couldn't stop the bottle or the damage it had inflicted. From the time he was six he had tried and failed. By the time he had arrived at his father's place, it had been too late. The old man's heart had already lost the battle. Delaney couldn't go through the nation, the state or even the town of Moosehead Falls breaking every bottle of whiskey for causing years of misery and his father's death. But he could kill a wolf. He'd gladly kill the wolf.

He reached over and turned on the bedside lamp. Light flooded the room. He glanced down and studied the woman sleeping so peacefully in his arms. The light didn't seem to bother her. Thick black lashes fanned her cheekbones, hiding the greenest eyes he had ever seen. Her nose tipped up charmingly, and her chin had a stubborn tilt to it. Even in sleep she could be stubborn. It was her mouth that held most of his attention. Lord, what those lips could do to a man should be against the law. He brushed back a lock of her hair and allowed his fingers to rest against the side of her neck. The strong, steady beat of her pulse thundered under his fingertips.

He wondered what kind of childhood she had had. The total opposite of his was his guess. Upper middle class, a set of doting parents and a younger brother to spoil. The perfect family, his dream family.

Delaney gave a heavy sigh and pulled her closer. Only now it wasn't so perfect. Her parents were half the world away and her brother had disappeared under mysterious circumstances. Laura was left shouldering the load, and she was doing it amazingly well. She'd examined all the facts, weighed the options and then picked up her rifle and tranquilizer gun and followed him into the forest.

Miles of rough terrain hadn't made her utter one word of complaint. Outdoor facilities and bedding down in his father's dilapidated cabin hadn't made her quit. Even after the horrid scene at the Spellings' ranch and the eerie howling in the dead of the night, still she was willing to go for more. Why? Was the love she felt for her brother that strong?

He'd never experienced that kind of love. Maybe when he was a little boy he'd loved his parents like that, but he couldn't remember. His father's abuse over the years had killed any affection he might have had for him. If Kathleen, his ex-wife, had been missing during their marriage he would have searched for her as diligently as Laura now searched for her brother. But out of responsibility, not out of love. When he married Kathleen it was out of friendship, trust, great sex and, he had thought, a future. She was to be the woman to build a family with. Kathleen had shattered that trust and illusion. If Uncle Sam had asked him to go out and hunt the wolf and not come back until it was dead, he would have without a question. That was what he was being paid to do—follow orders. None of it would have had to do with love. Love was an illusion that never really was there. People saw it for no other reason than they wanted to see it.

Did Laura feel love for her brother, or was it responsibility? Hadn't she promised her parents she would look out for Marcus? That was why she was hiking all over northern Minnesota, looking for her brother. Responsibility. Delaney gave her slender shoulder a gentle shake. Her brother should be the one looking out for her, not the other way around. If he had a sister—younger or older, it wouldn't have mattered—he would be the one looking out for her. "Laura," Delaney whispered as she scrunched up her face. "Time to wake up."

She gave a moan and buried her face against his chest. Delaney held back his laugh and shook her shoulder a little harder. "Laura, we have to be getting up."

"Why?" was mumbled into the thick curls covering his chest.

"We should have been downstairs by now." Her groan only made him feel guiltier. If it hadn't been for him, she would have had a lot more sleep last night. "George probably has breakfast ready by now."

Laura glanced up and squinted against the light. She hated waking up in the morning, but she didn't mind it so much when she was in Delaney's arms. Her mind refused to function without a cup of coffee, but her body obviously didn't have that problem. She could tell by the rigid bulge against her thigh that Delaney was happy, very happy, to have her draped across his body. If she played her cards right, maybe she could convince him to spend the day in bed with her and she wouldn't have to get up. She gave the bulge a gentle nudge. "Are you being chatty again?"

Delaney swept her up into his arms and carried her into the bathroom. "*Lady,* you could tempt a saint!" He carefully stood her on her feet and started the shower.

Laura grinned. Mornings weren't that bad after all. Who needed caffeine, when Delaney stood directly in front of her, naked as the day he was born. Only older, much older. "After last night, no one could ever refer to you as a saint, Delaney."

He groaned and steered her toward the shower. "Behave, woman!" A light slap landed playfully on her rear. "Be downstairs and ready to leave in fifteen minutes."

Her grin only grew as he walked out of the room and closed the door. Delaney had been tempted. Some things in life Mother Nature never intended to hide. She glanced at the counter and found the first fault with Delaney's lodge. Hunting lodges that catered to men, very rich men, didn't supply shower caps to their guests. She grabbed a washcloth, rolled it up and used it to tie her hair up into a ponytail. There wasn't time to blow-dry her hair.

Keeping her hair away from the spray, she stepped into the shower and reached for the soap. A strong, masculine arm reached around her and took the soap from her.

"Allow me."

She glanced over her shoulder and grinned at Delaney. "I thought you left."

He slowly lathered a white washcloth and rubbed it across her back. "Never even made it out of the bedroom." White bubbles coated her back, her buttocks, the top of her thighs.

Laura leaned against him as warm water pelted them both. "I have a feeling we're going to be late for breakfast."

Delaney kissed the top of her shoulder as his hands slid around to the front of her. Plump breasts overflowed his hands as his mouth skimmed up the side of her neck to nibble on her earlobe. "Count on it."

Laura entered the kitchen forty minutes later and tried not to blush. Delaney was already in the room, poring over maps and drinking coffee. She didn't know which excited her more—him or the prospect of her first cup of coffee. Delaney gave her a quick look before turning back to his maps. She couldn't read the expression in his gaze. George was busy setting two plates piled high with food at the end of counter. She placed her backpack next to Delaney's and their rifles.

Lucy broke the silence as she handed her a cup of coffee and a cheerful greeting. "Good morning, Ms. Kinkaid. I hope you slept well."

Laura studied her coffee as if it contained the secrets of the universe. "Fine, wonderful." She glanced at the two plates George had just set down. "Something sure does smell good."

George waved his arm at the plates. "Eat before it gets cold."

Laura heard an *again* in there, even if he was too polite to say it. She quickly sat on the farthest stool and waited for Delaney. George and Lucy knew where Delaney had spent his night. In her bed. When they had finally emerged from the shower and dried off, Delaney had given her a kiss to remember, then told her that her clothes were in the sitting room. When she questioned him on how he knew that, he shrugged into his robe and said that Lucy had delivered them before dawn. Thankfully he had disappeared through her patio doors, to head on back to his room downstairs, before she could expire of humiliation on the spot.

She shifted uncomfortably on the stool as Delaney sat next to her. He gave her a questioning look, but she refused to meet his gaze. As soon as Delaney picked up his fork, she dug into the meal. With Delaney leading the way through the forest, Lord knows when she would get another chance to eat.

"We won't be doing a lot of hiking today," Delaney said. He dug into his breakfast.

Laura watched Lucy make an enormous pot of coffee and begin arranging bowls of fresh fruit. George manned the stove and started cooking a small mountain of food. The two worked efficiently together. She turned back to Delaney and munched on a crisp strip of bacon. "Why not?" It wasn't that she wasn't glad not to be hiking practically into Canada, but she was curious about why not.

"We're going to try to outsmart him." He pulled a map closer and showed her an area of roughly five square miles. "This is where he was headed after he left the Spellings' place." He tapped a small area highlighted in yellow, showing Frank and Melinda's place.

Laura chewed another strip of bacon and studied the map. "What if he changed directions?"

"There's a lake on this side, and I don't see him trying to slaughter a bunch of trout." He moved his finger over in the opposite direction. "Nothing's here except rugged terrain, no livestock. And I don't see him backtracking. He's killed everything behind him." His finger moved to the area outlined in red. "So that leaves here."

She finished her coffee and thanked Lucy as she refilled the cup. A frown pulled at her forehead as she drank the fresh hot brew and contemplated the map. The outlined area didn't appear to be too heavily forested, and a couple of little squares and roads caught her attention. "What is it?"

"Cordel McMichael's cattle ranch." He broke open a buttermilk biscuit and took a bite while studying her reaction.

"It's perfect for him, isn't it?" She pushed away the plate. Her appetite disappeared.

"I don't know if I would use the word 'perfect,' but it's a logical assumption that he might be close by." Delaney pushed away his empty plate and folded the map. "George packed us lunch and some food just in case we don't make it back here tonight." He stood up and walked over to their packs.

Laura watched as he picked up both packs, leaving her the rifles. He gave George some last-minute instructions and then walked out of the room. He cared! Since she'd strolled into the kitchen he had done nothing that would indicate how he was feeling toward her and what they had shared. His uncharacteristic move of shouldering her pack spoke volumes. By the look on George's face and Lucy's, she would say they'd noticed it, too, and approved. She smiled at the couple, really smiled. The fact that Lucy had entered her room and knew that Delaney was in her bed didn't bother her any longer. Delaney cared! She hurried across the room and picked up the rifles.

"Thanks, George, for the delicious breakfast." She glanced at Lucy. "Thanks for the coffee and the clothes. I left them upstairs on the bed. Was that all right?"

"Fine. Now that I know your size, I'll see if I can find you something better to wear for tonight."

"That wouldn't be necessary. I'm hoping I can convince Delaney to stop at my brother's house so I can grab some more clothes and check on things."

Lucy nodded. "You two be careful out there."

## Chapter 9

Delaney stepped from the Jeep and stared down at the valley below. The activity there gave him the answer he needed. His assumption about the wolf had been right on the money. The animal had headed straight for the McMichaels' place. Only problem was, judging by Cordel's reaction, he had been there, done his damage and now was gone. Delaney watched as Cordel kicked an oversize tire on his truck while two of his sons walked between a couple of dead calves, shaking their heads.

Laura joined him on the ridge and followed his gaze. "We're too late, aren't we?"

"Seems that way." He continued to survey the area below but couldn't detect any sign of the animal. The McMichaels' house and main barns were out of sight, over the next hill. The fences, designed to keep the cattle in, looked to be in good shape. A herd of cattle grazed peacefully a couple of hundred yards away from Cordel and his sons. If the wolf was still in the area, the cattle would know.

"Are we going down?"

"Yes. I want to see what damage he did, and to follow his trail. First, though, I want to condense our packs into one. No sense in both of us lugging a pack."

Laura pulled some essentials from her pack and handed them to Delaney. He handed her a bundle of clothes in return. She frowned as he undid his sleeping bag. "What if we're caught out in the dark?"

"We won't be. By the look of the slaughter, I'd say our friend might not care that we're human. I don't know about you, but I'm not about to take any unnecessary chances." He zipped his coat, secured the pack and locked the Jeep. He gave Laura the Winchester and the tranquilizer gun but kept his own rifle. "Are you sure you're going to be warm enough?"

Laura zipped her coat and flipped up the collar against the wind. She pulled a thick red knit band from her pocket and placed it around her head so it covered her ears. She patted the other pocket, where her gloves were, and smiled. "Short of a blizzard, I'll be fine."

Desire rushed through him when she smiled. She looked beautiful this morning. Hell, she looked radiant. The sun had barely risen, and he was contemplating heading back to bed. Sleep wasn't the priority, loving sweet Laura was. How could she make him want her so badly without doing anything? Standing on a blustery hill, wearing an olive green hunting jacket and clunky hiking boots, with a Winchester strapped across one shoulder, shouldn't have made her look desirable. But it had. If Cordel hadn't already spotted them standing up there, he'd be tempted to roll out his sleeping bag and watch her purr. Laura made sweet, delectable little sounds in the back of her throat when they made love. He wanted to hear those sounds and make her burn. Instead he headed for the valley and the carnage below. "Come on, the sooner we get started, the sooner we can get back." Tonight she would purr.

Ten minutes later, Laura glanced away from a dead calf and felt her breakfast start to churn. She took a couple of deep breaths and slowly leaned against the front fender of the McMichaels' truck. How could one animal cause so much destruction? She wanted to believe an entire pack of bloodthirsty wolves had attacked the herd last night, but she knew it wasn't true. One lone wolf had viciously slaughtered seven cattle. Five had been mere calves, but two had been full-size beasts. The destruction was everywhere. The dying grass of autumn was stained red.

"Are you all right, ma'am?"

Laura glanced at Brent McMichaels, one of Cordel's sons, and gave him what she hoped was a smile. It felt more like a grimace of pain. "I'm fine. Thanks for asking." It was more than what Delaney had done. So far, after introducing her to Cordel and his sons, he'd virtually ignored her. She glanced over to where he was kneeling by one of the calves. He had pulled on rubber gloves and he and Cordel were examining the poor dead animal. She turned away. She wanted to keep her breakfast down and her dignity intact.

Brent McMichaels glanced between her, Delaney and the dead animals. "It isn't a pretty sight, is it?"

She noticed how pale he looked for a rancher's son. Working outdoors all summer long should have left the eighteen-year-old Brent bronzed and healthy. His hands were tanned, but his face appeared pinched and pasty. She had a feeling she wasn't the only one in danger of losing breakfast. "You should have seen what he did to a flock of sheep yesterday." Had it only been yesterday afternoon that they'd arrived at the Spelling place?

"Bad, huh?" Brent concentrated on the worn toe of his boot.

"Worse than this. He killed the entire flock." She buried her hands in the deep pockets of her coat and raised her face toward the sun. The temperature was above freezing, but the wind had kicked up something awful. But it wasn't the windchill that was making her so cold. It was the knowledge that her brother might have something to do with all this that caused the freezing hollow in the center of her soul.

"How many were there?"

"Over a dozen." She kicked up a small cloud of dust beneath her boots. All those sweet-faced sheep, killed. For what? "I think there were fourteen."

"Did he eat them?"

"No. Just killed them. One right after another. They couldn't run. They couldn't escape." Tears of frustration were building behind her eyes. She couldn't cry now. If Delaney saw her blubbering like a baby, he would surely leave her with the McMichaels until he returned. More than likely, he would be carrying a dead wolf. She couldn't chance Delaney's leaving her behind.

"That's the weird part, isn't it?"

"What's the weird part?" To her way of thinking, everything was the weird part. Nothing was how it should be.

"That he doesn't eat them." Brent made a helpless gesture. "I understand about the food chain and the survival of the fittest. We had the occasional wolf kill one of the herd before. Usually it's in the dead of winter and food is scarce. What I don't understand is this senseless slaughter." He gave her a long look. "Is the wolf rabid?"

"We don't think so." Rabies would explain some of the wolf's unusual behavior. But there would be signs if he had the disease. Delaney hadn't noticed any foaming at the animal's mouth. Rabies also would have left the animal in a weakened condition—days, if not hours, away from death. A wolf was not on the decline if he'd just taken down twelve hundred pounds of beef. Laura shivered and rubbed her forehead where the beginning of a headache was forming. What was she doing here? The tracks imprinted in the soft earth were clearly those of a wolf. The barbarity of the attack was surely that of an animal, not a man. Marcus was not responsible for this savagery, no matter what enzymes he'd injected into his body. So why was she here?

"Are you one of them zoo ladies?" Brent asked.

Laura stared at Brent. "Zoo ladies?"

"Yeah, one of those people what go around protecting all the wild animals and screaming about the environment." He glanced at the tranquilizer gun she had stood against the bumper of the truck.

"No, I'm not a wild-life specialist, but I do my fair share of screaming about the environment. I work with plants and trees and discover some of their secrets. Many of which could help mankind if we'd only take the time to look, instead of burning down rain forests and bulldozing everything else under so we can have another mall."

"So, what are you doing hunting the wolf with Thomas?"

Laura glanced at Delaney, who had joined them. "I'm just a concerned citizen."

"There are a lot of concerned citizens," Brent said. "Sheriff Bennet's discouraging all of them from forming hunting parties."

"That's right, Brent," Delaney said. "He has his reasons. First of which is safety. You get a bunch of yahoos out in these woods and someone is going to end up being shot accidentally. And it won't be the wolf."

"Dad said he would sit at home as long as his herd wasn't in danger." Brent glanced at a corpse of a slain steer and raised one eyebrow as his father and elder brother, Carson, joined them.

Cordel McMichaels glanced around him. A deep sadness pulled at his features and dulled his eyes. "Looks like I won't be sitting home now."

"Are you planning on hunting the wolf?" asked Delaney.

"Are you planning on stopping me?" replied Cordel.

"I can't stop you, Cordel. Every man has to do what he thinks is best." Delaney looked at the man, who was only a couple of years older than him. "I'm asking you not to, though." His gaze shot off into the direction the wolf had taken. "This isn't your ordinary wolf."

"I already figured that out for myself." Cordel pulled a pack of cigarettes from his shirt pocket and lit one up. "Want to tell me about it?"

"Not right now. I'm working with a bunch of assumptions. Something I'm having a hard time doing." Delaney gave Laura a glance, which she rightfully interpreted. He wasn't going to tell the McMichaels about her brother, or his theories about werewolves.

Cordel blew a stream of smoke into the air. "Want to enlighten me on some of those assumptions?"

"No."

Laura held her breath and waited for Cordel's response. Her gut opinion of Cordel and his boys told her they weren't used to being excluded, especially when it concerned their ranch. Cordel appeared to be a couple of years older than Delaney, but both men looked to have been raised outdoors. Hard physical work wasn't a stranger to either one of them.

Cordel took another pull on the cigarette. "Do you have any idea how much money is lying slaughtered on the ground?"

"I have a rough idea, but I'm sure you could tell me to the exact dollar. Ranching is a tough way to make a living, and every head of cattle makes a difference."

"So, I'm supposed to shrug off the killings and allow you to take care of the situation." Cordel dropped the cigarette to the dirt and ground it out beneath his boot. "You're a better hunter than me, Thomas, I'll give you that."

"You're a better rancher than me." Delaney continued to lock gazes with the older McMichaels. "I know what I'm hunting. How about if I stick to what I'm good at, and you stick to what you're good at?"

"I'll give you a week. If the wolf isn't killed by then, me and my boys will be joining up with the other ranchers and setting out on our own. We won't be asking you or Sheriff Bennet for permission, either."

"Fair enough." Delaney pulled on his backpack, which he had taken off to examine the cattle. "One week." He picked up his gun, motioned to Laura to follow and headed in the same direction the wolf had taken.

"One more thing, Thomas," Cordel called. "If the wolf so much as looks at any more of my cattle, the deal's off."

Delaney nodded, but didn't reply.

They had been traveling for twenty minutes before Laura broke the silence. "Maybe you should have told him about Marcus and his theory. He might have understood." The McMichaels seemed like a nice family to her.

Delaney glanced over his shoulder. "Are you out of your mind, too? Cordel would have called Bennet and had us both hauled away to a funny farm." He gave her a look that spoke his disappointment. "That is, if Cordel could have stopped laughing long enough to dial a phone."

"It's not that crazy," snapped Laura. She didn't like the way he'd said *too*. Marcus wasn't crazy, just a little eccentric. At one time, people thought Columbus was crazy for thinking the earth was round. "You read his journal and you believed."

"I don't believe he turned himself into a werewolf, Laura."

Laura's chin rose an inch as she stared across the few feet that separated them. "Then what do you believe?" There were a whole lot of questions buried in that one simple one.

Delaney sighed and turned back around. "I believe we are wasting valuable time standing here arguing." He started forward and never turned around again to see if she was following.

She knew he could hear her behind him, but it still irked her that he didn't bother to check. *After what we shared last night and this morning you would think the man would at least turn around to make sure I was coming.* If he didn't believe Marcus had changed into a wolf and was the one responsible for all this butchery, then why was he allowing her to tag along? Delaney hadn't struck her as the type of man who did things out of the goodness of his heart. Then again, he hadn't struck her as a sensitive, passionate lover, either, until last night. The man had made her feel things she'd never thought possible. Not only had he stroked her body to a shattering climax, but he had touched her heart.

Was it possible to fall in love with a man like Delaney? It was rotten timing if she was. He had been the one making very clear there were no promises, and she had accepted him into her bed under those conditions. She just couldn't change the rules in the middle of the game. What was she going to do now? She was falling in love for the very first time. She never hid from anything in her life, but confronting Delaney in the middle of the woods seemed inappropriate.

Laura stepped over a fallen log and narrowly avoided stepping on a dry twig. Tromping through the forest like an elephant would not only alert the wolf if he was within hearing distance, it would give Delaney a reason for leaving her behind. She shook Delaney and his motives from her mind and concentrated on what she was doing. There would be plenty of time later to question him, both on Marcus and their relationship.

Delaney finished his sandwich and can of fruit juice. Laura was getting to him. Since they had stopped for lunch she had done nothing but stare at him and quietly eat her lunch. Problem was, he could see the wheels turning in her head. There were a thousand questions burning in her green eyes. Questions she wasn't asking. Any other woman would be hounding him, but not Laura. She just sat there quietly munching on a thick chicken-salad sandwich George had fixed for them. Laura had made an impression on both George and Lucy. He had never seen George bustle around the kitchen before dawn, whipping up a seven-course lunch for him. Delaney usually got leftovers from the night before, or whatever else the hunting parties were taking along. Laura comes along, and wham, freshly made chicken-salad sandwiches, celery and carrot sticks, individually wrapped gooey buns, and boxes of raisins. Where in the hell had George come up with little boxes of raisins with smiley faces printed on the box? It had to be Laura's presence. He'd never had smiley face raisins packed in his lunch before.

He nodded at her lunch. "How's the food?"

"Great. George is worth his weight in gold."

Delaney chuckled as he visualized George. "That's a lot of gold."

Laura munched on a carrot stick. "Want to tell me what you did to make him and Lucy so devoted?"

"I'm a great employer."

"There's more to it than that."

He concentrated on opening the tiny box of raisins. He was uncomfortable talking about himself. "They had a problem, and I helped them fix it."

"It must have been some problem." She bit into a crisp piece of celery and frowned as the noise echoed around them.

Delaney shrugged. It wasn't his problem to discuss. If George and Lucy wanted anyone to know, they would have to be the ones to tell. Besides, the problem wasn't all that difficult to handle, and everything had worked out well for everyone concerned. It was now Laura's brother who had a problem, and Delaney wasn't about to put any money on everything working out for the best. So far the trail was scattered with unanswered questions and dead animals. Ranchers in this area didn't take kindly to having the throats of their livestock ripped out. "Looks like your brother has the problem now."

"True." She nibbled on the celery for a moment. "Are you going to help him?"

"I think we have to find him before we can help him."

"We're on the right track." She nodded in the direction they had been hiking.

"No, Laura." He stood up, paced to a large aspen tree and gazed at a small valley below. When he had finally called a halt for lunch he'd picked this spot thinking

Laura might enjoy the view. He had been pushing hard all morning, and sight-seeing hadn't been on his agenda. So far she hadn't even bothered to look. "We aren't following your brother."

"Then what are we tracking?"

"In all likelihood, we're following the wolf your brother experimented on, XYZ."

Laura shook her head. "Marcus's journal said that XYZ wasn't fully grown and was dark gray. You said this wolf was abnormally large and black."

"Your brother also did some experimenting with growth hormones on XYZ. They could have altered his size in a short period of time."

"How do you explain the color difference?"

"When Marcus classed the animal as dark gray, he might not have been referring to the coloring at all. Almost all wolves belong to a species called the *gray wolf*. There are two main types of gray wolves—the timber wolf, which we are tracking, and the tundra wolf. When Marcus said the wolf was dark gray, "dark" could have been referring to the black coloring and "gray" to the species." It was a long shot, but the other alternative was unthinkable.

"Marcus has jet-black hair, just like the wolf."

Delaney whirled around. "Can he also rip a twelve-hundred-pound steer apart with his teeth?"

"But the injection . . ."

"But nothing, Laura. The most powerful mind-altering drug available couldn't make a man rip apart a steer." He shoved his fingers through his hair before jamming his fists into the pockets of his coat. Why must she be so stubborn and unrealistic? "For the last time, there are no such things as werewolves!"

"Says who?"

"Says me!"

Laura tilted up her chin. "The world laughed at Columbus when he said the earth was round. They laughed at the Wright brothers when they said man would fly. Forty years ago—" she thrust out her empty hand

"—who would have thought there would be computers that could fit in the palm of your hand?"

"Are you comparing your brother with the Wright brothers and IBM?"

"No, all I am saying is his ideas are theoretically possible. Can't you at least entertain the possibility?"

"It would be like believing the moon is made out of cheese."

"No, it won't. We've already landed on the moon and proven it isn't made of cheese." She rewrapped the remaining celery and carrot sticks and placed them back into the lunch bag along with the plastic bag her sandwich had been in. "Is it a question of my intelligence?"

"Your intelligence? What does that have to do with your brother?"

"You're obviously questioning my intelligence for believing in the possibilities."

"Your and Marcus's intelligence were never in doubt. What I am questioning is your brother's sanity."

"Gee, that sounds a whole lot better." Laura stood up and shoved the lunch bag back into Delaney's pack and mimicked his deep voice. "I don't think you're stupid, just insane."

Delaney couldn't help himself. He smiled. Really smiled. For the first time in long time he had something to smile about. He had Laura. Funny, sexy, intelligent and stubborn Laura. A woman with grit. A woman who wasn't afraid to stand up to him and speak her mind. A woman who could make him lose control and burn hotter than the sun. Lord, what a novelty she was.

Laura glared at Delaney. "What are you grinning about?"

"You."

"Me?"

He closed the few yards separating them and tenderly cupped her chin. "You take a man's breath away."

"Me?" Her voice had a squeaky, disbelieving quality to it.

"Yes, you." He slowly rubbed his thumb over her lower lip and marveled at the way her eyes darkened instantly with desire. She felt it, too. This powerful pull between them. *Attraction* didn't begin to describe the pull. *Need* was a more appropriate word. He needed Laura, and his gut was telling him it was more than just physical. "I left the sleeping bags back in the Jeep so I wouldn't be tempted to lay you down and make love to you all afternoon." His lips brushed the sweet softness of her mouth. "I thought I'd be immune to your charms." His mouth lingered and stroked. "I failed to allow for your humor." It was the one charm he hadn't been prepared against. Humor was a rare commodity in his life. Grit, humor and fiery passion all in one woman. No wonder Laura overwhelmed him.

Laura reached for his mouth as it left hers. "Who needs sleeping bags?"

Delaney chuckled and took a step back. "You're a dangerous woman, Laura." He kissed the end of her nose and backed farther away. "About a quarter mile ahead of us is a turning point for the wolf. Either he'll head north into the swamps, or west. There are a couple of small ranches in the west. It's my guess that's where he's headed."

"So we're going west?"

"No, we're hiking till we see which way he heads, then we are turning around and going back to the Jeep." The pout pulling at her lower lip was delightful. He wanted to nibble on that lower lip until the pout changed into a smile. "With any luck, we'll be back at the lodge for dinner."

"What about our differences concerning the wolf?"

"Let's just agree to disagree, okay?" He didn't want to get into another argument about the wolf with her. He strapped on the pack and picked up his rifle.

Laura smiled as she hauled the rifle straps over her shoulder. "Okay, but I will be expecting a full apology from you when we finally catch the wolf."

Delaney shook his head and chuckled as he started off into the woods. Leave it to Laura to have the last word.

Laura leaned against the bathroom door and sighed. So much for spending a quiet evening at Marcus's house with Delaney. She had managed to talk him into driving to her brother's house instead of the lodge. On the twenty-minute ride to the house he had called Sheriff Bennet and suggested they get together. By the time they had arrived, the sheriff, Deputy Bylic and two men, who were later introduced to her as local ranchers, were already at the house.

Their meeting had gone on for over an hour, when she mentioned food. She didn't know about anyone else, but she was starved. The three pots of coffee she had made were long gone. Since it was her brother's table they were all sitting around, she figured it was her duty to bring up the fact that it was way past dinnertime. Lunch had been six hours and a seven-mile hike ago. Delaney immediately suggested they call the only pizza shop in Moosehead Falls and have pizzas delivered. Ben's didn't usually deliver, but since it was the sheriff's department doing the ordering, they made an exception this time. Within half an hour four large pizzas arrived. Laura good-heartedly pulled out all the soda she had in the refrigerator and started another pot of coffee.

She sat at the counter, eating her pizza, and listened to the men argue, agree, insult and compliment one another. The sheriff wanted the wolf caught no matter what, but agreed with Delaney on restraint. Deputy Bylic hung on every word Delaney uttered. The ranchers wanted to go after the wolf with everything they could get their hands on. By the sound of some of their threats, she had to guess they could get their hands on quite a lot. Delaney wanted the privilege of capturing the wolf. Since he was a hunter by trade, he had the best chance of getting the wolf. He didn't want the woods crowded with trigger-happy ranchers ready to shoot at anything that moved.

Delaney had invited the two hotheaded ranchers to the meeting to make them a deal—they would stay out of the woods and he would keep them posted on which direction the wolf was headed. Ranchers then could be notified to take precautions, and if their livestock couldn't be brought into barns, then they had the right to stand guard and protect their herds. She had glared a hole into the back of Delaney's head for that remark, but he never turned around.

By the time maps had been hauled out and strategies started to fly she had had enough. Not once had anyone asked for her opinion. Wasn't she one of the two people who, for the past three days, had been hiking over half of Minnesota trailing the animal? The testosterone in the room was stifling. She was exhausted and dirty, and she'd be damned before she'd start another pot of coffee. With a mumble about locking up when they left, she'd headed for the shower.

Laura stepped out of the shower and wrapped her brother's robe around her. She toweled her hair dry, somewhat ran a comb through it and slipped into the master bedroom. The men were still debating the merits and disadvantages of bringing in helicopters to aid in their search. She closed the door and curled up in the center of the bed and opened her brother's journal. They could argue all they wanted to out in the kitchen. She had a feeling the answers were in the journal.

With a huge yawn and two fluffy pillows beneath her head, she started to read the journal from the beginning.

Delaney opened the door and peered at the woman sleeping in the center of the bed. Lord, she was lovely. A thick cloud of black hair was spread out across light-blue sheets. The ridiculously large robe had fallen open to reveal one pale breast, tipped with a dusty nipple, and one incredibly long leg. He leaned his tired body against the doorjamb and stared. He was in trouble. Big trouble.

Easing the physical ache with Laura hadn't helped. If anything it had only made things worse. It used to be he was aware of her as soon as she walked into the same room. Now he knew the moment she walked out of the room. He missed her. Just looking at her now, sleeping so beautiful, made him hard as granite. When she'd left the kitchen earlier it had made him edgy. Instead of concentrating on the wolf, he wondered what she was doing. When he'd heard the shower start, he'd remembered every detail of their shower together that morning. Bennet had appeared quite amused by his distraction. The third time Bennet had to say his name to get his attention, he realized how useless he had become. He'd called an end to the meeting, told Bennet where the wolf was heading so that the ranchers could be warned and bade everyone a good-night. By the time everyone had cleared out, the doors were locked and the kitchen put back into order, another half an hour had passed.

Delaney pushed away from the jamb and headed for the shower. Laura looked too peaceful to disturb. After a day of hiking, she had to be exhausted. Especially since neither one of them had had a whole lot of sleep last night. The least he could do was allow her one good night of rest. Marcus Kinkaid was one lucky man. To have a sister—or anyone else, for that matter—love him the way Laura did was a gift. A gift every man wasn't fortunate enough to receive.

Ten minutes later, Delaney gently removed Laura's robe and slipped her in between the covers. He found Marcus's journal under her arm and carefully set it on the nightstand. She never even stirred. Guilt riddled his body as it responded to her nakedness. He was the reason she was so exhausted. He had pushed her too hard today. After seeing which way the wolf was heading—westward—he should have turned around and gone back to the Jeep. Instead he'd followed the trail another mile uphill, just to make sure the animal hadn't backtracked or veered off toward the north. Laura hadn't complained, but that wasn't unusual. She never so much as grumbled politely about the hike or the rough conditions. Her need to find the wolf only matched his need to kill it. Laura was never going to forgive him if he shot and killed the wolf before she had a chance to examine the animal. For some strange reason, which he had a hard time understanding, she believed in Marcus's theories.

Delaney quietly turned off the light, dropped the towel wrapped around his hips and eased into bed. He pulled Laura's warm body against him and smiled as she snuggled up to his chest. His fingers wove their way into her hair. The scent of coconut shampoo teased his nose.

He wondered what it would be like to have a woman believe in him so unconditionally. He knew Laura wasn't the type of person who normally went around believing in werewolves, or any other creatures of the night. A lot of what she was feeling toward Marcus was guilt. He had read the first page of the journal, where Marcus had effectively laid the seeds of blame on Laura's doorstep for sparking his interest in werewolves. It was a rotten thing for a brother to do. But he didn't think all of Laura's belief came from guilt.

She honestly thought there was a chance that her brother had succeeded with his experiment. *A chance!* That was what she had said—a chance. She had been hiking through northern Minnesota because of those two words: *a chance*. Returning to her job in Saint Paul wasn't going to locate her brother. Sitting in his house all day, waiting, was fruitless. So she had strapped on a backpack, and hiked her muscles into agony, all because there was a chance. Who was he to discount her chance? Her brother was obviously an intelligent man, and most of his theories, as Laura pointed out, seemed plausible. So who was he to discount them as the ravings of a madman? As Laura had said, most of the world's greatest discoveries were made by someone the world at one time considered a madman.

Delaney silently chuckled. Laura now had him believing in chances. She wasn't a woman, she was a witch.

"Delaney?" mumbled Laura into his chest.

"Shhh...go back to sleep." He slowly ran the palm of his hand up and down her smooth back.

Laura's hand curved around his hip. "What time is it?"

"Time for you to go back to sleep." He ground his teeth as her hot little hand slid over his hip and up his thigh. He was going to be a gentlemen and control his desires, even if it killed him. Laura needed her sleep.

She nuzzled the curly hair covering his chest with her cheek and smiled drowsily. "All of a sudden, I'm not sleepy any longer."

She was killing him! Inch by inch, as her fingers skimmed higher, his control was once again shattering. "Laura!" he groaned as she tenderly cupped him.

"Are you getting chatty on me again?"

The amusement in her voice was his undoing. In one sure thrust, he turned her onto her back and entered her. He brushed the hair away from her eyes and waited until she adjusted to his size. "Are you awake?"

"I am now." She arched her hips and smiled dreamily.

Delaney felt her silken thighs wrap around his hips and knew he was lost. He allowed her heat to pull him in deeper. He burned. Her sweetness surrounded him, the way nothing else ever had. In a matter of minutes they reached the peak of their desires and together they went tumbling over the edge.

He lay spent and satisfied on cool cotton sheets with Laura's moist body resting on top of him. She had done it again. Made him lose his control. And this time he wasn't sure if she had been totally awake. He brushed a damp curl away from her forehead and asked, "Are you all right?"

"Couldn't you tell?" she mumbled sleepily.

He could feel her smile against his skin and dropped a kiss onto the top of her head. When she didn't raise her head or move he knew she had fallen back to sleep. "Laura?" he whispered into the dark. He wanted to at least wish her a good-night.

She snuggled closer and softly muttered, "I didn't mean to."

He raised an eyebrow and looked at the woman sleeping in his arms. "Mean to what?" he softly asked.

Her reply was so low he barely heard it. "Fall in love with you."

Delaney stared at her in shock. She appeared sound asleep. Had she even known what she said? Laura was falling in love with him! It was the last thing he wanted. What had happened to the no promises, no future? How could she be falling in love? She knew nothing about him.

It wasn't supposed to happen. No one was supposed to be hurt. He didn't want to hurt Laura. It was the last thing he wanted to do. Laura believed in love and in families sticking together, no matter what. To him, love didn't exist and the idea of families sticking together was about as alien as werewolves roaming Minnesota.

If he had one ounce of dignity he would leave right this minute. Plop a goodbye note on the kitchen table and disappear from her life. Before the hurt grew.

So why was he lying in her bed, cradling her body as if it were a fragile piece of crystal? Why were his hands trembling and a film of moisture coating his eyes? And why was his heart beating a thousand times a minute, threatening to burst through his chest?

# Chapter 10

Delaney dropped his pack by his desk and headed right back out the door. Laura let him go without a word. The frustration of waiting all day for a wolf, who never showed, had been evident in every line on his face. Delaney was ready to explode, and she didn't want to be anywhere near him when he did. For three days the wolf had been playing games with them. It sounded ridiculous, but it was the only explanation she could come up with. For the past days they had known which direction the wolf was headed, and staked out the obvious destination as soon as it was light enough to see. They had spent a day in a dilapidated barn overlooking a small penned-in area of sheep and the wolf had attacked a lone milk cow two miles away. Yesterday they hid between boulders in the middle of a cow pasture as the wolf raided a small henhouse at the next ranch. The wolf seemed to know every move they made.

Today had been the worse. Seven hours of crouching beneath pine trees with a freezing drizzle pelting them all afternoon had taken its toll on Delaney. The wolf hadn't disturbed the cattle grazing below them. He had at-

tacked and killed two hunting dogs chained up about a
mile and a half from where Delaney and her had been
waiting. When Sheriff Bennet had broken radio silence
to give Delaney the news, it had been nearly dusk. They'd
left their position and driven to the home where the incident had occurred.

Laura couldn't bring herself to go around to the back
of the house, where the dogs had been. Instead she'd
surveyed the front side of the house. Nothing. Over the
past couple of days she had been getting pretty good at
picking up the wolf's trail. Delaney had taught her a lot.
But she hadn't been able to spot any sign of where the
wolf had come out of the woods in front of the house.
The house was a nice, small, one-story dwelling. A man
named Hank Ansel lived there alone. There hadn't been
any barn or livestock. Only his two hunting dogs. When
he had arrived home from work, he found the dogs and
called the sheriff.

She had leaned against the front fender of the Jeep,
trying to ignore the rain slipping beneath her collar, for
ten minutes before Delaney rejoined her. He turned on
the Jeep, started the heater and told her to wait inside for
him. He would be right back. Forty minutes later he had
returned, soaked and angry. During the drive to the lodge
he told her he'd followed the wolf's trail to within forty
yards of where they had been concealed beneath the
pines. The wolf had known where they were!

Delaney had taken the knowledge that the animal had
once again tricked them as personal. He somehow felt
inferior to the wolf. In a way, she could understand his
frustration. The wolf had an uncanny ability to stay one
step ahead of them, but she didn't take it personally.
Maybe it was a male thing, this need to conquer, outsmart and dominate.

Right now she was too miserable to care. She was wet
and cold, and every muscle in her body ached from being motionless under a tree all day. She needed to soak
for a long time in a very hot tub, and that was exactly
what she was going to do. She hung her wet coat on the

coat rack and placed her damp boots by the heating element. Later she'd start a nice fire and curl up on the couch with a good book or Delaney. For now, she'd go warm up in the tub and let Delaney cool off. It was frightening how much she was beginning to understand the man.

She walked into the bathroom and started to fill the tub. Ever since she and Delaney had become lovers, they'd alternated the nights between Marcus's house and the lodge. Marcus's house gave them total privacy, but Delaney's apartment in the lodge gave them comfort. She loved the fireplace, George's cooking, the hot tub built for two and, especially, Delaney's king-size bed. She also loved Delaney.

There, she finally admitted it to herself! She loved Delaney. For days she had been convincing herself she was just *falling in love* with Delaney, not actually *in love*. A person who was falling usually could stop herself at any time. What she felt for Delaney was unstoppable. In fact, she had already landed. She was in love. Wholeheartedly, unconditionally, in love for the very first time in her life. And there wasn't anything she could do about it. She was in love with a man who desired her, yes, but love? There was so much about Delaney that she didn't know, and he wasn't the type of man who liked to talk about himself. Getting Delaney to reveal anything remotely personal about himself would take an act of Congress.

With a weary sigh, she turned off the faucets, dropped her wet clothes into a neat little pile and climbed into the steamy tub. Bubbles! That was what she needed. Bubbles always made her feel better.

Delaney quietly pushed open the bathroom door and grinned. Laura was lying in a tubful of bubbles. A thick white towel was wrapped around her hair and bubbles covered every inch of her, from her chin on down. His hot tub never looked so inviting. He chuckled as she lifted one foot and five little toes emerged from the white froth.

Laura cracked open one eye and glanced at Delaney standing in the doorway. "Are you human yet?"

"Barely." He removed his flannel shirt and it landed somewhat haphazardly near her pile of laundry.

"You didn't yell at George, did you?"

"Relax, your dinner is safe and at this moment sizzling away under the broiler." His insulated undershirt landed on top of his flannel shirt. "I started to voice my frustrations to him, but I got no sympathy."

"Poor baby," cooed Laura. She raised her foot higher and wiggled her toes. White bubbles slid over her foot, passed her ankle and pooled around her calf. "What did he do? Threaten to burn your steak?"

"No, he told me to leave the kitchen or he was going back home and I could finish fixing dinner for fifteen people." His socks, jeans and underwear hit the floor in a sodden mess.

"It took you an awfully long time to get back here." She raised her arms and smiled seductively as the water and bubbles slipped over her skin.

"I went over to Jake Stoner's place to check up on business." He frowned as he stepped into the tub. "Everything is running smoothly."

She moved her feet so he could sit down. "Why so glum, then?"

"I guess I just realized they don't need me. I haven't been here to run the place for well over a week, and nothing major happened. No emergencies. No cancellations. Hell, Jake even booked a ten-men hunting party for Thanksgiving weekend." He sat down and sighed as the warm water covered his cold body. Cold weather had never bothered him before and visions of his hot tub had never caused him to hurry home before. He looked at Laura sitting across from him, all pink-cheeked and sexy. Maybe it wasn't the weather or the tub. Maybe it was the company.

Laura ran her toes up the inside of one of Delaney's thighs. She stopped dangerously close to a very sensitive area and grinned. "Are you feeling unloved?"

Delaney chuckled and removed her foot. "Dinner will be here in about fifteen minutes."

Her foot immediately returned to the same spot. "Haven't you ever heard of a quickie?"

He felt her small, delicate foot gently brush up against him and knew he would once again lose the battle with his control.

Delaney smiled as he sat down on the couch and placed Laura's bare feet on his lap. It was a disgusting shame what she had done to him. Now even her toes turned him on. By the time he and Laura emerged from the bathroom, dinner had to be reheated in the little microwave he had in his kitchen. After the meal, Laura, still dressed in a robe, had curled up on the couch with a book while he went to check on things to make sure everything was okay for the night. He had also spent fifteen minutes on the phone with the sheriff and poring over maps. The last tracks of the wolf he had spotted, before it became to dark to see, showed that the animal was headed back toward Moosehead Falls. The direction he had been going led past numerous small ranches and homes. The only chance he had of picking up the fresh trail was to be up and out of here before dawn. With any luck, he'd be able to spot tracks in the morning dew before it was burned off by the sun. Morning was going to be coming early.

Laura closed the book she had been reading and looked up. "Everything okay?"

"Fine. The sheriff is sending two of the deputies out to warn the people living in the area the wolf was heading toward tonight. We have an early wake-up call. After what happened to Ansel's dogs, there's a lot of talk about group hunts. They aren't going to wait much longer for me to bring the wolf in, Laura." He gently squeezed her foot. "In three days, there are no bookings at the lodge till the weekend. Jake and Clint, George's son, will be coming out with us to hunt the wolf. Jake and Clint could get in front of him, and with me and you in the rear, we could trap him."

"Will they be using tranquilizer guns?"

"No, it wouldn't be safe for them." His heart did a funny little turn in his chest as she lowered her gaze and stared at the book still clutched in her hand. He couldn't read the title, but he knew it was one of the half-dozen or so books she had brought with her from Marcus's house. He waited for her to start arguing, but she didn't. She just stared at the book. "I'm sorry, Laura. They are doing this because I asked them to. I can't have them put their lives in danger. Tranquilizers are unpredictable and there's a time element involved. In those precious seconds it takes for the dart to take effect, this wolf could do a lot of damage. I am willing to allow you to try to use the dart, if it appears safe, only because of the scientific value the wolf might have."

She jerked her head up. "Then you do believe me!"

"Not about Marcus's theories. I was thinking more along the lines of seeing what your brother did to XYZ."

"What if it isn't XYZ?"

"Then the wolf should definitely be examined. It could have some contagious disease, or even a new type of rabies. A hundred different things could be wrong with it. Without the wolf, or at least his body, there's no way of knowing."

"You won't even consider Marcus's theory, will you?"

Delaney shoved his fingers through his hair. "Laura," he groaned in exasperation. He wanted to say yes, just to please her, but he couldn't.

"Forget it." She lowered her gaze back to the book.

"All right, Laura. I'll give Marcus's theory a million-to-one chance, okay?" In this crazy mixed-up world in which they lived, he guessed anything could be possible. Not probable, but possible.

She slowly raised her head and smiled. "I'll take those odds."

"Why?"

"People have won the lottery on worse odds than that."

Delaney laughed and tried to grab her feet, but she yanked them out of his hands and tucked them under her robe. He glanced at the book she had been holding. "What are you reading?"

"It's a book on transformations." She gave him an impish smile. "You ought to read it. It might make you change those odds to a million to two."

He tugged the book out of her hand and opened it up. Sure enough, the book was on transformations. He skimmed the titles of the chapters: Shapeshifters, Werewolves, Native American Legends, Vampires, Other Creatures of the Night, to name a few. He closed the book and handed it back to Laura. "I'll wait for the movie."

She chuckled and dropped the book onto the end table. "It's already been done—a couple hundred times." She sat up and stretched. "The other night at Marcus's, I heard Deputy Bylic mention something about you being in the military. Which branch?"

"Marines." He kicked off his shoes and plopped his feet on the table. He really didn't want to get into a discussion about his past with Laura. It wasn't the highlight of his life. The only thing he had to show for his thirty-six years of living was this lodge, and the success he had made of it. Laura had already seen his only achievement; everything else was a downhill slide. "I enlisted the day I graduated from high school." Laura had the right to know about the man she was sleeping with. "I spent thirteen years in the service, most of which were in a sharpshooter outfit." He didn't have to tell her that he was in command of that outfit for seven of those years.

"So you aren't just pulling my leg when you say you can hit what you aim at?"

"If I'm aiming, I'll be hitting it."

Laura nodded. "No wonder Deputy Bylic thinks you're the greatest hunter since Daniel Boone and Sheriff Bennet has so much confidence in your abilities."

"Doesn't take much to impress people around here."

"Just being a highly decorated sharpshooter?"

"How did you know?" No one around there knew about the medals he had tucked away in some drawer except George and Lucy, and they wouldn't tell.

She grinned. "You just told me." She chuckled at his look. "I couldn't imagine you being some lowly old soldier for thirteen years. My guess is you had a chest decorated with ribbons and list of promotions when you left."

The sweet naiveness gleaming in her eyes almost undid him. For days he'd thought of nothing but her sleepy declaration of falling in love with him. He didn't think she remembered saying it, but that wasn't the point. She shouldn't be falling, or even contemplating falling, in love with him. It could never be. She deserved so much more out of life than what he could give her. If a person honestly thought she was in love with someone, then she should be loved in return. He didn't believe in love. Desire, yes. Need, yes. He could admit to himself he needed Laura. A person could need another person. But it wasn't love.

He had to make Laura see him in another light, one less honorable than what she was seeing now. She was romanticizing the medals and the glory. "I left the military under unfavorable circumstances." *Unfavorable circumstances! What a way to put it.*

"Unfavorable to whom? You or them?"

"Everybody." He couldn't bear to see the innocence in her eyes shatter, so he turned and faced the blazing fire. "I spent seven months in a military prison."

She sat up straighter, but didn't move away. "What was the charge?"

"Treason." He gave a rough chuckle. "Treason against the United States of America." It doesn't get any worse than that. To be charged with betraying your own country. Even in a time of peace, it was the worst offense a soldier could be charged with.

"Impossible! You would never do such a thing." She frowned and started to chew on her lower lip. "At least not knowingly. Was that it? Were you tricked into something?''

Delaney jerked his head around and stared at her. She believed his innocence! Without even hearing the facts. ''If only my wife had had that much faith in me.''

''Your wife?'' This time Laura did move away. She also gripped the front lapels on the robe until her knuckles turned white.

''Excuse me, my *ex-wife*.''

''You were married?'' Her grip relaxed.

He turned away from the sadness dulling her eyes. He had disappointed Laura. Not with the charge of treason logged against him, but because he had been married. Damn! She hadn't flinched when he told her he had spent seven months in jail, but mention his ex-wife and she looked ready to cry. ''It only lasted two years. Seven months of which I was behind bars.''

''She divorced you because you were charged with treason?''

''Hell no.'' He stood up, faced the fire and then swung around to face her. ''I divorced her because she was sleeping with the military lawyer who had charged me with it!'' He flinched at the sound of his voice echoing through the room. He hadn't meant to yell, but talking about the betrayal had rekindled the pain.

''Oh...'' She worried her lower lip for a moment. ''You must have loved her very much.''

Delaney laughed for the first time while remembering the worst seven months of his life. ''How did you manage to come up with that one?''

''You seem awfully upset about something that happened five years ago.'' She nervously wrapped the sash of the robe around her finger. ''Besides, you married her, didn't you?''

Delaney shook his head at her reasoning. Marrying someone and loving someone didn't necessarily go hand in hand. He walked over to the mantel and stared down into the flames. ''I meet Kathleen DuVal in one of the local bars right off base.'' She had been looking for a man, any man. He had been looking for a warm, willing woman. "We immediately hit it off. We had a lot in common." They had both came from abusive homes and had been depending on themselves most of their lives. Both of them had been lonely. "We became friends and lovers. Within a month, we decided to get married. I wanted a family—she wanted security. We both could have done a lot worse than each other. Love never entered the picture."

"So what did you base the marriage on? Family and security?"

He grimaced, but didn't turn around. Love happened in fairy tales, and life was not a fairy tale. "There have been plenty of marriages based on less than that." He picked up the poker and jabbed at a burning log. "I thought we had trust and respect."

"What happened?"

"Being a military wife wasn't as glamorous as Kathleen thought it should be. The money wasn't great, my assignments sometimes took me out of the country for weeks and I kept pressuring her about starting that family." He had found out later on that while he thought Kathleen was trying to conceive his child, she had been secretly taking birth control pills. "One day, while I was out of the country, some polished military lawyer trying to make a name for himself tripped over a stack of false information, and came up with treason."

"How—"

"By finding a gullible source and planting the information. While this lawyer was bumbling around questioning everyone, he stumbled across Kathleen. She took one look at his fancy title, decided it would be more rewarding being married to a lawyer than a soldier and fed the guy the answers he wanted to hear. As soon as I landed back on the base, I was hustled off to prison in handcuffs and disgrace." He stared at the fire for a long time as the memories came flooding back. It still hurt remembering how the military had taken the pompous lawyer's word over his own. The faces of his men as they'd watched him being handcuffed still haunted him. When he'd finally learned of Kathleen's betrayal, days later, he had gone berserk and trashed his cell. The military had kept him in that trashed cell for weeks, before his own lawyer threatened the commander of the base with a countersuit.

When Delaney didn't continue, Laura asked, "What happened then?"

"Two of the men who served with me, Sean Peterson and Dev Bradley, worked with my lawyer. They believed in my innocence. It took them months to uncover the truth, but they finally did." Sean and Dev had kept his hopes up during those months. To this day, he would trust his life to either one of them, without question. They were the only two people in the world who had believed, unconditionally, in him at the time. Since then, only George and Lucy had crossed the boundary of friendship and become more. Laura could very easily slip over that boundary if he let her. He wasn't about to. "The military disbarred the lawyer and cleared my name of any wrongdoing. The lawyer dropped Kathleen and I divorced her. I couldn't stay with the military after that, so I opted for an early retirement. I took my life savings, bought the lodge and started all over again."

It all sounded so simple: *I took my life savings, bought the lodge and started all over again.* How was it possible to condense a man's life into one short sentence?

"If Kathleen had loved you, she would never have betrayed you."

Delaney chuckled sadly and shook his head. Laura still believed in fairy tales. "I knew Kathleen didn't love me the day I asked her to marry me. Our relationship was based on mutual need, not love."

"Why didn't you marry a woman you loved?"

He turned around and faced her. Laura had to learn the truth sometime. It might as well be now. "Because there is no such thing as love, Laura."

She tilted her head and studied him. "Who told you such poppycock?"

"No one had to tell me, Laura. I learned that the hard way." Twelve years of being raised by an abusive, drunken father. Thirteen years of listening to the military's propaganda concerning loyalty, honor and respect, only to have it fall apart on the weakest evidence. And a wife who'd betrayed him with another man and practiced nothing but deceit throughout their marriage. These had all taught him the lessons.

"What about your family? Didn't you love your father?"

He glared at her. At one time he might have loved his father, but it was so long ago he couldn't remember.

"What about the children you said you wanted with Kathleen? Were they going to be born to a father who didn't love them?"

Delaney started to sweat. He'd never thought about that. Was he as guilty as his father? How could he contemplate bringing a child into the world without love? Laura had a point. A point he would rather not face. "There weren't any children." Nor would there ever be any children. Dreams of a family had died behind those prison bars.

"You would have loved them," she stated knowingly.

"How do you know what I would have felt?" He ran his fingers through his hair in frustration. She had hit a sensitive nerve when she questioned his feelings for children. "How do you even know there is such a thing as love?"

Laura glanced down at her hands for a moment, then slowly raised her gaze to his. "Because I love you."

Delaney felt the blow to his chest clear across the room. She loved him! Laura loved him! He wanted to cry for the wasted years when he would have given anything to hear those words. Now it was too late. "Laura, don't." He walked toward her and stopped a couple of feet away. "I don't want to hurt you." He reached out and tenderly cupped her cheek. "Hurting you is the last thing I want to do."

She leaned her cheek into his hand and closed her eyes. "It's okay, Delaney. I knew the rules when this started." She turned her face and pressed a kiss into the palm of his hand. "I thought you said we had an early start in the morning." She stood up and headed for the bedroom.

He felt his gut split open. She wouldn't meet his gaze. "Laura?" They had to discuss this now.

"Not tonight, Delaney. We'll talk later." She kept her face turned away. "Are you coming?"

"In a minute. I have to bank the fire and shut off the lights."

"Okay." Laura walked into the bedroom.

Delaney heard his bathroom door close and felt like a jerk. She was crying. He had heard how her voice had broken when she asked if he was coming. After all his good intentions and honesty, he had hurt her just the same. He couldn't give her what she wanted—his love. There wasn't any to give. Every time in his life he had reached out to people, they had failed him. He couldn't reach out again, no matter how badly he wanted to. It would kill him to be abandoned again. When things got tough, he was always the first person people discarded. His father, his wife, the military. He couldn't add Laura's name to that list.

There was so much unsettled business between them that life was bound to get tougher. The wolf was their immediate obstacle. Soon, perhaps as early as tomorrow, they would corner the animal. How would Laura react if he had to kill it before she had a chance to use the tranquilizer gun on it? She honestly believed there was a chance this savage creature was her brother. If she had to choose between the wolf and him, he wouldn't want to wager any money on the outcome. Life had taught him who the winner would be. The wolf.

With vicious pokes, Delaney squatted in front of the fire and cursed the unfairness of life. The fire was a mound of embers by the time he placed the fire screen in front of it, turned off the lights and went to join Laura in his bed.

* * *

Two days later, Laura stood in Delaney's office and
listened to the complaining. Once again she was being
politely ignored and it was starting to get to her. A group
of six highly incensed ranchers were demanding to know
what Delaney was doing. Sheriff Bennet was trying to be
civil to the vocal group, but they were pushing their
complaints into the threatening category. By the dull red
sweeping up Delaney's jaw, she would guess he was ready
to take his frustration about the wolf out on the ranchers. She leaned against a file cabinet, crossed her arms
and waited for the explosion.

The ranchers deserved whatever Delaney dished out.
How dared they question his integrity or his devotion to
capturing the wolf? She had been with him every minute
for over a week, and no one knew better than she—the
man was relentless. For two days helicopters had circled
the area, searching for the wolf. The animal seemed to
know when they were there and hid. Not once in more
than twenty hours of air time had there been a spotting.
As soon as the air search was called by darkness the wolf
struck. Delaney was perplexed by the wolf's intelligence.
It was now a matter of honor that he get the wolf.

With every act of intelligence from the animal, the
more her conviction grew. Marcus and this creature just
might be one and the same. What other explanation
could there be? Delaney kept trying to rationalize the
wolf's behavior, but even he was having a hard time. The
theory of lycanthropy seemed more realistic than half of
Delaney's excuses.

Laura tried to smother a yawn, but knew Delaney had
spotted it. He noticed everything she did. She wondered
why he didn't seem to notice how ticked off she got when
she was ignored just because she was a woman. Tonight
he would insist they call it an early one because of that
yawn. For a man who professed not to believe in love, he
sure had a caring side. She loved that caring side and
every other side he possessed. She loved him.

The other night after she declared her love, all she'd gotten in return was his guilt. She had locked herself in the bathroom, had a good cry and then had given herself a pep talk. It started with the famous line, *'Tis better to have loved and lost than never to have loved at all*. But then she realized she hadn't lost. At least not yet. Delaney and she were still together. Somehow she had to make him see there was such a thing as love. The main question was, how? For two days she had pondered that question, and so far she hadn't come up with a satisfactory answer.

When Delaney had finally joined her in bed, he'd tenderly pulled her into his arms and held her through the night. There hadn't been anything sexual in his hold, just a warm, loving embrace. How could a man who had done that not know the meaning of love? His ex-wife's behavior had at first shocked, then horrified her. The military lawyer who'd charged him with such a crime should have been sent to prison, along with being disbarred. The marines should hang their heads in shame for allowing the travesty of justice, but in the end they had been punished. They were the ones who had lost Delaney. Men like Delaney would only be an honor to the service, never a burden. No wonder Delaney didn't believe in love. All he had ever known was betrayal. It was interwoven with the concrete wall surrounding his heart. The one she was determined to break through.

Laura grimaced as one of the ranchers used a four-letter word suitable only for the gutter. Delaney's face flamed purple. All eyes in the room glanced her way. Her presence finally had been noticed. It wasn't the kind of attention she wanted. She would have preferred being asked her opinion on the hunt. She had two choices: she could stay and watch Delaney rip the man's tongue out, or she could take the safer route. She pushed herself away from the cabinet. "If you all would excuse me . . . I need to check with George about dinner."

"I'm sorry, ma'am, if I offended you," mumbled the rancher as he looked sheepishly at his boot.

"Apology accepted." She walked to the door and opened it. "I understand about the pressure everyone has been under lately." She gave Delaney a meaningful look. "When you are ready to hear my opinion about the wolf and where he might be headed, just ask." She closed the door behind her and walked down the hall.

She smiled all the way to the kitchen. The look on Delaney's face had been priceless. He now knew she was miffed about being excluded from the strategy sessions. Good, let him stew with that for a while. She had more important things to do. Like pump George and Lucy for information. Maybe they could supply the key to unlocking Delaney's heart.

Five minutes later, she was amazed how easy it had been. Then again, George and Lucy had practically tied her to a stool at the counter, poured her coffee and started to relate everything they could about the man.

George had known Delaney's father and was aware of the abuse Delaney suffered as a boy. The picture George drew with his words wasn't pretty. No wonder Delaney had only glared at her when she asked if he loved his father. Nevil Thomas should have been arrested for child abuse and neglect. There hadn't been a loving family. No nucleus where Delaney could have given love and received love in return.

"George, I don't mean any disrespect, and I appreciate the information, but I think Delaney should be the one who tells me about his father." It was too personal to be discussing his childhood behind his back over a cup of coffee. "What I had in mind was something more recent."

"Recent?"

"Like what he did for you and Lucy?"

George rubbed at an imaginary spot on the counter with a towel. "He gave me and Lucy a job."

Laura reached into the bowl of fruit sitting in front of her and snapped off a stem of grapes. She popped a grape into her mouth. "There's more to the story than that, George." She wasn't going to push the issue.

Lucy refilled her empty coffee cup and shared a meaningful glance with George before answering. "He helped us when no one else would." She glanced at Laura, who continued to eat grapes. "It's no secret around these parts, so you might as well know. Our son, Clint, got himself into trouble the year he graduated from high school. He wanted to go to college for forestry, but we didn't have the money, and his grades weren't good enough for scholarships." Tears filled her eyes, but she continued to speak. "He took a job at one of the lumber mills and started to hang around with the wrong crowd. Eight months later he was arrested on drug charges and sent to prison. George lost his job as a cook for one of the camps because he got into a fight with Clint's so-called friends. We were living on my salary as a part-time maid for an owner of one of the mills."

George put a comforting arm around his wife. "I came to Delaney as our last hope. I had heard he was opening up a hunting lodge," George said. "By then we had sold our house to pay for Clint's legal expenses and he still wasn't out of jail. I was blackballed from the logging camp because of the fight, and Lucy's hours had been cut. We were living with Lucy's sister and could barely pay for our own food."

"Delaney gave you both a job and the cabin to live in, right?"

"He also got Clint a better lawyer and paid most of the legal expenses," Lucy said. She gave a delicate sniffle and dabbed at her eyes with the hem of the apron tied around her middle. "Within a month, Clint was released from prison and was working for Delaney as a guide."

Laura knew it would be something like this. Delaney had a heart the size of Lake Superior under his tough facade. The grape she was chewing tasted like tears. How was she ever going to burst through the concrete wall that surrounded his heart? She stood up, went over to Lucy and George and gave each a big hug. "You both deserve what Delaney did for you. You both loved your son unconditionally." Delaney had witnessed the power of love and had even helped it along. Maybe there was hope for him and her.

"We can never repay Delaney for what he has done."

"Is Clint happy being a guide?"

"He is almost as good as Delaney himself," said George proudly. "He stays out of trouble and takes a few college courses when he has the time. One day he will be a forest ranger, the way he always dreamed."

Laura smiled. "I think Delaney got the better end of the deal." She gave Lucy another hug. "He ended up with the best cook in northern Minnesota, a first-class housekeeper and a guide."

A flush swept up George's jaw and Lucy burst out laughing at the sight. "Lord have mercy," cried Lucy. "I haven't seen him blush since our honeymoon!"

Laura joined Lucy laughing just as Delaney stepped into the kitchen. He took one look at the women and asked, "What's so funny?"

She wasn't about to answer that question, but Lucy had no qualms about teasing her husband more. "George is blushing."

George, who had turned back to the stove when Delaney entered, looked over his shoulder. "Am not. It's the heat from the stove. Darn fool woman has been away from the stove for so long she forgets how hot it can get."

Delaney raised an eyebrow, stared at the older man, but didn't make a comment. He then glanced over at Laura. "Did you see about dinner?"

"George says it will be ready in about ten minutes." She nodded to a small table in the corner of the room. This was Delaney's lodge and theoretically his kitchen, even if George did all the cooking. It would be nice to sit down to a meal in the casual atmosphere of the room and share a meal with George and Lucy. "We'll be eating it in here tonight."

"You want to eat dinner in the kitchen?" He glanced around the room as if seeing it for the very first time.

"Sure, why not? Millions of people across the country eat dinner in their kitchen every night." She had a feeling he had isolated himself from everyone at the lodge. From George's and Lucy's watchful expressions, she knew she had been right in her assumption.

Delaney continued to stare at the table, as though trying to figure out what to do now. Laura winked at Lucy. The woman knew exactly what she was trying to do. ''If you show me where the plates are, I'll set the table.''

# Chapter 11

Delaney slowed down as the silhouette of a pickup truck parked on the side of the dirt road came into view. Who would be out here, in the middle of nowhere, at this time of the morning? The sun hadn't risen, but the sky was turning from black to a murky gray. He pulled up next to the truck and muttered a curse.

"What's the matter?" Laura asked.

"That's Glen Barnes's truck." He slowly drove onto the grass in front of the truck and turned off the Jeep.

"Who's Glen Barnes?" Laura glanced over her shoulder at the dented, rusty truck.

"Glen's the county troublemaker. If there's a fight, Glen is guaranteed to be in it. If the sheriff says stop, Glen is the first to go. And wherever there is booze, there's Glen." Delaney frowned at the truck behind them. It appeared empty, but there was always a chance Glen was passed out on the seat. He prayed this was so and Glen was not out looking for trouble. Twice Sheriff Bennet had hauled Glen in for hunting the wolf. Both times he hadn't been anywhere near the animal. Now, with the sheriff going around notifying everyone where the wolf was heading, it wouldn't be difficult for Glen to locate the general area. Glen's truck was parked directly in the middle of last night's designated "wolf zone."

"What does that have to do with us and the hunt?" She followed Delaney out of the Jeep and walked to the truck.

He shone his flashlight into the cab of the vehicle. It was empty except for the dozen or so beer cans littering the seat, the dash and the floor. The gun rack behind the seat had only one gun in it. Delaney's gut burned—the other slot was empty. The beam of his flashlight swept the bed of the truck. Nothing but old tires, rusty tools and more empty beer cans. "Glen's been giving the sheriff a hard time about not being able to hunt the wolf." He started to walk around the truck, looking for tracks. "He also has been raising a stink with the ranchers about forming hunting parties and putting a bounty on the wolf."

"A bounty?"

He hadn't told Laura about the bounty because it would sound as if they were putting one out on her brother, not the wolf. "Glen wants a reward offered so he can make some drinking money." The beam of light picked up some footprints leading from the truck into the woods. Delaney swore.

"Is Glen a rancher?"

"Are you kidding? Ranching would require actually working for a living. Glen doesn't believe in work. He likes to hunt only because it gives him a perverse pleasure in watching a helpless animal die."

"Sounds like a real *pillar* of the community." She grimaced and wrinkled her nose as she surveyed the truck.

"Right now, we have a problem." Delaney returned to the truck after following Glen's tracks for a couple of yards. "Glen's heading for the woods."

"That's the area the wolf was headed in last night, isn't it?"

"Yeah, but that's only the first problem."

"What's the second?"

"By the way Glen was staggering all over the place, I'd say he had a little too much to drink."

"By the look of his truck, I'd say it would be a miracle if Glen wasn't drunk." She followed Delaney back to the Jeep and watched as he hauled out his pack.

He handed Laura her guns. "If I asked you to stay in the Jeep, would you?"

"No."

"I thought you would say that." He handed her a brilliant orange vest and knit hat. "If you are coming with me, put these on." He strapped on a vest, then the pack. "Hopefully Glen is passed out somewhere and won't be mistaking us for the wolf."

Laura snapped the vest and pulled the cap over her ears. "Are we going to be trailing the wolf or Glen?"

"Glen. He'll be easier to find and I want him out of the woods. I don't want to be worrying about him taking potshots at us all day." He locked the Jeep and started in the direction Glen had taken. The sun was starting to rise, and Glen's weaving boot prints were as easy to spot as a neon sign. He glanced over his shoulder at Laura. The bright-orange hat covered most of her black hair. Only a thick braid hung down her back. It was one of the things he worried about; some half-blind hunter would see that black hair, think she was the wolf and shoot. "Stay close to me—don't fall behind." He slowed his pace until she caught up.

Delaney followed the conspicuous trail into the woods. The way Glen was staggering and stepping down on dry twigs, if the wolf was anywhere near this area he would have heard. Glen had about as much of a chance of shooting the wolf as Castro had of becoming the next president of the United States. Delaney stopped about a quarter of a mile into the woods and studied an area of dirt. He couldn't prevent the chuckle from escaping his throat.

Laura glanced at the marks in the dirt for a moment. She leaned close to Delaney and whispered, "What is it?"

"Glen fell." He pointed to a partial handprint. "By the looks of it, I'd say he fell smack on his face." He shook his head at an empty beer can lying nearby and continued on. For the next fifteen minutes he followed the trail of boot prints, scuff marks in the dirt and empty beer cans. Hansel and Gretel left bread crumbs; Glen Barnes left beer cans so he could find his way back home.

Laura, who was scanning the surrounding area, walked directly into Delaney's back. Her nose smashed into the pack and she almost lost her grip on the tranquilizer gun she was carrying. The Winchester was strapped over her shoulder. "What the—"

"Shh...." Delaney turned around and gently gripped her by the shoulders. He moved her so she was facing the way they had just came. "Don't say a word—just guard my back," he whispered.

Laura silently lowered the tranquilizer gun to the ground and swung the rifle off her shoulder. She held Delaney's gaze for a moment before clicking off the safety and concentrating on their surroundings.

Delaney gave her shoulders a light squeeze before continuing down the path to where he had spotted a rifle lying on a bed of dry leaves and twigs. The rifle looked old and neglected, just like the other one in Glen's truck. The sweet smell of blood was in the air. So was the stench of death.

A couple of yards away from the rifle a brown worn boot stuck out from behind a bush. Delaney silently swore as he scanned the surrounding area for any sign of the wolf. Problem was, a leg was still attached to the boot. He stepped closer and peered around the clump of bushes. Glen Barnes wouldn't be needing the trail of empty beer cans to follow home. Glen Barnes was dead, and he hadn't gone gently into the night. The wolf had ripped the man's throat out, and just as casually as he

had done to the sheep and cattle, he had left it within a
yard of the body.

Delaney had seen a number of men die over the years,
even his own father. None of those deaths had prepared
him for this act of savagery. He felt his breakfast churn
and quickly looked away. Glen wasn't his favorite person in the world; in fact, Glen wasn't anyone's favorite
person. But he hadn't deserved to die like this. Alone, in
the middle of nowhere, with his throat ripped out by a
wolf.

Delaney looked at Laura as she guarded his back, and
wanted to smile. She had taken his order like a soldier.
Somehow she'd known this wasn't the time to favor the
tranquilizer gun over the Winchester. She also had known
not to ask a bunch of questions. Laura had shown more
grit in the past couple of minutes than most soldiers
demonstrated during their stint in the military. Her back
was straight and proud, and she appeared able to handle
anything that came her way.

Delaney's gut was telling him the wolf was gone and
they were safe for the time being. He scanned the area
again. He wouldn't jeopardize Laura's safety on his gut
feeling. When nothing moved or seemed out of place, he
walked over to Glen's rifle and picked it up. With a swift
examination, he determined that it was still fully loaded.
Glen never had time to get one shot off. In Glen's condition, it wasn't surprising. What was surprising was that
the wolf had attacked and killed a human.

A chill slipped down his back. The other day the wolf
had tracked them to where Laura and he had been hiding under a tree overlooking a pasture. The wolf could
have attacked, and in their vulnerable position probably
have killed them both. But it hadn't. Why? The wolf had
obviously had no qualms about killing Glen, so why not
them?

Delaney hoisted Glen's rifle onto his shoulder and rejoined Laura. "Let's go."

"Where?" She glanced at the strange rifle swung over
Delaney's shoulder.

"We have to return to the Jeep and call the sheriff." He looked behind him, but Glen's body was out of sight behind the clump of brushes. "Glen's dead."

Laura glanced from Delaney's ashen face, to the dirty rifle, to the clump of bushes that held his attention. She bit her lower lip, swallowed hard and asked, "How?"

He held her gaze. "The same way the sheep and cattle were killed." He didn't want to go into detail, but he wanted Laura to know the truth. The wolf was now a man killer. The rules of the hunt had just changed. He could no longer chance her coming along with him. Tranquilizing the animal was out of the question now. The woods would now be filled with righteous ranchers protecting their livestock and avenging Glen's death. Chaos was about to reign in Saint Louis County, and he didn't want Laura anywhere near the insanity.

She shivered and glanced once again at the clump of bushes. "Are you sure it was the wolf who did it?"

"Yes." There wasn't a doubt in his mind. It would be unfair to Laura to give her a sliver of hope, when there wasn't any. He eyed the wolf's tracks. He would know those tracks anywhere. Not only did he think about them all day long, they now haunted his dreams. Those tracks were leading him away from Laura. The wolf was pulling him one way, Laura the other.

"Come on," Delaney said, "we have to go notify the sheriff." He reached for her hand.

"Shouldn't one of us stay here?"

"Barnes isn't going anywhere." He started to tug her in the direction that the Jeep was parked.

"How about if I go call the sheriff on the phone in the Jeep, while you stay here?"

"No, Laura. You are not walking through these woods without me."

"I can take care of myself." She dug in her heels and glared at Delaney.

He saw her fear and confusion behind the grit. Who could blame her? First it was a missing brother, then slaughtered sheep and cattle, now a dead man. In the past several weeks Laura's peaceful life in Saint Paul had been completely turned around. Nothing was how it seemed. She'd come to Moosehead Falls searching for a brother and ended up hunting a wolf. The worst thing, though, was that her brother had conveniently laid it all at her door with his first entry in the journal telling how she had fascinated him with tales of werewolves, vampires and ghosts.

Marcus was a young man with a serious problem, and instead of taking responsibility for his experiments, he'd blamed Laura for childhood tales. Delaney had already witnessed the immensity of Laura's love. Marcus had played upon that weakness. Even the most loving families had their flaws. Was that what love was all about—finding someone's weakness and then using it against him or her? Maybe he was the lucky one, never having known this emotion called love or having had a family.

He tenderly cupped her cold cheek. "I know you can take care of yourself, Laura." His thumb brushed her jaw. "It's me who can't stand the thought of you being out of my sight right now. It has nothing to do with your abilities to protect yourself. It's me." He gave her a crooked smile. "I need to know you are safe."

She pressed her cheek farther into his hand and gave him a smile that would surely light the heavens. She didn't bother to glance back at the spot where Glen lay, as she held Delaney's hand and headed for the Jeep.

Twenty minutes later Laura cringed as Sheriff Bennet, Deputy Bylic and Deputy Randal, all in different vehicles, came barreling up the dirt road to where she and Delaney waited.

Sheriff Bennet stepped out of his car and glared at Deputy Randal, the donut-eating deputy from her first night in town, as he got out of his squad car without turning off the siren. "Shut that thing off," barked the sheriff.

Laura sighed as Delaney muttered something about the racket, and the wolf being across state lines by now. She had to silently agree with him. Deputy Randal had made enough noise to drive every woodland creature into Canada. The wolf would be harder to track now. Delaney might have some ridiculous idea about her not accompanying him on the hunt, now that the wolf had proven deadly against a human, but she wasn't buying it. She needed to be with Delaney. Not only to find the wolf, but to make sure he was safe. Her heart had nearly exploded with joy when he told her how he needed to see that she was safe. It was exactly how she felt toward him. She called it love. Delaney was still fighting that notion.

The sheriff looked at Delaney, and he nodded in the direction that the body lay. "Are you sure he's dead?" asked Sheriff Bennet.

Delaney didn't say a word; he just raised one eyebrow.

"I think if Thomas says Glen's dead, he's dead." Deputy Randal flinched at the look the sheriff sent him. "Sorry, sir. I was just trying to be helpful."

"If you want to be helpful, call the coroner and give him our location." Bennet went to the trunk of his car and started to remove a roll of yellow plastic tape, a bunch of clear bags for evidence and a pair of thin plastic gloves. He slammed the hood of the trunk before barking another order at the overweight deputy. "If the coroner gets here before we get back, bring him to us."

The deputy's jaw dropped open as far as his five chins would allow. "But how will I find you?"

"Think!" The sheriff turned his back on the flustered deputy and approached Delaney and Laura. "This is not going to sit well with the ranchers." He shoved his fingers through his hair in frustration. "Damn fool. What was he thinking going after the wolf alone?"

"I'd say he wasn't thinking," Delaney said. "From the number of empty beer cans marking his trail, I'd guess his brain cells were too pickled to think." He handed the sheriff Glen's gun. "I found this about two yards from the body. He never got a shot off."

The sheriff frowned, but took the gun. "Any idea how long ago?"

"Three, four hours tops."

"He was out here in the dead of night, hunting the wolf?" The sheriff glanced between Glen's battered pickup and the woods. "Why would he do that? Why not wait until dawn?"

"I think I know the answer to that, Ray," Deputy Bylic said. "When I made my nightly stop at Orville's Place, Glen was there, drinking heavily. He was with a bunch of ranchers and they were talking about putting a bounty on the wolf." He rubbed the back of his neck. "A pretty big bounty."

The sheriff and Delaney both swore. "Why didn't you tell me sooner?"

"This is the first time I've seen you since then. I didn't think it was as important that I needed to wake you out of bed at two in the morning."

"You're right, Rick," Ray said. "I wouldn't have done anything about it last night." He glanced off at the woods. "Glen obviously had a different idea." He returned his attention to Delaney. "Are you two ready to show me where he is?"

"Laura's staying here," Delaney said. He leaned away from his Jeep and pulled on the pack. "If one of you could give her a ride back to her brother's house, I'd appreciate it."

Laura smiled sweetly at the sheriff and his deputies. "If you would excuse us for one moment." She tugged on the sleeve of Delaney's coat, until he followed her a couple of yards away from the vehicles. "What in the hell is this all about?" she hissed.

Delaney kept his voice low. "You can't go back into the woods. It's too dangerous."

"Why, because the wolf killed Glen?"

"There's that. But also because the ranchers have put a bounty on the wolf. Every hunter within a hundred miles will be combing the woods, hoping to get that bounty."

"What does that have to do with me going with you?"

"Laura." Delaney sighed in exasperation. "It will be too dangerous. I can't allow you to come."

"Fine." She gave Delaney her sweetest smile. "I'll have Randal drive me back to Marcus's house."

"Good."

"There I will pick up another pack and my car. Within an hour I will be out in the woods searching for the wolf." She continued smiling as his expression turned dark and dangerous. She was playing with fire, but she had no intention of getting burned. "I can either accompany you, or I'll go alone. Either way, I'll be going."

"That's blackmail," growled Delaney as he took a threatening step closer.

Laura held her ground. "No, it's a choice, Delaney. Your choice."

"Can't you understand that I want you home, where you will be safe?"

"*Can't you* understand that I want *you* home, where you will be safe?" She parroted the question right back at him. Couldn't he understand that she had fears about him hiking through these woods with all those ranchers carrying guns with bigger calibers than their IQs? "Is this some sort of male thing? Is this where the big strong male tries to protect the fragile little woman?"

"No, this is where I care what happens to you, Laura. It has nothing to do with big and little or male and female. It has to do with Delaney Thomas caring about Laura Kinkaid."

Laura relaxed. It wasn't a declaration of love, but it was close. Caring for someone was a big step in the right direction. "Doesn't it occur to you that I might care just as much about what could happen to you?"

The dark and dangerous edge he projected left. A slight flush swept up his cheeks. "I can take care of myself, Laura."

She noticed that flush and wondered how many times in his life someone had expressed concern for his safety and welfare. From what she had heard regarding his background, she doubted if anyone ever had. "The way I see it, Delaney, is two very capable people who can both take care of themselves could pull together and hunt the wolf. Or they could go their separate ways and be distracted by worrying about the other one all day long."

Delaney studied her face for a long while before sighing. "You win." He started to walk back to the vehicles and the sheriff.

Laura's low voice stopped him in his tracks. "I didn't know we were playing a game."

He turned back around and gazed at her face. "No, I guess we're not."

"Are you coming, Delaney?" called Ray.

"Yeah, we both are."


Laura stood a good forty feet away from the men and the gruesome body they were studying. The clump of bushes blocked her view of the body, which was fine with her. She didn't want to see the corpse. Just looking at Deputy Bylic's pale complexion was enough to turn her stomach. Why had the wolf attacked Glen? From what she had seen of the man's hunting abilities, he hadn't been a threat to the animal. Glen's trail through the woods was impossible to miss. A herd of buffalo would have left less of a trail. The wolf would have heard Glen's approach a mile away and had plenty of time to leave or hide. From the number of beer cans Glen had left in his wake, she would hazard a guess that he wouldn't have been able to spot the wolf, let alone actually hit it if he had gotten off a shot.

Had Glen just been unlucky enough to stumble across the wolf at the wrong moment? Or had the wolf been the hunter? From what she had read about wolves in Marcus's personal library on the subject, there hadn't been one case in North America where a healthy wolf had killed a person. Either that meant this wolf was unhealthy, or the record had been broken. Wolves avoided people whenever possible. So what had happened here? She glanced around the area, but could not detect anything amiss besides Glen's lifeless body. There didn't appear to be any signs of a struggle. Even the clump of bushes near the body looked normal—no broken branches, no snapped limbs and no smashed leaves. Had the whole thing happened too fast, or was Glen so drunk he hadn't known what was happening? She prayed it was the latter. She didn't know Glen, had never even heard of him till this morning, but no man deserved to die like that.

Delaney walked away from the sheriff and the sick-looking deputy and joined her. "Are you ready?"

"Whenever you are." She nodded at the two men standing over the body.

"Are you sure you don't want to go back to Marcus's house?" He tucked a lock of black hair that had blown across her face back behind her ear. "I'll meet you there around dark."

"Forget it, Delaney." She smiled up at him. "Either I go with you, or I head out on my own." She nodded westward. "He went that way." The wolf's tracks had been easy to spot, now that she knew what to look for.

Delaney raised one eyebrow and shook his head. "I'm afraid I created my own monster."

Laura grinned. "I had to do something while following you over half of Minnesota." Her grin widened and her gaze lowered to his backside. "Not that the view was all that bad." She chuckled softly as a tide of pink flooded his cheeks and he headed off in a westward direction. She repositioned the strap of her rifle on her shoulder and followed him deeper into the woods.

Laura glanced at the rancher who had given her and Delaney a ride back to the Jeep, and smiled. "Thanks." She didn't know what smelled worse—the manure he had been shoveling out of the barn, his cheap after-shave or the cigarette he was smoking.

"Thanks, Norman," Delaney said, as he climbed out of the cab of the pickup and helped Laura out.

"Shame you didn't catch the wolf, Thomas." He blew a smoke ring and watched as it disintegrated against the windshield. "Hal and Emmitt called right before you two showed up at my place. They wanted to know if I'd join their hunt. Bounty's up to a couple of hundred dollars. We would split it three ways."

"I can't tell you what to do, Norman." Delaney reached into the bed of the truck for their rifles and his pack. He looked back at the driver through the open passenger door. "This isn't your ordinary old wolf, Norm. He's a thinker and a killer. There can't be a more deadly combination than that."

Norman released another smoke ring and nodded. "It's been mighty cold these past couple of days." He rubbed his knee and sucked in another lungful of smoke. "Arthritis has been acting up lately."

Delaney nodded in understanding. "There are a lot of easier ways to earn, what did you say, about seventy-five bucks."

"Sixty-six dollars and sixty-six cents," muttered Norman. "This old man has had his days of hunting. Besides—" he puffed on the cigarette "—you can't eat the damn critter."

Laura turned away and pretended a great interest in the tip of her boot. *Eat the wolf!* As if today's events hadn't been enough to turn her stomach. She wanted to go soak every ache out of her body in Delaney's hot tub. She wanted to have a good cry. But most of all, she wanted Delaney to hold her tight and tell her everything was going to be all right. Today had been the worst day of the hunt. They had run into three other hunters, all looking for the wolf. The news about the bounty had traveled throughout the county. By tomorrow, hunters would be tripping over one another trying to claim it.

Delaney said goodbye and thanks again to Norman before hustling her to the front seat of the Jeep. The ride back to the lodge took place in silence. Laura stared out the side window and wondered about her brother, the wolf and her parents. How in the world was she ever going to tell her parents that Marcus was missing? She had promised them she would take care of him, and she'd failed. She had never failed at anything before in her life. When she failed, she failed royally. She'd failed at seeing Marcus's obsession with lycanthropy. She'd failed by being so caught up in her own career that she hadn't been there when he'd really needed her. And now she was failing every day when she and Delaney went out in search of the wolf and came home empty-handed. Defeat was a humbling experience and she wallowed in it on the twenty-minute drive back to the lodge.

Delaney pulled the Jeep into a parking space and turned off the engine. He looked over at Laura and drummed his fingers against the steering wheel. "Want to tell me what's bothering you?"

She shrugged. The good cry she had been wanting was a lot closer than she would have liked. "Do you think the wolf will kill again?" The thought of her brother actually being this creature was repulsive.

"It's always a possibility." Delaney picked up her cold hands from her lap and briskly rubbed them between his palms. "I tried the best I could to keep the others away, Laura. I don't like the idea of the woods overflowing with hunters any more than you do. But the rules have changed. The wolf changed the rules, Laura, not me and not you."

"I don't want anyone to shoot him."

"I know."

She chewed on her trembling lower lip. "I don't want him to kill anyone else."

"I know that, too." He moved as close as he could and pulled her into his arms. "It's been a rough day."

Laura pressed her face against his coat and nodded. Tears had overflowed, but she didn't want Delaney to see them. She ignored the gear shift pressing into her hip and buried her face deeper.

Delaney tightened his hold and kissed the top of her head. "I'm afraid the days are going to get rougher still, until this is over."

Laura jerked back and swiped at her eyes. "Don't you mean until the wolf is dead?"

"Possibly." He frowned at the tears. "What do you want me to do, Laura, lie to you? Tell you the wolf didn't rip a man's throat out this morning? That he's just a misunderstood German shepherd puppy searching for a good home? How about if I lie to you and tell you all those hunters are out today because it's the opening of squirrel season?"

"No, I don't want you to lie to me, Delaney." She gave a delicate sniff and wiped the last tear rolling down her cheek. "I want the truth, no matter how painful. If I know the truth, I can handle it."

"Then the truth is, there's a very real possibility that one of those hunters will run across the wolf before we do." He squeezed her hand. "Those hunters aren't carrying tranquilizer guns, Laura."

"I know." She gave a deep sigh. Why was she arguing with Delaney? It wasn't his fault she was so upset. "I just feel so helpless."

"What you need is a long soak in the tub, one of George's delicious meals and a good night's sleep." He brushed a soft kiss over her mouth. "Everything will look a lot better in the morning."

"What if he kills again?"

"I don't think anyone will be hunting for him in the dark after what happened to Glen. Besides, Bennet is talking to the ranchers to see if they will drop the bounty."

"Do you think they will?"

"No, but it's worth a try." He slowly ran his hand up her thigh. "Come on, let's get you warmed up. Whatever happens tonight happens. We'll worry about it tomorrow, okay?"

"Okay." She removed his hand from her thigh and smiled for the first time in hours. If it had climbed any higher, she would have gone from warm to meltdown.

* * *

Hours later, Delaney closed the book he had been reading. For the past two nights he had been going through some of Marcus's books, hoping to find some clues to Laura's brother's behavior. What he had discovered was intriguing. He could now see where Marcus had obtained some of his ideas about lycanthropy. History had been full of stories about werewolves since as far back as ancient Rome. The word *werewolf* meant man-wolf. Native Americans had many stories about creatures that were giant half man-half wolves who roamed the forests and who could devour a man. There had been many theories on the actual transformation, but none could equal what Marcus had attempted. Marcus theorized that with so much written about the subject, so many tales, over such a long period of time, there had to be some grain of truth buried beneath the legends. He had been searching for that grain.

Delaney glanced over at Laura, who was sitting on the other end of the couch, poring over more books. While he had been indulging himself on the legends and tales, she had been trying to decipher the scientific element in what Marcus had done. Her mouth was pulled down in a pout and her teeth were worrying her lower lip. It was an endearing trait, one he was beginning to know only too well. Something was troubling her.

"What are you reading?" He tried to see the cover of the book she was studying, but her hands were blocking the title.

Laura looked up and blinked. "Did you say something?"

"I asked, what has you so perplexed?" He could tell she had been a million miles away from him. He didn't like that feeling at all.

"I'm trying to understand all of this." She waved her hand at the book in her lap. "But it's all beginning to sound like Greek to me."

He moved closer and glanced at the open book. It was all words, except for a few diagrams of what appeared to be cells. "Blood cells?"

"Blood enzymes, to be more precise." She closed the book and leaned her head against the back of the couch. "If I can't understand what he did, how am I going to reverse the procedure?"

"Aren't you putting the cart before the horse?"

"What do you mean?" She peered at Delaney from beneath lowered lashes.

"Shouldn't we find Marcus first, then figure out what we ought to do?" Even after reading all those tales of werewolves, the assumption that Marcus was one still went down the wrong way. Whatever the wolf enzymes did, they didn't turn him into a werewolf. His money was on Marcus's having found a willing woman and a large bottle to forget his troubles. Marcus wasn't running crazy through the woods, thinking he was a wolf. After all their hiking and now with every man who owned a gun searching the woods, someone surely would have either spotted him by now or run across his tracks. Why Laura was worried about blood enzymes was beyond him. She should be contacting the best head doctor in Saint Paul. Then again, if he kept reading all those books of Marcus's and agreeing with a lot of what was written, he'd be the one needing the head doctor soon. Why did life have to be so complicated?

"What's that supposed to mean?"

"Just that you should find your brother before working yourself all up over enzymes."

"You still don't believe, do you?"

"Do you believe it one hundred percent?" He tossed the book on Native American legends onto the coffee table and stood up. Laura had to be the most stubborn female he'd ever had the misfortune to cross paths with. "Honestly, Laura, one hundred percent?"

"One hundred percent? No." She gripped the book on her lap and watched as he paced in front of her. "Ninety-eight percent, yes."

"Why?" he shouted in frustration. "Why would such an intelligent, levelheaded woman believe her own brother had turned himself into a wolf?"

"Because," shouted Laura right back as she stood up, "it's the only hope I have." She glared at Delaney until tears filled her eyes. Without saying anything else, she turned, walked over to the French doors leading from the living room to the balcony and stared out into the night.

Delaney felt his frustration wither and die. How could he have been so cruel to her? He kept forgetting he wasn't just dealing with a wolf—he was dealing with a creature Laura thought was her brother. As ludicrous as it seemed to him, she believed it. She had to believe it. It was her hope.

He stood behind her and gazed at the pale reflection of her face in the glass. This love she had for her brother was alien to him. He couldn't comprehend it. To love someone so much, you were willing to believe the impossible. And Marcus was only her brother. How deeply would Laura love a man? She'd professed her love for Delaney, but in truth he hadn't believed it.

He had chalked her declaration up to lust, need and desire, not love. He moved away from her and stood before the fire. "You love your brother very much, don't you?"

"Yes."

Her simple answer said it all. Love did exist. It was a hell of a time in his life to figure that one out. "Sometimes I forget that in your eyes, I'm talking about your brother when I mention the wolf."

She gave a sniffle and a watery smile, but didn't turn around.

"That's understandable."

"I never had a brother or sister to share the good times or the bad times with." In his life he could count on one hand the good times. "My mom died when I was little and I don't remember her much. My father preferred the bottom of a bottle to a son who reminded him of his dead wife every time he looked at the boy. If I'd had a brother or sister, it might have been more bearable.''

"Brothers can be a pain in the butt sometimes." She turned around and watched Delaney frown at the flames.

"I imagine they could, but it would have been nice to have a pain in the butt around anyway." He could still feel the loneliness of his childhood pull heavily on his soul. His childhood had made him what he was today. The days he'd spent alone in the woods, pretending he was the greatest tracker who'd ever lived, had paid off. By the time he was twelve he could track any creature. Many were the times he had had to go out and catch dinner because his father had blown what little money they had on booze. "My only family was a drunken old man who refused to be a father."

"Didn't you have an aunt or uncle you could have gone to?"

"No. There was only me and Nevil Thomas. From the time I was six until I left home at eighteen, I tried to make him if not love me, then at least respect me. It didn't work." Pain tore at his heart for the twelve years he had beaten his head against a stone wall. Nevil Thomas hadn't shown one ounce of caring toward his son. He hadn't been there the night Delaney had graduated from high school, and he hadn't shown up at the bus station when Delaney had left for boot camp. "While I was away for thirteen years, I wrote twice a year and sent a Christmas present. Nevil never wrote back or called. He never even showed up for his only child's wedding, and I'd sent him airline tickets and money for a new suit."

"Some people were never meant to be parents, Delaney."

He gave her a ghost of a smile. "I can't argue that." The sweet sadness dulling her eyes pulled at his heart. He wasn't looking for sympathy or pity. "I don't understand this love between you and Marcus, Laura. Families and love have never gone together for me. For the past five years I have taken care of my father the only way he would allow me. I stopped by once a week with groceries and lectures on drinking and to make sure he was alive. He never appreciated any of it." Laura cringed. "Family to me means responsibilities."

"I can understand where you got that idea from, Delaney. In my own way I feel responsible for Marcus. I'm older and I should have been there when he needed me."

Delaney nodded. Laura would think herself responsible for her brother. It was who she was. "Then you will understand when I tell you Nevil Thomas called me 'Son' as he lay dying in my arms." He looked away from tears pooling in her eyes. "He also asked me to do something for him. It was the first and last time he ever requested anything from me."

"What was it?"

"To kill the wolf." With those four words he knew he would destroy whatever feelings Laura had for him.

# Chapter 12

Laura paced Marcus's kitchen and listened to the shower run in the other room. She had already taken hers, and now Delaney was taking his. Another day of hiking up one hill down another and trekking through half-frozen mud had yielded them nothing. They had followed the wolf's trail until it had become too dark to see. Luckily the trail had skirted a half-dozen small ranches and they had gotten a ride back to where Delaney had parked his Jeep. She had been willing to continue following the trail or to camp in someone's barn so they could get a head start come dawn, but Delaney wouldn't hear of it. He claimed it was too dangerous, a point she had been reluctant to argue. Besides, Clint and Jake were joining the hunt at first light. Delaney had a plan to squeeze the wolf between his guides and himself. Jake would be coming from one direction, Clint another and Delaney and her from a third. The wolf would have nowhere to run, and she could possibly get a good shot at tranquilizing it. Seemed like a reasonable plan to her, except for one factor. Delaney wanted to kill the wolf.

Laura shuddered and checked on the tray of frozen lasagna cooking in the microwave. Store-bought lasagna could never compare with one of George's meals, but it was the best she could come up with on such short notice. Delaney should be tickled pink that she didn't slap down a jar of peanut butter and a jar of jelly with a loaf of bread and call it dinner. The man wanted to kill her brother! Laura opened the refrigerator and pulled out the fixings for a salad and slammed them down on the counter. That wasn't right, either. Delaney wanted to kill the wolf, not Marcus. Only, in her eyes they were one in the same, or could be. She was the one who thought the wolf was Marcus. Not Delaney.

She rinsed off the lettuce, tomato and two lone carrots and started to chop them into two salad bowls. Gourmet cooking had never been high on her list of priorities in life. She gave the lasagna a half turn and set the timer for another six minutes. When she heard the shower shut off she went to the laundry room and started a load of laundry. She needed clean jeans for the morning and her coat was covered in mud.

An hour later she and Delaney were sitting in the living room. Dinner, such as it was, was done and the kitchen was clean. The first load of laundry was in the dryer and another was washing. Delaney had a couple of maps spread over the coffee table and he was frowning.

"Problems?" she asked. Delaney wasn't much for asking other people's opinions on the hunt, but it would be nice if just once he confided in her.

"Yeah." Delaney sighed as he rubbed the back of his neck. "Our friend's changing direction."

"He isn't headed for Moosehead Falls?" She could have sworn they were moving in that direction this afternoon.

"Yes and no." Delaney unfolded part of the map. "See here—" his finger skimmed the paper "—this is the trail we followed today."

The course did seem to be heading for town, except it veered off to the east more. "If he had kept in the original direction, straight for town, he would have bypassed all these ranches and homes.'' Her fingers drifted across the map in a straight line. She counted at least half a dozen ranches the wolf could have attacked.

"Exactly." Delaney studied the map and frowned. "Why do you suppose he skirted the area?"

"You want my opinion?" she asked in surprise. The great Delaney Thomas was finally asking her for some input.

"You don't have to sound so shocked about it." He pulled out another map.

"Well, the first thing that comes to my mind is, he's on to us. He knows the ranchers are all out gunning for him and he's avoiding people and ranches as much as possible."

He raised his head and looked at her. "And the second thing that comes to mind?"

She bit her lower lip. She should have known he would pick up on her slip. Since he was asking for her opinion, she might as well give it to him. "I have noticed one very strange thing."

"What's that?"

"The wolf hasn't attacked any animal since he killed Glen Barnes. He's had plenty of opportunities, and we have trailed him right past ranches loaded with vulnerable livestock."

Delaney tapped a pen against the map. He appeared to be following the wolf's trail from where Glen's body had been found. "Why do you think that is?"

"Honestly?"

He looked up and seemed to be searching her eyes. "Honestly."

"I think he's sick of killing." There, she'd said it. It had been bothering her for two days now. The wolf was changing. Which could mean if it was her brother, he could be changing back. The effects of the injection could be wearing off. It was a hope. A deep-seated hope she had buried within her heart.

"Wolves can go for very long times without eating, Laura."

"I know." She glanced at the bookshelf crammed with books on the subject. "But this wolf never ate his victims, only slaughtered them. So why stop now?"

"Good question." Delaney lowered his gaze back to the map. "A question, I'm afraid, I don't have an answer for."

"I didn't expect you to. You asked for my opinion—I told you."

"Okay, but why is he headed for this area?" He pointed in the direction the wolf was taking. "It's nothing but hills, rocks and cliffs. There's nothing up there."

"I don't know." She glanced at the area. Delaney was right. The section of land was sparsely covered with trees, leaving the wolf with very little concealment. The ground was a broken mass of hills and cliffs. If they trapped the wolf on one of those hills, he wouldn't be able to escape unless he jumped over the side of the cliff, which would only lead to his death. "Maybe there's a cave or den he's searching for."

"Possibly, I hadn't thought of that." Delaney shook his head. "I'm pretty sure our wolf is a male, so why head for a den, unless he has a mate?"

"Do you think he does?"

"No. He's been away for too long. There haven't been any signs of other wolves in the area. I'd say our fellow is a lone wolf."

"We could trap him easier if he heads for those hills."

"I know." He refolded the maps. "That's what I'm hoping for. Jake and Clint will be coming in from the west and north. We're picking up his trail from where we left off and will be coming from the south. East is the river, so we should be able to flush him out."

Laura nodded. Maybe by this time tomorrow night it will all be over.

Delaney stacked the maps into a neat pile and reached for her hands. "Laura, about the wolf."

She gave him a small smile. "I understand why you want to kill him, Delaney. I can't blame you. If a wolf was responsible for causing my father to have a heart attack and die, I would want to hunt it down and kill it, too."

"I don't want to hurt you."

"I know." She gave his hands a squeeze. The anguish in his face was enough to break her heart. She didn't want to pull him apart, but she was. Delaney cared about her, really cared. He knew that if he shot the wolf, it would hurt her. But the promise he had made to his father was stronger. She didn't want to compete with a deathbed promise, but to possibly save her brother, she had to. "There's something I want you to see." She got up and walked over to the bookshelf.

A moment later she returned to the couch, carrying a photo album. "I want you to see Marcus as I see him." She opened the album. A chubby little newborn filled the first page. "This is Marcus the week he was born." She turned page after page and reminisced. Their parents were in many of the photos, but she was in nearly every one. Anyone looking at the album couldn't fail to notice how close she and Marcus were.

Delaney seemed fascinated by the little girl who graced nearly every picture. "This was me on the first day of kindergarten, and there's Marcus crying. He didn't want me to leave him alone at home." The memory of that incident was gone, but the pictures retold the story.

She turned the page and felt tears constrict her throat. Marcus was dressed up for Trick-or-Treat as a vampire; she was a fairy princess. Even at the age of five, he had shown his fascination with the unusual. "I remember he begged, pleaded and cried to my parents until they gave in and bought him the cape and fake fangs. They wanted him to be Einstein, but he wanted Dracula. My father told me to knock off the bedtime stories or else."

"Or else what?"

Laura gave a watery chuckle. "He never said." Pictures of Christmases, Easters and summer vacations filled the next several pages. An anguished cry escaped her throat as she turned the following page. In full color and enlarged to a five-by-seven was her brother at age ten, dressed for Halloween. He had been a werewolf that year. Tears filled her eyes as she blinked at the picture. He had been so proud of his costume. Why hadn't she remembered that Halloween before now? He wore that face mask everywhere for months afterward. "It's my fault, isn't it?"

"No, Laura." Delaney tried to remove the album from her trembling fingers, but she wouldn't let go.

"This is the 'or else,' isn't it?"

"Parents say that all the time. They were probably worried Marcus would have nightmares or become afraid of the dark."

"Yeah, not too many parents worry about their son growing up and becoming a werewolf, do they?" The tears were now overflowing. She couldn't stop them. She didn't want to stop them. Her finger tenderly traced the half smile, half snarl on Marcus's face. "It's all my fault."

Delaney took her shoulders and forced her to face him. "No, Laura. Men choose their own destinies. What Marcus did in his lab was his own doing. Children have been hearing vampire and werewolf stories for centuries. It doesn't mean they want to grow up and become one."

"But..."

He gave her a gentle shake. "There are no buts, Laura. What Marcus did or didn't do was his own choice." He tugged the photo album out of her hands and closed it.

Laura used the sleeve of her sweatshirt to wipe her eyes. "Delaney?" she said softly.

"What?"

She had bitten her lower lip so hard a tiny drop of blood had appeared. She gazed at him and sobbed, "I don't want my brother to die!"

Delaney pulled her into his arms and held her tight. "Shhh...honey, I know you don't." He gently rocked her as she wept.

Laura soaked the front of his shirt with her tears and cried, "But you're going to shoot him."

"No, Laura, I'm going to shoot a wolf."

"But..."

He pushed her a few inches away and forced her chin up so he could see her face. "Listen to me, Laura. Everything is going to be all right. I promise."

"How?"

"First we have to catch the wolf, then I will help you locate your brother." He wiped away a tear clinging to a lash.

"But..."

"No more buts, Laura." He tenderly cupped her face and brushed his lips across her mouth. "Everything will work out." His next kiss was longer. When he lifted his mouth he said, "I promise."

Laura believed him. Delaney would make everything all right. He had to. She didn't have anywhere else to turn. With a sigh, she melted into his arms and allowed him to love her.

Laura stood in a rock-filled clearing and anxiously watched the small patch of trees and underbrush Delaney had just disappeared into. Her heart pounded in her throat as she waited for the sound of gunfire. None came.

All morning long they'd trailed the wolf and kept in touch with Jake and Clint by radio. The wolf had veered more to the east and was now in the area of the high cliffs overlooking the river. It was where Delaney wanted him. They had just taken a break for lunch when Delaney heard something in the trees and went to investigate.

Laura glanced around the area. It would have been breathtakingly beautiful if it hadn't been for the mission they were on. The wind was whipping across the open area, but the sun was shining brilliantly. The river was a ribbon of shimmering blue a couple of hundred feet below them. Rocks and sparse pine trees dotted the terrain. If the wolf was here, the only cover he would have was the section of trees that Delaney had just entered. Laura gave a sigh of relief when no thundering gunshot split the air. Delaney had to be through the small section of trees by now. It had probably been some cute squirrel gathering the last of his booty for the winter ahead.

She sat back down, opened the pack Delaney had been carrying and pulled out the lunch she had packed for them this morning. A low chuckle vibrated in her throat—peanut butter-and-jelly sandwiches. She had just pulled out two cans of soda, when she caught the flash of something out of the corner of her eye. She turned her head, and every ounce of blood drained from her face. The wolf was standing on a huge rock not more than a couple of yards away from her. The oddly gold glare of his eyes held nothing but madness.

Her life flashed before her eyes. Her parents, with their comforting love. Marcus and his absentminded smile. The red bike she had gotten for her fifth birthday. The day she'd made the breakthrough that had led to finding the wrinkle-reduction cream. And the love she'd discovered for Delaney, always Delaney. Everything flashed in a second, yet the wolf didn't spring. She hadn't expected that. All she had known about the wolf had prepared her for a quick, violent death, yet he didn't move. He just stood there staring at her.

Laura forced her body to obey the frantic shouting of her mind. *Move!* Her guns were directly behind her; all she had to do was reach for them. She slid six inches back and reached behind her. Her fingers closed around the cold barrel of a rifle. In one fluid motion, she stood up, swung the rifle around and aimed. The wolf never moved. He just stood there staring at her with those eyes. Weird eyes. Insane eyes. Eyes that had seen hell and knew what awaited there.

She squinted her left eye and aimed with the right. At this range, it would be impossible to miss. Even if the wolf leaped now, all she had to do was squeeze the trig-

ger and he would be dead before he hit the ground. When
she had reached behind her for a gun, she had grabbed
the Winchester, not the tranquilizer gun. In her haste to
stand she had knocked the other weapon over, and it had
slid a couple of feet down the smooth rock. The tranquilizer gun was now out of reach. She would have to kill
the wolf or be killed.

She aimed the rifle right between his eyes. Her mind
was frantically giving her finger the command to pull the
trigger, but her heart was studying the eyes. They seemed
to be begging her to pull the trigger. How could that be?
Wolves didn't understand the concept of suicide; they
only understood survival. Suicide was a human option,
and this wolf couldn't have human options, unless...

Could this foul-smelling creature with the stench of
death surrounding him be Marcus? The physical appearance was that of a wolf. Not one human trait was in
evidence. Yet the eyes. The eyes tugged at her heart. They
seemed to be pleading with her to pull the trigger.

The wolf gave a growl as Laura's mind and heart battled. Her heart won; she couldn't shoot the animal. Not
even to protect herself. The wolf took a threatening step
closer, and Laura backed up. The cliff was less than a
yard behind her. If she backed up any more, she would
fall to her death. Laura planted her feet firmly and kept
the Winchester aimed at the wolf. Suicide might be a human option, but it wasn't hers.

Out of the corner of her eye she spotted movement
behind the wolf. Delaney! He must have trailed the wolf
through the small wooded area, over the rocks and cliffs
and directly back to her. She kept the gun aimed at the
wolf and didn't glance in Delaney's direction. The wolf
moved to the right and took a step closer to her. More
movement told her Delaney had stepped to his right. So
why hadn't he shot yet?

The wolf danced again to the right and issued a
threatening growl. Laura watched as he tensed, but he
never broke eye contact with her. It took her a moment
to realize what was happening. The wolf knew Delaney

was behind him, and was purposely moving so that she was always directly in front of him. If Delaney fired and the wolf moved, Laura would be straight in the line of fire. The wolf was using Laura for protection and Delaney couldn't shoot for fear of hitting her.

From the blur out of the corner of her eye she could tell Delaney was moving in closer to the wolf. He was practically on top of the animal. Laura shot a quick glance at Delaney just as the wolf turned and leaped at him. The thunderous sound of the gunshot split the air and a piece of rock flew through the air directly in front of Laura. When the wolf had leaped at Delaney he had knocked the rifle out of his hands and sent it sailing. Delaney's shot had gone wide.

Laura froze at the sight of blood. Delaney's blood! The wolf had managed to bite the arm Delaney had thrown up to protect himself. Blood seeped through the tear on the sleeve of Delaney's coat. She couldn't tell how bad the wound was, but Delaney was obviously favoring the arm. He had pulled it against his side and was staring at the wolf.

She could taste blood. Her own, from where she had sunk her teeth into her lower lip. Delaney was now unarmed against the wolf and wounded, and only she could save him. She looked away from Delaney and the pain etched into his face, and focused on the wolf. The animal was about ten feet in front of Delaney and a good twelve feet from her. Laura stepped to the right and froze as the wolf turned his head toward her. He seemed to be waiting for her to pull the trigger. She took a deep breath and stepped once again to the right. She wanted to make sure Delaney wasn't anywhere near her line of fire if she had to shoot. But she was also inching her way closer to the tranquilizer gun.

The wolf stared at Laura for a moment, then threw back his head and howled. The unearthly sound nearly caused Laura to drop the gun and cover her ears to block out the horror of it. The animal sounded as if he were in pain, inhuman pain. As the haunting howl died, the wolf took a threatening step toward Laura with teeth bared. She kept the rifle aimed right between his eyes, but didn't pull the trigger. The wolf turned his head and looked at Delaney, then back at Laura. He seemed to be thinking. He took another aggressive step toward her. When she didn't squeeze the trigger, he changed directions and took a flying leap toward Delaney's throat.

The sound of the shot was deafening to her ears. Laura absently felt the powerful kick of the rifle against her shoulder as she watched the wolf's body tense in mid-flight and then fall lifelessly to the ground. She lowered the gun, but continued to stare at the animal.

Delaney stared in wonder at Laura. She had killed the wolf to save his life! A man would have to be blind not to see what had just happened. Laura, even when the wolf had threatened her and moved closer, couldn't bring herself to pull the trigger. The wolf had stood there, seemingly perplexed, and then made a leap for him. The wolf had known Laura wouldn't shoot to protect herself, but would to protect him.

The pain in his arm where the wolf had managed to bite him was intensifying, but he ignored it. Laura was more important to him at this moment. Wounds could heal; Laura might not. She had believed the wolf was her brother. He took a step toward her. "Laura?"

She glanced away from the huge body of the dead wolf. A patch of blood soaked the fur where the bullet had entered. She glanced up when Delaney called her name and blinked back the tears. "In the movies, if it was a were-wolf he would change back to his human form now."

Delaney glanced at the wolf and grimaced. He should have been the one to kill the beast, not Laura. When he had tracked the animal through the trees and then as it had started to circle and head back to where Laura was waiting, he thought he would die. The wolf was heading for Laura, and he wasn't there. When he had stepped around an outcrop of rocks and spotted the wolf no more than a couple of yards away from her, his heart had stopped beating. It wasn't until he had the wolf in his sights that he realized how dangerously close Laura was to the cliff behind her. That, added to the fact that if the wolf moved a fraction the bullet could strike Laura and possibly send her over the edge, was enough to plague him with doubts. He'd never doubted his ability before. That hesitation had nearly cost him his life and Laura's. The wolf had made the first attack at the height of his uncertainty. He should be counting his blessings that the animal only managed to nip his arm and knock the gun out of his hand. If the wolf's jaws had locked around his forearm, he would have lost the limb and most likely his life.

He glanced at the dead wolf, then back at Laura. "It's only a wolf, Laura." He took a step closer to the wolf and rolled it onto its back. The animal's tongue lolled out of its mouth, but that was the only movement. No metamorphosis occurred. The wolf remained a wolf. A dead wolf. "We'll have it tested for rabies and other diseases. We'll also see if it's the wolf your brother experimented on—XYZ." He pushed the wolf onto its side so it wasn't facing them. "It's not your brother, Laura."

She looked away from the mound of black fur. "How's the arm?"

"I'll live." He glanced down at the sleeve of his coat and frowned. The entire sleeve was soaked in blood. He hadn't realized he was bleeding that badly.

Laura glanced at his arm and gasped. "Take off the coat and let me see."

"I'll be fine, Laura."

"If you tell me it's just a scratch, I'll shoot you with the tranquilizer gun."

He studied her face and had to chuckle. She apparently meant it. "See what we have in the first-aid kit." He eased off his jacket and swore as it moved his right arm. He slowly lowered himself onto a rock.

What little color Laura had left in her face fled with one look at the arm. She immediately started to rummage through the pack for the first-aid kit. She opened the blue plastic box and located the small pair of scis-

sors. With a few snips she had Delaney's flannel shirt and
thermal undershirt split to nearly his shoulder. The
wound was a good six inches in length and by the amount
of blood, she would hazard a guess, clear to the bone.
She glanced up and studied Delaney's face. He appeared
pale. Without making a comment she reached for the
sterile dressing and placed it directly on the wound. With
her free hand she grabbed another bag containing a
bandage, ripped the bag open with her teeth and started
to wrap the bandage around his arm. "You've lost a lot
of blood."

"I'll make it." He leaned his head back against a huge
rock behind him and closed his eyes.

Laura reached for the radio. Delaney's color didn't
look good, and she could never carry him. She pressed
the button. "Jake, Clint, somebody answer me."

"I'm here, Laura. Where's Delaney?" Jake Stoner's
voice was easily recognizable. "I heard a shot."

"Same here," came Clint's voice.

"The wolf's dead, but Delaney has been injured. The
wolf tried taking a chunk out of his arm and he's lost a
lot of blood."

"Where's your location? From the sound of the shot,
I don't think you're too far away from me." Clint was
anxious. "Is Delaney conscious?"

"Barely." Laura glanced at Delaney. By the way his
jaw was set, she knew he was still awake. "We're up on
the cliffs." She looked around the area, hoping to spot a
landmark or something else she could use as a focal
point.

"Tell them Suicide Ridge," whispered Delaney.

"Delaney said to tell you Suicide Ridge." She refused
to look at the wolf lying behind her. How could an animal know that the locals called this place Suicide Ridge?

Clint's voice emerged from the black box in the palm
of her hand. "Jake, since you are closer to them, hike on
up there. I'm heading for the Stanely place to use their
phone. I'll have a medevac dispatched to the clearing

about a mile north of Suicide Ridge. Jake, you're going to help Laura get him there if possible."

"Right," snapped Jake. "On my way."

"Laura," Clint said. "If you can, apply pressure to the wound and elevate his arm above his heart to slow down the bleeding."

"Tell him I'm not dead, just bleeding a little," growled Delaney. "I'll be hiking back down in a few minutes."

What was he crazy? He had lost more blood than she had in her entire body, and now he wanted to hike down this mountain. If it wasn't for the fact that she was scared to death he'd die, she'd let him try. Laura turned her back on Delaney. "Tell that chopper to hurry up. I think he's getting delusional."

"Roger," snapped Clint.

The radio went silent in her hand. She glanced back at Delaney. He was applying pressure to the wound and trying valiantly to raise the wounded arm. The fatigue etched in his face told the story. She immediately dropped the radio and went to help him.

Four hours later, she quietly entered the hospital room where Delaney lay. The helicopter ride to the hospital had been frantic, yet uneventful. Delaney had lost consciousness by the time she and Jake half carried, half dragged him to the clearing. Within ten minutes the helicopter had landed and a few moments later she and Delaney were on their way. Jake had stayed behind on Delaney's orders. He had wanted the wolf's body brought down and taken to a vet for examination.

The minute they had landed, Delaney had been rushed off to the operating room. A surgeon was needed to repair the damage the wolf's teeth had done to the muscles in his arm. A hour and a half ago, the surgeon had greeted her in the waiting room with great news. Delaney was expected to make a full recovery, and the doctor didn't think there would be any permanent damage to his arm. Laura had spent a tense ninety minutes more pacing the room until they released Delaney from the recovery room and put him in a regular room.

She softly entered the room and closed the door behind her. Delaney appeared to be sleeping, but she was glad to see some color back in his face. Quietly she pulled a chair up next to the bed and held his left hand. She could have lost him today on that cliff. Tears overflowed her eyes and rolled down her cheeks. The man she loved could have died because of her. She should have shot the wolf the first time she had the chance. It was all her fault that Delaney had been bitten. The tears flowed faster.

If she believed the romantic version of the werewolf theory, then she had to believe the wolf would turn back into its human form once dead. The wolf she had killed this afternoon was just a wolf, nothing more. It wasn't Marcus. Her brother was still missing, but she could live with that. If she could spend the past weeks hunting a wolf and then finally killing it, she could locate one missing brother. Delaney would help her find Marcus. He had promised, but that was before she had allowed him to be attacked. How could Delaney forgive her now? She reached for a tissue from the box sitting on the stand next to his bed and blew her nose. Three tissues later, the tears were still flowing and the shock of everything that had happened that afternoon was finally sinking in.

Delaney opened his eyes when the gentle sound of weeping became unbearable. He would give anything for whoever was crying to stop. It was breaking his heart. It took a moment before Laura came into focus, and then he wished she would go away. He couldn't stand to see her like this; it was worse than the weeping. He was looking at a woman whose heart seemed to be breaking, and it was all his fault. Because of him, she had killed the wolf. The wolf she thought was her brother. So in essence, she had killed her own brother to save him.

He ran his tongue over his dry lips and said, "What are you doing here?"

She hastily wiped at her eyes and tried to smile. "How are you feeling?"

"I'd feel a lot better if you weren't crying all over the place." He didn't mean to sound so rough, but her tears were ripping him apart and his voice was harsh and scratchy. Laura could never forgive him for the choice she had had to make, so why drag out the goodbyes?

She tried to stop crying, but only managed a sick-sounding hiccup. "I don't understand."

"There's nothing to understand." He glared at the door as Clint and Jake walked into the room. "About time you two got here." He nodded at Laura. "Would you guys take her back to her brother's house outside of Moosehead Falls?"

Clint and Jake exchanged a strange look. "Sure, if that's what you want."

Laura blinked at Delaney and then at the two guides, who only shrugged at her silent question. "I can stay longer, Delaney."

"I'm tired and I need to get some rest." He clutched the white blanket and for the first time he noticed that he was in some stupid hospital gown.

Laura stood up and glanced around the room. "I can wait down the hall until you wake up."

"No, thanks, I would rather you go on home." He glared at Jake and Clint, until they started to move toward the door. He couldn't look at Laura. His one look since he'd woken up told him everything he needed to know. She was riddled with guilt over shooting the wolf.

"I'll come to see you tomorrow." Laura picked up her coat. "Is there anything I can bring you?"

"Don't bother coming." He continued to glare at Clint, who was holding the door open for Laura. "I'll see you around."

Laura swallowed hard. "You'll see me around?" Delaney nodded but didn't look at her. She took a step closer to the door. "All right, Delaney, we'll play it your way for now." She brushed by Jake. "Never let it be said that I forced myself upon you when you were in some weakened condition." She left the room with her head held high and tears clinging to her lashes.

Delaney watched the door close behind her and the two men. He wanted to call her back and apologize, but knew this way was for the best. He'd known from the beginning that it would never work out between Laura and him, and he had been right. He closed his eyes and her face came into focus. Not with the childlike expression she had when something amused her; or with the soft, womanly glow she had after they made love; or even with the passionate heated intensity etched in her features when he was deep inside her. It was the face he'd seen when he'd woken a moment ago. The face that had given him the strength to send her away. It had been a face filled with guilt.

# Chapter 13

Delaney prowled the halls of the lodge. He paced his lonely apartment. He hiked for miles around the lodge. Nothing helped the pent-up feeling of frustration building daily within him. He needed to perform some simple physical tasks, such as split a cord of wood, run in a marathon or dig a moat around the lodge. Anything! With his right arm in a sling and the doctor's strict orders not to use the arm, it was impossible to do anything but mope around the place. Books held no appeal; movies were worse. For the past two nights he had even eaten his meals in the kitchen with George and Lucy so he wouldn't have to face his own company over his dinner.

Since he'd come home from the hospital over a week ago, Lucy had been mothering him to death and George had done nothing but cook his favorite meals, hoping to spark his appetite. He didn't want to eat, and he didn't want Lucy's mothering. He wanted Laura. Sweet, sexy and filled-with-grit Laura. When she'd pulled that trigger and saved his life, she had proven one very important thing; the vein of grit he'd always suspected wasn't a vein—it was the mother lode. Laura hadn't failed him when the going got tough. She had stuck it out to the end, only to have him toss her out of the hospital room. He was the one with the flawed grit. He hadn't stuck it out to the end. He, in essence, had betrayed Laura's love.

*Laura's love.* She had claimed to love him, something no one else had ever claimed. His father had barely tolerated his existence and his ex-wife, Kathleen, had been too busy loving herself to make room in her heart for anyone else. He had never felt love before Laura. Now he knew what he had been missing. She had wrapped her love so sweetly and securely around him that he never knew it was there until he pushed it away.

Delaney walked past the darkened reception area and glanced around at the empty room. Every stick of furniture, every paint color, even the curtains, had been handpicked by him. The overall affect was masculine, yet comfortable. Five years of his life and practically every cent he had ever saved had gone into the lodge. It was his home, his life. So why was it feeling so empty now?

He made sure the front door was locked and then went into the bar. The clients who patronized his hunting lodge liked someplace to unwind, down a few cold ones and brag about the day's hunt. The huge screen television connected to the satellite dish behind the lodge could pick up every single sports event televised. That didn't hurt, either. It wasn't even midnight, yet the bar was empty. Dawn came mighty early to the hunters.

Delaney didn't bother to turn on any of the lights. The small light connected below the bar top and above the sink area gave off just enough light for him to see. He reached into the small refrigerator and pulled out a bottle of light beer. Even when he was sinking into the bowels of hell, he couldn't bring himself to drink alcohol. With a heavy sigh he sat down on one of the bar stools to contemplate his lonely life, which stretched out endlessly in front of him.

Three empty bottles later, George quietly slipped into the room and perched on the stool next to him. Delaney got up and, without saying a word, retrieved two more beers from the refrigerator. He was through half the bottle before he asked, "Did Lucy throw you out?" He never thought for half a second that Lucy would. George and Lucy were the perfect couple, if there was such a thing.

"She's worried about you." George tilted back his head and downed half the bottle in one gulp.

"Me?" Delaney said with a chuckle. "You can tell her to stop worrying. The doctor assured me my arm will be fine."

"That's not what she's worried about."

Delaney studied the wet ring his beer bottle had left on the bar. With the tip of his finger he slowly outlined the circle. Lucy was concerned because of his recent behavior. Who could blame her? Ever since he'd come home from the hospital he hadn't been himself. He didn't want to be himself. The heartless man who had tossed Laura from his hospital room was gutless. After he'd seen the guilt she was feeling, his first reaction had been to break all ties before she could hurt him. But how could she hurt him if he didn't love her? The answer was so simple it scared him to death. He loved Laura. Maybe that was the main reason he'd pushed her away.

He took another gulp of beer and studied the fancy array of bottles behind the bar. "I've got a lot on my mind lately, George."

"Want to talk about it?"

"You know a lot about women?" Women befuddled him. They thought differently from men. They were prone to be more emotional, softer and unpredictable. There wasn't a man alive who could honestly say he understood the female species one hundred percent.

"Can't say that I do," muttered George. He got up and fetched two more bottles of beer. "I've been married to the same woman for twenty-four years and she can still surprise me." He twisted the top off his bottle and grinned. "Some of them surprises make for the best memories." He glanced at Delaney and the smile slipped. "What happened between you and Laura?"

"Nothing," he mumbled and twisted off his bottle top. "Life." He raised the bottle up. "Everything." Delaney downed the nonalcoholic beer.

"That doesn't sound like you, boss."

"What doesn't sound like me?"

"You're giving up." George sadly shook his head. "I never thought I'd see the day when you surrendered."

"What exactly am I giving up on?" He wasn't giving up on anything. The decision had already been made the second Laura pulled the trigger. In her mind she had killed her own brother to save him. Even if there was some outside chance their relationship could continue, there was no way she could ever forgive him for that.

"You're giving up on the woman you love." George ignored Delaney's protest and continued. "That little gal was totally smitten with you, and you were five times worse."

"Me?"

"I've seen the way you looked at her. I might be old, but I'm not blind. You love her or my name's not George Randal Whitecloud." He continued to shake his head. "There, I said my peace. I'm not the kind of guy who goes around sticking his nose where it don't belong, but you asked why Lucy's upset and I told you. We both are wondering why you are sitting around here twiddling your thumbs while Laura's getting away."

"She's not getting away. I pushed her away." She was probably back in Saint Paul by now, getting on with her life.

"Pushed her away? Why?"

"It's a long, complicated story." It also borders on unbelievable.

George settled his large frame more comfortably on the stool. "I ain't going anywhere."

It took Delaney two full minutes to decide if he should tell George everything. He had never had a male friend before, a confidant. Sean Peterson and Dev Bradley, the two men from his squad who had collected all the information needed to prove his innocence against the treason charge, were the closest friends he had. He could still remember the day George and Lucy had come to him with their problems and how he had helped them to solve them. George had never betrayed his trust; maybe now was the time to share his burden. He started to tell George about Marcus and how he'd met Laura.

Half an hour later George still sat on his stool, with wide eyes and slack jaw. "Lord, Delaney, that's some story."

"Yeah, life is full of strange things."

"So was the wolf her brother, XYZ, or just some other wolf?"

"The sheriff faxed me a copy of the wolf's autopsy report this afternoon. All that was listed was the cause of death—one bullet shot directly into the brain. All the blood work and specialized tests we ordered will take a couple more weeks. They did rule out rabies." He waved his arm in the sling. "Which I was happy to hear."

"So you don't know if it really was Marcus Kinkaid or not?"

"George, there're no such things as werewolves."

"You even admitted to giving the subject more than a second thought." He shivered and finished whatever was left in his bottle. "Imagine, a werewolf prowling the woods outside."

"George," groaned Delaney. He didn't need another person believing in werewolves.

"So if it wasn't Marcus, where is he?"

"I haven't the foggiest notion." Delaney played with the empty bottle in his left hand. "Laura has checked everywhere she could think of."

"He's got to be somewhere. Everybody is somewhere."

"Yeah, everybody is somewhere." Delaney debated getting another drink, but decided against it. Talking to George had helped somewhat. It hadn't solved anything, but it had helped. He stood up and stretched one-handedly. "It's getting late and morning comes awfully early around here." He wasn't really tired, but he didn't want to spend another hour with George, hashing over what a fool he was. He already knew that.

George stood up, rinsed all of the empty bottles and placed them in the plastic recycle bin under the bar. "That's it?" He started to walk toward the door with Delaney. "You're just giving up like that?"

"I'm not giving up anything," growled Delaney as they stepped out into the deserted reception area. Didn't the man see how hopeless the situation was?

"You're giving up the woman you love without a fight!" snapped George. He shook his head and headed for the rear entrance. Halfway down the hall he turned and repeated, "I never thought I'd see the day when you surrendered."

Delaney stood there in the dark and watched as George disappeared through a doorway. The old man didn't know what he was talking about. He wasn't surrendering. There wasn't anything to surrender. He turned and walked to his lonely apartment at the other end of the hall.

He opened his door and frowned. Every time he entered the rooms he expected to see Laura there or smell the floral scent of the bubble bath she loved to use. He closed the door and wearily leaned back against it. More than once he had ended up smelling like a greenhouse himself. He loved that scent. He loved Laura.

It was a hell of a time to realize he was capable of love. He had waited for this emotion for thirty-six years. Now that he was finally experiencing it, it brought him nothing but pain. How was it he felt nothing but pain without love? Now he was feeling the pain once again. This time he was the cause of it. He had been the one to push Laura away. She and Jake had half carried him to the helicopter landing site; she had clung to him during the ride and she had been the one pacing the waiting-room floor. Dr. Grenly had asked every time he came in to examine him where the beautiful brunette was who had been tearfully awaiting the results of the operation. Delaney had done nothing but bark at the doctor. Laura had shown so much love, and all she had gotten for it was to be tossed out of his hospital room without even a proper explanation.

How could he explain about the guilt that had been on her face? He knew how she felt. He also knew he was the cause of it. If it hadn't been for him, she never would have shot the wolf. He was at a loss to explain why the wolf hadn't immediately attacked Laura. But what really baffled him was when the wolf had stood between them and seemingly known Laura wasn't going to shoot to save her own life. The wolf had then leaped for his throat, and only the bullet from Laura's gun had prevented his death. Defenseless and wounded, he wouldn't have stood a chance against the beast.

He pushed away from the door and wandered the room. George was right; he had given up without a fight. He had never told Laura how he felt. It seemed pointless now, especially since she honestly thought she had killed her own brother. But she hadn't. He still couldn't bring himself to believe in werewolves. He had seen that wolf up close and real personal. You couldn't get any more personal than having the creature sink its teeth into your forearm. The wolf couldn't have been a man at one time, enzyme blood transfusions or not. The physical differences were too great. That wolf was either XYZ or some other wolf, not Marcus Kinkaid. It was going to take weeks before the blood work came back, and then who was to say they would be conclusive enough for Laura to rule out the wolf's being a werewolf?

There was only one way for Laura to believe she hadn't killed her own brother, and that was to find Marcus. Delaney glanced down at his arm in the sling. How was he ever going to find Marcus, when he couldn't even drive? For the first time in over a week, a spark of excitement gleamed in his eyes as he surveyed the computer, fax and phone over by his desk. He had all the tools right at his fingertips. All he needed to do was stop moping and get busy.

If he could locate Marcus, Laura wouldn't feel guilty any longer. There was always a chance she wouldn't forgive him for the way he had pushed her away, but he was willing to live with that chance. There hadn't been any chance of Laura and him working things out the way he had been going. At least this way, there was a chance.

It was well after one in the morning. There was nothing he could do tonight, but come first thing tomorrow morning he was finding one lost brother. His step was lighter and a trace of a smile lingered on his mouth as he turned off the lights and headed for bed.

Laura very carefully replaced the receiver. If she allowed her emotions to dictate her actions, she would throw the phone against the wall. Another dead end. It was as if her brother had disappeared off the face of the earth. In the two weeks since the wolf's death she had done nothing but try to locate her brother, and failed. The wolf hadn't been her brother, so that left one very important question: where was he? If the werewolf theory had been hard for her to swallow, UFO abductions were an impossibility. Marcus had to be somewhere, the question was where, and why hadn't he returned home?

She had to concentrate on finding Marcus—and not concentrate on Delaney. She had called every day while he was in the hospital to check on his condition. Dr. Grenly had finally taken pity on her and personally assured her that Delaney would make a full recovery, even if he was signing himself out of the hospital two full days before the doctor wanted him to. Delaney was a stubborn man, but she had already known that. Pride had kept her from phoning the lodge and talking to Lucy or George. If Delaney wanted to talk to her, he knew where to find her.

During the day she kept herself busy pestering the sheriff and anyone else she could reach. There was a saying that the squeaky wheel got the oil. She had indeed been the squeaky wheel, but so far she hadn't received one drop of oil.

The nights were the worst. Everywhere she looked, she remembered Delaney. The big queen-size bed in her brother's room had brought back too many memories, so she now slept in the guest room on the narrow twin bed. More nights than she cared to remember, sleep had been late in coming, and then she'd awaken before dawn, reaching for Delaney's warmth, only to discover cold, empty sheets.

She hadn't given up on Delaney and she loved him more with each passing day, but he needed time. Time to forgive her for not shooting the wolf sooner. If she had shot the wolf the moment she'd seen it, Delaney never would have been bitten. And he knew it. There was no other explanation for his behavior in the hospital that day. She knew she must have looked a sight when he'd finally awakened, but she didn't think Delaney had sent her away because her clothes were dirty, her face pale and her eyes bloodshot and swollen from crying. He couldn't even meet her gaze.

Jake and Clint had tried a couple of times to start a conversation on the way home, but it took every ounce of concentration she possessed not to begin crying again. Both men had obviously been bewildered by Delaney's behavior, but who could blame them? They didn't know what had happened up on the ridge; only she and Delaney knew. She'd choked. She had had the wolf pinned, and they both had known it. Only she couldn't fire. Every time she met the wolf's glowing eyes, it seemed to be asking to be put out of its misery. It was too much of a human plea and it had caused her to ponder what she was doing. Even when the wolf had turned on her and growled, she couldn't squeeze the trigger. It was only when the wolf leaped for Delaney the second time that she knew she had no other option. It was either the wolf or Delaney, and she would have willingly given her own life to save the man she loved. Instead, for one second, she thought she might have given her brother's. When she saw the wolf lying in a dead heap she had known without a doubt it wasn't Marcus. She didn't know how, she just knew. It was quite possible, if not probable, the wolf was XYZ, the poor creature her brother had experimented on.

So now she spent her days searching for Marcus and her nights dreaming of Delaney. She had spent some hours tying up some business ends on the deal she had signed just before this whole thing started. It was just as easy to tie them up here as it would be in Saint Paul. Her work in the lab had come to a standstill, but she didn't like the idea of using Marcus's lab. After what he had been doing down in the basement, the place gave her the creeps. The thought of gathering some samples from the surrounding area for future testing was growing more appealing every day. Northern Minnesota was a lot more densely forested than the southern portion of the state. There were species of plants and trees here that she didn't have access to down in Saint Paul.

She should be thinking about taking a trip back to her apartment to check on things there and to pack some more clothes. She couldn't bring herself to abandon Marcus totally. The thought of returning home and picking up her life where she had left off was unthinkable.

Before she went, though, she wanted to talk to Delaney. Everyone he had ever known had abandoned him. His father had left him for the bottom of a bottle. His ex-wife had lied to him, then cheated on him with a man she thought had more prestige. Even the military had betrayed him by showing their lack of faith. She wasn't about to abandon him and return to Saint Paul. She loved him. It was as plain and simple as that. One day, hopefully, he would forgive her, and they could pick up where they'd left off. There was so much love inside Delaney, if only he would lower the barriers around his heart. She knew the instant he was redeemable, that the concrete was just surrounding his heart, not embedded into it. Delaney had told her he had asked his wife for children. A man incapable of love would never ask for children, especially a man with Delaney's background.

With his father as a role model, Delaney would never consider children, and he wasn't the kind of man to have a child just to prove to the world he could raise one better than his own father. Delaney wanted a child so he could love somebody and have someone love him in return. All he had to do was open his eyes, and he could have seen the love she had for him. Delaney had been so busy keeping the barriers in place he'd forgotten to open his eyes. All she had to do now was gain his forgiveness and make him see.

It was a tall order for her, but defeat wasn't in her vocabulary. She glanced down at the sheet of paper in front of her and made a deal with herself. There were six more names on the list of people Marcus used to work with. If she managed to contact every one of them this afternoon, she'd get all dressed up and drive up to Delaney's lodge tonight. With renewed determination she picked up the phone and punched in seven digits.

Three hours later, she was slowly giving up on the idea of confronting Delaney tonight. It was nearly dark and she had only managed to contact four of the names. Why was it scientists were so suspicious of every question? All she wanted was information on her brother, not government secrets.

A car door slammed outside just as she replaced the receiver after trying to reach a Carter Granite for the eighteenth time. The man was never home or in his lab. Maybe he'd disappeared off the face of the earth, too. She stood up and stretched the muscles in her lower back. It was probably the sheriff or Deputy Bylic. Both had a habit of checking in with her at least once a day.

She was halfway across the living room, when the front door opened and Marcus stood there. At least she thought it was her brother. He appeared to be twenty-five pounds thinner and pale, but he never looked so damn good to her. She let out a loud cry and threw herself straight into his arms. She and Marcus would have crumpled to the ground if whoever was behind Marcus hadn't caught both of them.

"*Marcus!* Where have you been?" She steadied herself and then helped her brother, who seemed to be having problems getting his balance. "Are you all right?"

"He'd be a lot better if you'd stop throwing yourself at him," drawled an amused voice behind him.

Laura spun around and stared at the man. "Delaney!"

"Don't throw yourself at him, Sis." Marcus chuckled weakly. "I'm in the middle and I couldn't withstand another blow like the last one." His crooked smile belied his words.

Delaney gently took most of Marcus's weight and helped him to the couch. A small, rounded man with thick glasses followed them into the room and closed the door.

Laura ignored the man and rushed to her brother's side. "What happened?" Marcus looked terrible. His hair was still the same jet black and full, or she would have guessed he had been going through chemotherapy or radiation treatments.

"Let him catch his breath, Laura." Delaney gave her an encouraging smile and patted her hand. "Why don't you just sit here and look at him while I go make everyone a cup of tea?"

"Tea?" Laura was afraid Delaney had lost his mind. She'd never seen him drink a cup of tea, let alone make one.

"Splendid idea," cried the little man. "I'll help."

Both men left the room, leaving Laura alone with her brother. He appeared so frail and weak she reached out and took his hand and gently squeezed.

Marcus's attempt to squeeze back was feeble at best. He chuckled softly at his own weakness. "I guess I look pretty rotten to you."

"You look beautiful to me." She loosened her grip when she felt his fingers tremble. "I'm going to call a doctor as soon as I'm done looking at you."

"Please, Sis, no more doctors. I just got out of a hospital this morning."

"Hospital? What for?" she cried. "What hospital? I tried every hospital in northern Minnesota. No one had ever heard of you."

"Delaney wasn't lying then when he told me what you have been going through."

"Let's not talk about me. What happened to you?" She'd deal with Delaney later, in private, but now she needed some answers from her brother.

"Delaney tells me you found my journal and read it. He also said you killed the wolf and saved his life." Marcus glanced toward the kitchen. "He seems like a great guy to me, Sis." He looked down at his trembling hands and sticklike legs. "Of course, you're going to have to wait until I'm up and around more for me to give my complete approval."

Laura flushed, but refused to be sidetracked. "Out with it, Marcus. What happened after you injected yourself with those enzymes?"

"When I couldn't reach you, I called an old colleague, Carter Granite. He arrived about six hours after the injection. If it hadn't been for him I probably wouldn't be here today."

"Why?"

"I went a little crazy—or to be completely truthful, I went a lot crazy. I guess I was crazy before the injection. You don't do something like that if you're sane."

"Is that Carter Granite?" She nodded toward the kitchen, where the man had disappeared with Delaney.

"Yes." Marcus leaned his head back and closed his eyes.

"He got you to a hospital?" It seemed impossible that such a man could physically contain her brother while he was in a rage, let alone drag him to a car.

"I keep forgetting to add his title. He's Dr. Granite and he specializes in toxic poisoning." Marcus gave his sister a ghost of a smile. "He sedated me and drove me to a private clinic in Wisconsin."

"That's why I couldn't locate you!"

"Not too many people know about this clinic, and even if you had managed to contact them, they would have denied ever hearing my name. It's on the hush-hush, and the government uses it a lot. Carter knows a lot of people in all the right places."

"Why wasn't I notified?"

"Carter didn't know that I tried reaching you and left a bizarre message. If he had, he would have gotten in touch with you somehow. He didn't want to contact our parents and panic them. They couldn't have visited me, and he didn't know what to tell them. He decided to wait until I was out of the woods. For the first couple of weeks, it was touch and go."

"Oh, Marcus." She tenderly leaned against him and allowed the tears to fall. Her brother had almost died, and no one had even bothered to call her. "Why didn't you phone me?"

"I was out of it, Sis." He bent and brushed a kiss over her cheek. "Carter did everything he could. If I had known you were here worrying, we would have gotten a message to you. I figured you were still in New York, wheeling and dealing."

The simple act of kissing her had tired him out. He was nearly asleep. "Marcus, one more question. Are you all right now?"

"Yes, big sister, don't worry. I know I look like hell, but I'll live."

That was all she wanted to know. Marcus was going to be all right. She brushed back a lock of his hair, which had grown since the last time she had seen him. "How did you manage to be with Delaney?"

"He found me," Marcus said on a chuckle, but he kept his eyes closed. "Here Carter thought we were untraceable, but your Delaney located me and managed to contact Carter."

She ignored the *your Delaney*. "He drove to Wisconsin?"

"As soon as he had Carter's decision that it was safe for me to travel, he was there the next morning to bring me home." He reached for her hand and gave it one last squeeze. "I'm sorry, Sis—" his voice was a mumble "—for giving you such a scare."

She squeezed his back and gently whispered, "You'll pay later, little brother." She doubted if he had even heard her. He was sound asleep.

Delaney, followed by Carter Granite, walked into the room carrying a tray loaded with teacups. Dr. Granite walked over to Marcus and studied him for a moment. "You and the trip appear to have tired him out, Ms. Kinkaid."

"Call me 'Laura,' please." She stood up and shook the doctor's hand. "From what Marcus told me, I have a lot to thank you for."

"Nonsense, Laura." He flashed her a grin that showed a wicked sense of humor. "Your brother has a lot to thank me for." He glanced at Delaney. "Could I impose again on you for some assistance in getting my patient into bed?"

"I'll help!" cried Laura. Delaney's arm was no longer in a sling, but it still couldn't have completely healed.

"Laura, go turn down his bed and see if you can find a pair of pajamas for him," Delaney said. With minimal fuss, he and Dr. Granite were half walking, half dragging Marcus down the hall.

Laura hurried in front of them and yanked down the comforter and sheet. She fluffed a pillow and watched nervously as her brother was lowered to the bed. When he appeared to be still asleep she shook her head and gazed at the doctor. He didn't seem too concerned about Marcus's health. She walked over to a bureau and located a pair of navy blue pajamas and placed them on top of the dresser.

Delaney gently pushed her from the room. "He's fine, Laura. How about giving him a little privacy?"

She stomped off toward the living room and her tea. Five minutes later Delaney joined her. "I have to bring in a bunch of stuff."

"What kind of stuff?"

"Doctor stuff. Medical stuff. I don't know. Whatever Dr. Granite felt your brother needed was packed." He headed for the door.

"I'll help." She rose from the couch and helped Delaney unload the entire truckful of equipment into Marcus's bedroom. Her brother never stirred. Dr. Granite became busy setting up all the fancy equipment. Laura and Delaney quietly left the room and closed the door behind them.

They returned to the living room and the now-cold tea. Laura took a sip and grimaced. "How about if I put on some coffee?"

Delaney glanced into his teacup as if it contained poison. "Sounds great." He carried the tray back into the kitchen and dumped everything down the drain. "I only offered to make tea because your brother isn't allowed coffee yet."

Laura finished measuring out the grounds and dumping in the water before turning to Delaney. He was less than a yard away from her and his after-shave was playing havoc on her senses. Lord, how she missed him. "I want to thank you for finding my brother." She took a step closer.

"You might not want to thank me."

"Why not?"

"I stopped at the sheriff's office on the way here. Marcus and the doctor stayed in the car, but I went in and told Ray what Marcus had been doing in his lab. I also mentioned my suspicions that the wolf you killed was the one he had been experimenting on. Ray will be pressing charges against your brother for cruelty to animals, threatening an endangered species and anything else he can think up."

"I see." She bit her lip. Her brother was now a criminal in the eyes of the law. "I'm still thankful, Delaney."

"I did talk Ray into allowing your brother to recuperate here at his house. He's coming out tomorrow to formally press charges and place your brother under house arrest until he is well enough to go to court."

"Sounds fair to me." She took another step closer. "Why did you do it?"

"Stop at the sheriff's?"

"No, go through a lot of trouble to find my brother."

"He's important to you." He glanced somewhere over her left shoulder. "I didn't want you going through the rest of your life thinking you shot your own brother."

"I knew the wolf wasn't Marcus the moment I shot him."

"You did?"

She nodded. He sounded shocked by that. "I was wrong all along, Delaney. There are no such things as werewolves."

"Then why the guilty look in the hospital?" He ran his fingers through his hair. "I came to, and there you were, looking so damn guilty and ashamed."

"I was guilty and ashamed."

"About what?"

"Not shooting the damn wolf sooner!" She balled her hands into tight little fists. "If I had shot the wolf the first opportunity I'd had, he never would have attacked you. There you were, bleeding all over the place, needing to be flown off the ridge, and then there was the two-hour surgery on you arm. I had a lot to be guilty and ashamed about. If I had missed the second time he went for you, you would have been killed!" The horror of that moment flooded her voice.

"Why didn't you tell me?"

"As I recall, you didn't give me a chance to say two words, not even goodbye." Tears pooled in her eyes, but she refused to cry. It seemed all she ever did around Delaney was cry. Well, from now on, she wasn't going to shed one tear.

"I thought you were feeling guilty for thinking you killed your own brother to save my worthless neck."

She reached out and caressed his neck. "It's not worthless." He hauled her into his arms and gave her a such a hug she feared for her back. "Priceless, maybe, but never worthless."

"I've been going crazy without you, Laura."

She gave him an impish grin. "Good, that's what you deserved for tossing me out of the hospital room." She poked him in the chest with her fingertip. "But you're forgiven."

"But am I still loved?"

She caught her breath at the seriousness of his question. How could he think otherwise? She knew how, and vowed to make up his past with so much love that he'd think it was Christmas every day. "You don't stop loving someone, Delaney, just like that." She snapped her fingers. "I might have fallen in love with you that fast, but I won't fall out of love ever." She reached up and gave him a kiss that spoke not only of her love, but of her need, too.

Delaney pulled away from the hot kiss and groaned. "I learned one thing while I was in that hospital bed and wandering around the lodge, cursing everything in sight."

"What's that?"

"I love you." He brushed a tender kiss over her dewy soft lips. "I never believed in love, until you came along and proved me wrong." His mouth was more insistent the second time. "I love you, Laura Kinkaid. So where do we go from here?"

"Anywhere we want, Delaney. Anywhere we want." A fat tear rolled down her cheek and she hastily brushed it away. "Damn."

"What's wrong?"

"I promised myself I wouldn't cry around you anymore."

He traced the path the tear had taken with his thumb. "Cry all you want, Laura. As long as they're tears of happiness, I'll be here to dry them."

\* \* \* \* \*

# COMING NEXT MONTH

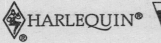 

*Silhouette*

SPECIAL EDITION™®

**is proud to announce the latest miniseries by SHERRYL WOODS**

AND BABY MAKES THREE

Discover how the Adams men of Texas all find
love—and fatherhood—in most unexpected ways!

Watch for the very first book in this series, coming in December:

**A CHRISTMAS BLESSING** (Special Edition #1001)

Luke Adams didn't know anything about delivering babies. But when
his widowed sister-in-law showed up on his doorstep about to give
birth, he knew he'd better learn fast!

And don't miss the rest of the exciting stories in this series:

**NATURAL BORN DADDY**
(Special Edition #1007), coming in January 1996

**THE COWBOY AND HIS BABY**
(Special Edition #1009), coming in February 1996

**THE RANCHER AND HIS UNEXPECTED DAUGHTER**
(Special Edition #1016), coming in March 1996

**HEARTBREAKERS**

We've got more of the men you love to love in the Heartbreakers lineup this winter. Among them are Linda Howard's Zane Mackenzie, a member of her immensely popular Mackenzie family, and Jack Ramsey, an *Extra*-special hero.

In December—HIDE IN PLAIN SIGHT, by Sara Orwig: Detective Jake Delancy was used to dissecting the criminal mind, not analyzing his own troubled heart. But Rebecca Bolen and her two cuddly kids had become so much more than a routine assignment....

In January—TIME AND AGAIN, by Kathryn Jensen, *Intimate Moments Extra:* Jack Ramsey had broken the boundaries of time to seek Kate Fenwick's help. Only this woman could change the course of their destinies—and enable them both to love.

In February—MACKENZIE'S PLEASURE, by Linda Howard: Barrie Lovejoy needed a savior, and out of the darkness Zane Mackenzie emerged. He'd brought her to safety, loved her desperately, yet danger was never more than a heartbeat away— even as Barrie felt the stirrings of new life growing within her....

INTIMATE MOMENTS®
Silhouette®

HRTBRK4

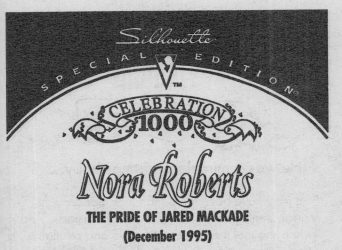

### Silhouette
#### SPECIAL EDITION
#### CELEBRATION 1000

# Nora Roberts

## THE PRIDE OF JARED MACKADE
### (December 1995)

The MacKade Brothers are back! This month,
Jared MacKade's pride is on the line when he
sets his heart on a woman with a past.

If you liked THE RETURN OF RAFE MACKADE (Silhouette
Intimate Moments #631), you'll love Jared's story. Be on
the lookout for the next book in the series, THE HEART OF
DEVIN MACKADE (Silhouette Intimate Moments #697)
in March 1996—with the last MacKade brother's story,
THE FALL OF SHANE MACKADE, coming in April 1996
from Silhouette Special Edition.

These sexy, trouble-loving men
will be heading out to you in
alternating books from Silhouette
Intimate Moments and Silhouette Special Edition.

NR-MACK2

## Silhouette SPECIAL EDITION

### Holiday Elopements

He was a miracle Christmas baby....

It may have been more than luck that brought
Mariah Bentley to the aid of a child in distress. And
when she met the babe's attractive and available
uncle, Aaron Kerr, it soon looked as if Christmas
wedding bells would ring!

Don't miss
**THE BRIDE AND THE BABY**
**(SE #999, December)**
**by Phyllis Halldorson**

It's a

### Holiday Elopements

—the season of loving gets an added boost with a
wedding. Catch the holiday spirit and the bouquet!
Only from Silhouette Special Edition!

ELOPE2